Praise for
Tandem

"Tracey Bateman delighted me with *Thirsty*, and I'm pleased to find the same unique tenor and rhythm in *Tandem*. Once again I enjoyed her style and treatment of story elements, scenes, and characters. She has both engaging plots and characters, and I look forward to seeing more from her."

—KACI HILL, co-author of *Lunatic* and *Elyon*

"Is it possible for a writer of Christian fiction to pen a vampire tale with an inspirational message? It is. And the proof is in Tracey Bateman's *Tandem*, a tale of love, revenge, and sacrifice that chills, thrills, and inspires hope."

—TAMARA LEIGH, author of *Leaving Carolina* and *Nowhere, Carolina*

"With characters so multidimensional, *Tandem* by Tracey Bateman is a real page turner. A suspenseful, provocative read that's truly compelling!"

—ROBIN CAROLL, author of *Fear No Evil*

"*Tandem* by Tracey Bateman captured me from page one. Layered characters and plot twists kept me hypnotized. Intense. Involving."

—LYN COTE, author of *Her Abundant Joy*

Praise for
Thirsty

"Bateman has written a page-turner with a compelling vampire character that will set evangelical Christian readers talking."

—*Publishers Weekly*

"Tracey Bateman has set out to write a vampire story that is both redemptive and relevant. I think Bateman does just that in her first foray into supernatural suspense."

—FictionAddict.com

"Deep, cutting an intoxicating blend of human and supernatural, of characters scarred by the past, drained by life. This is the book I've waited for."

—TOSCA LEE, author of Christy Award Finalist *Demon: A Memoir*

"*Thirsty* does exactly what a novel like this should do. It grabs you by the throat and doesn't let go. But it does more than that, deftly delivering truth and beauty in a way that transcends the genre."

—SIGMUND BROUWER, author of *Broken Angel* and *Flight of Shadows*

"*Thirsty* is one of those rare treats that not only delves deep into generational issues and addictive behaviors, but also keeps the pages turning. Tracey Bateman writes with a sensitive ear to dialogue and family dynamics, bringing a human, and ultimately redemptive, angle to the vampire story. Well done!"

—ERIC WILSON, author of *Haunt of Jackals, Field of Blood* and *NY Times* best-selling *Fireproof*

TRACEY BATEMAN
AUTHOR OF *THIRSTY*

tandem

a novel

WATERBROOK
PRESS

TANDEM
PUBLISHED BY WATERBROOK PRESS
12265 Oracle Boulevard, Suite 200
Colorado Springs, Colorado 80921

Scripture paraphrases are taken from the Holy Bible, New International Version®. NIV®. Copyright © 1973, 1978, 1984 by Biblica Inc.™ Used by permission of Zondervan. All rights reserved worldwide. www.zondervan.com.

The characters and events in this book are fictional, and any resemblance to actual persons or events is coincidental.

ISBN 978-0-307-45717-2

ISBN 978-0-307-45718-9 (electronic)

Published in the United States by WaterBrook Multnomah, an imprint of the Crown Publishing Group, a division of Random House Inc., New York.

WATERBROOK and its deer colophon are registered trademarks of Random House Inc.

Library of Congress Cataloging-in-Publication Data
Bateman, Tracey Victoria.
  Tandem : a novel / Tracey Bateman.— 1st ed.
     p. cm.
  ISBN 978-0-307-45717-2 —ISBN 978-0-307-45718-9 (electronic) I. City and town life—Ozark Mountains Region—Fiction. 2. Serial murders—Fiction. 3. Secrecy—Fiction. I. Title.
  PS3602.A854T35 2010
  813'.6—dc22

                    2010024544

Printed in the United States of America
2010—First Edition

10 9 8 7 6 5 4 3 2 1

To the memory of my beloved father-in-law, George Bateman

I miss you every day

PART ONE

Thanks to the human heart by which we live,
Thanks to its tenderness, its joys, and fears,
To me the meanest flower that blows can give
Thoughts that do often lie too deep for tears.

—WORDSWORTH

PROLOGUE

I've always despised smoke. Avoided the acrid smell, the burning eyes, stolen breath. The way it catches hold of fabric and hangs on with long, pungent claws.

And yet in my dream—my recurring, "Is someone trying to tell me something?" dream—I float blissfully through a wall of gray, wafting, vaporous smoke, blind to what lies beneath the dark expanse of haze. In this dream that so often robs me of sleep, I'm aware that I'm falling, falling far, and yet I'm not afraid. But then I awaken, sweat soaked, heart pounding, afraid to die alone.

CHAPTER ONE

She awoke to the creaking of hinges and boots falling heavily on stone steps. Sitting up straight, she pushed back her hair. Maybe if she looked nicer, he'd come more often.

At one time she'd been beautiful. So beautiful, men had fought duels over her. But now she bore the scars of a terrifying night of agony. She would never be beautiful again.

As the door fell shut, the breeze carried the rusty scent of blood. Hunger clawed violently at her stomach. She strained forward to see through the dark as his legs came into view, as greedy for the sight of him as for the nourishment he brought.

I fought for breath, gasping, choking on fear. Rushing toward the security desk, searching for anyone with a uniform, reality sliced through my last thread of denial. Nothing would ever be normal again, and my dad's well-being depended on my never, ever forgetting that.

Dad often became agitated and confused when too many people pressed in around him. But he'd always loved the holiday season at the mall. Every year we went to look at the decorations, eat roasted cashews, and sample fudge. I didn't have the heart to stop the tradition we had both treasured since I was a little girl. Even before everything changed.

As far back as I could remember, Dad would count down the days from Halloween until Thanksgiving night when he felt it appropriate to hang the Christmas lights and put up the tree. He was like a child, waiting and thrilling to the moment. His excitement was infectious and I loved those moments too.

I hadn't taken my eyes off of him. Not for one minute, until Starbucks beckoned. I left my dad at one of the tables next to the kiosk. Kept my eye on him as much as possible. But sometime between finding him a seat and walking back with my chai mocha latte (with an extra shot of espresso), he had disappeared.

Dad had been worse lately. He'd gone from talking to photographs and forgetting my name to calling me by my mother's name.

He was also beginning to suffer panic attacks as his mind convinced him of things that weren't true. Hallucinations. But that morning, he was lucid. He was excited about looking at the decorations, and because I had needed a day of normalcy, one day, I had let down my guard and left him alone. For just a few minutes.

What had I done?

My jacket was heavy over a thick hoodie and by the time I reached the security booth sweat slicked my forehead and dripped down my spine.

"My dad," I gulped around a throat full of fear and guilt, "wandered away. He has Alzheimer's and if he finds an exit..." My mind shut down at the possible outcome of this disaster.

"Calm down, ma'am." The mall cop was a middle-aged man with salt-

and-pepper hair and a beer gut. "We'll find him." He put in a mall-wide call describing my dad from the photograph I handed him. Then he paused and looked at me. "What's he wearing?"

I couldn't picture his outfit. What kind of daughter was I? I pressed my fingers to my brow and closed my eyes, trying to picture what I'd laid out for him that morning. "A brown corduroy jacket, jeans, and a Cardinals ball cap." The security guy nodded and something in his eyes gave me the confidence I needed to believe he would find my dad.

Almost immediately I heard over the radio that Dad had been spotted walking into the Hallmark store.

My head swam with relief as I pictured him drawn to the festive décor.

"Okay," the officer said, his voice full of authority. "Don't approach him, but be sure he stays confined to the store until his daughter arrives."

"Thank you!"

"No problem, hon. That's why we're here."

I tossed a backward wave as I rushed out of the office.

At the Hallmark store, I found my dad browsing through Christmas ornaments.

I rushed forward, breathless from my sprint back through the mall. "Dad, I was worried sick about you."

He turned to me, his eyes bright, full of conspiracy. "Let's get one of these for your mother." He held up an ornament of Scarlett O'Hara and Rhett Butler.

My mom was a huge *Gone with the Wind* fan, and in a guest room at home, there was an entire display dedicated to the famed romance. It was filled with knickknacks, music boxes, and more than a few copies of the book. But all those had been purchased when she was still alive.

I watched my dad, relief that he was okay sinking over me like a fresh-from-the-dryer bed sheet. Light and peaceful. Some experts say don't go along with the patient's fantasies. Set them straight when they lose track of their time line. But this wasn't a patient; this was my dad and I didn't want to crush his Christmas spirit.

I'd tried to be honest with him once during a blip in his memory, and the sadness in his eyes when he remembered was more than I could bear.

"You're right, Dad. Mom would love that."

His eyes lit with pride. When Mom was alive, she would have been happy with a paper airplane if given by his hand. He had no idea how little it would have taken to make her happy. If he had, it might have made a difference in the end.

I pulled out my debit card, and my bank account dropped another twenty-eight dollars.

Dad dozed during the forty-five-minute drive home, and I had plenty of time alone with my thoughts. I glanced over at him. He was hugging my mother's gift tight to his chest, his head resting against the cold window glass. The sight of him tugged at my heart. My dad was disappearing before my eyes. And there wasn't a thing I could do about it.

I settled him in for a nap and hid the gift with all the others, deep down in my hope chest. There were sparkly earrings, sweaters, books, bracelets, perfume, all the things he'd thought she would love.

My mother died when I was seven in a head-on collision with an oak tree. She swerved to miss a cat. The cat lived. The tree died.

No little girl ever loved her mama the way I loved mine. She was white teeth and cookie dough and warm arms. She was my run-to person. Kiss-my-skinned-knee person. Disney-cartoons-and-caramel-popcorn person. My every person.

At the funeral home, I stood next to the closed casket. My soul howled with rage and sorrow, but the pain was too deep for human expression so I remained dry-eyed and silent. Reverend Fuller squatted down and looked at me with gentle, sympathetic eyes. He told me she wasn't really in there. "You'll see her again, honey. God just took her home, that's all."

I jerked away and blinked at him, furious that no one had bothered to tell me. I threaded my way through friends—almost all my mother's exclusively—and left the funeral home. I ran all the way home, calling her name as I burst through the door. "Mommy!"

I checked every room twice. But she wasn't there. Wherever God took her, it wasn't home. I slipped her nightgown over my clothes, crawled up into the bed she shared with my dad, and laid my head on her pillow. The scent of Ralph Lauren Blue clung to the cotton pillowcase and knotted my chest so tightly I couldn't breathe. I cried from a place so deep no sound escaped.

White-faced and trembling, my dad showed up an hour later. He grabbed me, held me, made me promise to never, ever, ever leave him again. He'd lost my mother; he couldn't bear to lose me too.

Amede Dastillion sat in her garden surrounded by her plants and 150-year-old statues. Virgin Mary and the saints who had once brought her mother such peace. She sipped her tea and indulged in a few moments of e-mail and surfing the Web.

Despite her insistence that she would never allow a computer in her home, she had succumbed to progress. Not only had she reluctantly agreed to the technology, but she had also found she quite enjoyed the immediacy of online shopping and e-mail.

The french doors opened and Roma stepped onto the patio carrying the day's mail and a fresh cup of tea. Amede smiled at her friend and servant of fifty years. "Thank you, Roma."

"You're welcome." She hesitated as she set the tray down. "There's a large envelope from Missouri. Who do you know in Missouri?"

Amede lifted the envelope and checked the return address. Abbey Hills. "No one."

"Well, someone seems to know you."

Amede turned the envelope over, frowning. "It appears so." Roma waited until Amede stared up at her. "Do you need anything else?"

"Fine, you can open it in private and tell me later. I have to leave early today anyway. Gerald's appointment is in an hour."

"How is he doing?"

A shrug lifted Roma's plump shoulders. "The chemo is hard on him."

Amede took Roma's hand and gave it a squeeze. "Tell him I'm thinking about him, and if there's anything I can do, don't hesitate to ask."

"I will. Thank you. And don't forget Juliette will be filling in for me tomorrow and Monday. Gerald needs me to take care of him after chemo."

Amede pressed her lips together.

"Now, Amede. She's trying. It would give me a lot more peace while I'm taking care of my dying husband if you could refrain from scaring my grand-daughter half to death. She's next in line so you'd best learn to get along with her."

Amede fingered the envelope. "Never underestimate the power of the guilt trip."

Roma smiled. "Mission accomplished, then. All right. Do you need anything else before I go?"

Amede sipped her warm tea and shook her head. "I'll be fine. You go before you're late."

When Roma walked away, Amede lifted the large envelope. She pulled from it a stack of letters held together by a red ribbon. A frown puckered her brow and her stomach tightened as she read the familiar names, written in her own hand. Her heart raced.

She opened the top letter and fingered the creases in the yellowed paper with her index finger, remembering the nights she stayed awake, penning heartsick words of longing, never knowing if they had been received or read. Memories washed over her. Not many of them good. But she glanced down at the note in her hand and couldn't help but appreciate the kindness of this stranger who had taken time to send the letters.

To whom it may concern,

These beautiful letters were part of the estate of the late Markus Chisom. Incredibly, the dates are from the 1870s through just sixty years ago. I researched the Dastillion name and was delighted to find your New Orleans home still belonging to the same family. I realize the writer of these letters must be long deceased but felt they belonged with the Dastillion descendants and should not be auctioned.

Sincerely,

Lauryn McBride

McBride Auctions, Abbey Hills, Missouri

Amede read the note again, her hands trembling as she realized none of her other letters must have reached their destination after World War

II. The last address she'd had was in St. Louis, where these letters were originally sent.

She glanced back at the big envelope. Abbey Hills, Missouri. She typed the name of the town into her search engine. Scrolling through the real estate opportunities, the Wikipedia paragraph, and restaurants in Abbey Hills, she clicked on a link that seemed interesting.

The link led her to a page with dark, eerie graphics. The banner over the top of the page read, "Welcome to Things That Go Bump in the Night."

Amede was about to click out of the Web site when she noticed the word *vampires*. It was always an amusing distraction to read what humans thought about vampires. She gave in to a minute of indulgence.

Vampires in Abbey Hills?
July 2009

The *Abbey Hills Chronicle* reported that several animal slayings had occurred just before the so-called murders of Amanda Rollings, wife and mother, and, subsequently, student Carrie Grayson, daughter of Principal Grayson, days later. According to sources, throats were slashed and blood drained ritualistically.

But we've seen this before. Jergin, Illinois, two years ago ring a bell? Dallas, Texas, as recent as six months ago. If the police can't figure out how the murders fit together, perhaps it's time they admit something otherworldly is at play.

What sorts of creatures drink blood?

Think about it, folks.

There are vampires among us.

Perhaps we should welcome them into society and offer an alter-
native to murder.

Leave a comment. Tell me what you think.

If you've heard of similar killings, send me an e-mail and I'll
check it out.

mirandaK@gmail.com

Amede stared at the page for a minute before clicking out of it.

The girl had no idea how close she was to the truth. She smiled at the
naive thought that vampires and humans could coexist peacefully. Although,
the thought was definitely interesting. Her life might have been much easier
if she'd had the option of living in the open.

One thing Amede knew for certain. If Eden's letters were found in Abbey
Hills and there were blood-draining killings in Abbey Hills, Eden was there.

Or at least she had been.

She lifted the phone and pressed 1 on her speed dial.

Roma answered. "Amede? Everything okay?"

"Yes. I need to go to Missouri for a few days."

Hesitation on the end of the line. "Another lead?"

"Yes. And this time it's a good one. When can you go?"

"You know I can't leave Gerry."

Amede clenched her fist, digging her nails into her palms. How would
she ever make a trip like this without Roma?

"I don't understand why you can't just heal him. What good is practic-
ing voodoo if it doesn't heal your own family? That's not much of a religion."

Roma released a breath. "I'm not dignifying that with a response. Do
you want Juliette to come with you? I can call her for you. She'll have to take
days off school."

"Will she be able to?"

"She knows her duty, Amede."

Amede nodded. "All right. Tell her we'll leave for Abbey Hills as soon as arrangements are made."

She disconnected the call a minute later and stared out over her garden. Amede hated to leave New Orleans in the late fall, after hurricane season all but loosened its stormy grip and the rains gentled. Regardless, she knew she must leave her sanctuary and venture among the living. A place of torture, loneliness in the midst of a crowd.

CHAPTER TWO

In Abbey Hills, sports and band were all we had. Unfortunately, I had never been musically inclined and didn't have time for sports. Absent those two extracurriculars, "Loser" was pretty much tattooed on my forehead during my thirteen years in the public school system. I might have liked to play sports, but Dad didn't have time to drive me to practices and go to games. Occasionally, though, I skipped a day of school, if he was between auctions, and we'd drive to St. Louis and watch the Cardinals play. Those were the best days ever. Just the two of us. Hot dogs, the Arch, and a four-hour conversation each way.

Her own screams woke her. She had dreamed she was alone in the dark, captive of a madman. When she opened her eyes and realized the nightmare was real, she couldn't stop screaming.

F or the first time since I had hired her the year before, Cokie, Dad's home health care worker, was late. She rushed through the door, flustered and without lipstick, which was also a first.

"Sorry I'm late, Lauryn." Her lungs hauled air as she set her purse on the counter and pulled a pan from the cabinet to begin cooking Dad's breakfast.

"It's okay. I'm working at the house by myself today." I smiled. "No one to answer to." I frowned at the shadows under her eyes. "You sick? I can stay home if you need to—"

Cokie shook her head. "I'm okay. Just tired."

I was unconvinced but in a hurry, so I hugged her and went to find my dad.

When I'd first hired Cokie, my Dad fought me like a twelve-year-old, insisting he was too old for a baby-sitter. My heart broke. It was just as hard for me to give up even a little space between Dad and me. It had been just the two of us for so long. I resented even the idea of someone else in the house, cooking, helping Dad with the things I'd been helping him do since his decline. All my life, really. But after he wandered away from the house for the second time and the sheriff's department called me to pick him up, his doctor recommended Cokie.

I accepted her as quickly as I could. Dad not so much.

But Cokie, two hundred pounds, fifty years old, and deceptively soft-spoken, was a godsend. She entered our lives tough as nails—and she needed to be—when it came to making sure my dad stayed put. Later when things got worse, she made certain he didn't "do his business anywhere but the bathroom." She made sure his clothes were on properly, hair combed, teeth brushed, and shoes on the right feet.

Plus, I could almost always count on walking into a clean house after work and smelling something yummy for supper. She was just what we needed, and she knew she was indispensible.

I kissed Dad on the head. "Cokie's here, so I'm going to work. See you later." He patted me absently but stayed glued to the History Channel, one of the only stations Cokie allowed him to watch. He wasn't allowed cooking shows because of the knives and the ovens. The Weather Channel sent him running for the basement.

Ten minutes later I downshifted and inched my Jeep along the red bricks of Jackson Street until I braked in front of the Chisom house. I knew every brick, every tree and bush, every house on this street by heart. As far back as I could remember I dreamed of living in one of the Victorians in this neighborhood, made even more beautiful in the fall of the year.

I took a moment to enjoy the view. Overnight, it seemed color had burst over Abbey Hills. I closed my eyes and leaned my head back against the seat. In my mind's eye the images floated around me. The crisp leaves whispered in the breeze, and for a moment I allowed myself to rest.

My cell phone rang, drawing me from my mental sabbatical. I released a sigh before I answered.

I had missed my appointment to get my Jeep serviced.

As I exited the Jeep, phone held tight to my ear, I apologized to the receptionist, then turned down the offer to reschedule. I apologized again, disconnected the call, and shoved the phone into my bag.

Fallen maple and oak leaves formed a thick blanket across the yard. I kicked through them, loving the swishing noise they made. Such a shame to rake them up. But I knew it had to be done before the auction.

Looking at the Chisom home always gave me a thrill. Even when I was a child, before Markus Chisom bought the house, it was my favorite home in

Abbey Hills. It always seemed a little lonely to me, a little angry even, and I identified.

Markus had restored the home to its original design. Buttery yellow clapboard siding, authentic for the era, and white trim gave the home the look and feel of an elegant farmhouse. It was the perfect home for small-town middle America. But I thought it lost something in the sunny brightness.

Reclusive as he was most of his time in Abbey Hills, Markus Chisom respected the treasures that filled his house. I hated the idea of selling to someone who might not continue to care for them. But that was always the risk one took when dealing with antiques and vintage homes. Today a lovely Victorian, tomorrow an ugly quadplex. I'd seen it happen before.

I shoved aside the nostalgia and considered the practical possibility of auctioning off this gorgeous old dame. Commission from the house alone would keep McBride Auctions alive for another six months. And that's what was most important.

The key felt cool in my hand as I walked toward the steps. I loved the cased-in feeling that always came over me from being among the wrought-iron works and the vines that crawled and climbed among them, flowery in spring and summer and creepy in fall and winter.

This summer, overgrowth had taken a toll on the yard. Walking through it felt like a scene from *Hansel and Gretel* or another Grimms' fairy tale. Deliciously scary, conjuring up all sorts of images of witches and wizards and princesses in a castle.

There was a downside to the overgrowth, and I considered, not for the first time, whether I should ask the sheriff to provide security for the home. Once word got out about the valuables inside—and there really was no way to stop gossip from spreading like a plague in a town the size of Abbey Hills—the place could easily be burglarized.

My mind rushed to the killings Abbey Hills had experienced a few months before. Slayings, blood draining, ritual sacrifice markings. No one knew exactly what happened to resolve the crimes, except for the highway patrol's assurance that the house fire outside of town had taken care of everything. This was the same fire that killed Mr. Chisom, although the sheriff insisted he was a hero, not a killer.

For all of the sheriff's and the highway patrol's efforts, news of the ritualistic killings had leaked to news media, and almost overnight Abbey Hills had been overrun with newspaper and TV reporters and one very annoying Internet reporter who ran a paranormal Web site and insisted evil lurked in the one-hundred-year-old town. She'd never moved on.

I was about to reach for the doorknob but saw the curtain rise and fluff down. My stomach tightened and my heart sped up. Slowly, deliberately, I reached into my bag for the phone. But the door swung open before I could punch in any numbers. A man stood in the frame, barely fitting, he was so tall.

"Boo," he said.

Recognition connected me to reality just in time to avoid a humiliating scream. "Charley! You about gave me heart failure."

The deputy laughed, enjoying his trick. "I couldn't resist."

I shoved past him, shaking my head. "You're such a juvenile." I tried to be mad, but he seemed to be experiencing such pleasure from putting one over on me that I had to laugh it off.

"Hey, you would have done the same thing."

I wouldn't have, but I liked Charley. I was one of the few who did. There weren't many in Abbey Hills who could tolerate him. I was definitely the only person he liked in town. At least since his sister Amanda was killed months earlier in the killings.

I rolled my eyes. "Whatever. What are you doing here?"

He shrugged, following me through the foyer into the living room, where I set up my workspace for cataloging the auction items. "I have a few hours before I have to go to work. Thought you might need some help."

Sliding my laptop bag from my shoulder and setting it on the desk, I cut a glance at him. "Really? Because I could use some muscles to bring up some of the crates and trunks from the basement."

"Where do you want them?"

"Right in here, but not up against the walls. I don't want them scratched." I had already laid tarp to protect the wood floor, so I was all set.

"Okay, do you want all of them brought up?"

I shook my head. "I color-coded the crates according to content. Could you bring up two that are marked with red?"

"Sure." He flexed and kissed his bicep. "These guns are glad to be of service, little lady."

"Gross." I shook my head and turned to the desk I'd brought from one of the vacant offices at the auction house. I slipped the laptop from my bag and set it on the desk next to the printer.

While I opened the program and got my workspace ready, Charley lugged the crates up from the basement. He barely broke a sweat. "Looks like all that working out is paying off," I said.

"Noticing the bod, are you?" He grinned. "Anytime you say, I'm all yours, pretty lady."

"Good Lord, Charley. Like yourself much?"

He leaned back against the desk, facing me. I rolled the chair away just a little so I didn't feel so closed in by his hovering. Charley was lonely. He had no family with his sister gone and had latched on to me. Mostly I guessed because his brother-in-law, Pete, had taken the two kids and moved to California, where his parents lived.

But it worked both ways with Charley. I had never been a social dove, and since my dad had begun exhibiting signs of Alzheimer's, my social circle had shrunk even further. Impromptu meetings with Charley provided me with someone to talk to.

But I was itching to be alone so I could get some work done.

"So, how are things with Janine?" I asked, more to try to get rid of him than anything. But Charley was in a reflective mood, so my question brought out his talkative personality instead of the one that usually surfaced when Janine's name came up.

"Sometimes I think I should just go back to her." He crossed his feet and arms. His forearms bulged under the strain.

"Do you miss her?" They had dated all through high school, and Janine was there during his days of mourning after his sister's murder. Then for no apparent reason—he didn't even know why himself—Charley just broke up with her.

"Sometimes." He grinned a lecherous grin. "Especially in bed."

"You're such a pig."

He shrugged. "At least I'm honest."

"Well, she doesn't need you going back to her just for sex. Leave the poor girl alone and let her move on. I heard she had a date last week with some guy who works security at Silver Dollar City."

Charley nodded, trying to be nonchalant, but I could tell by the look in his eyes he wasn't happy. "I knew about it."

"Is that why you are thinking about getting back together?"

"Oh, probably." He sucked in a long breath and exhaled. "Let's talk about you. How's your dad?"

"I lost him in the mall Saturday, but otherwise, about the same."

"How'd you lose him? Were you sidetracked by the Victoria's Secret models in the window...oh, wait, that's me."

Charley did have his moments. I rolled my eyes. "I got sidetracked by the very sexy smell of coffee."

I told him what happened. "I don't know what I was thinking. He could have walked right out through an exit and gotten lost for good or hit by a car. I'm so not fit to be a caregiver."

Charley crouched beside me and put his hands on my knees. Any other time I might have questioned his motives, but I could tell by the sincerity in his eyes that he truly wanted to comfort me. "Don't beat yourself up. That could have happened to anyone. You've been great with your dad so far."

"So far." I snorted. "That means I have plenty of room to screw up later."

"Have you thought about putting him in a home?"

I frowned and shoved him away. "No way. He'd hate that."

He steadied himself and stood up. "I'm sorry. It was just a thought." He shook his head. "Never mind. You're so wound up. When was the last time you got to go out and have a good time?"

"Who knows?"

"Anise's party is coming up in a couple of weeks."

"You mean the 'un-reunion'?"

He gave a snort. "You thought that was dumb too?"

"Who wouldn't, except the person dumb enough to come up with it?"

"Anise," we said at the same time and laughed.

Charley stepped over to the desk and resumed his earlier pose. "Remember, she tried to have a five-year reunion two years ago but no one cared enough to come back, so she figured she'd market it this way."

I raised my eyebrows. "She's quite the thinker, isn't she?"

Anise Devort married the high school English teacher and stayed in Abbey Hills after graduation just like Charley and I did. She came up with the brilliant idea of throwing a bash over the Thanksgiving holiday when our high school friends would be making the obligatory return home for a few days.

"Are you going?" Charley asked.

"I don't know. I haven't filled out the RSVP. I guess it depends on finding someone to stay with Dad."

"Get a teenager from the church youth group. They're always looking for baby-sitting jobs."

I rolled my eyes. "I don't hire baby-sitters for my *father*, Charley." Charley could be so clueless. "He has to have someone from an agency. A professional."

Which meant big bucks.

An e-mail came in on the computer and I clicked it open. A thank you from the woman I'd sent the letters to down in New Orleans. Sent from her iPhone. I wondered for a second how she got my e-mail address, then remembered I'd attached my business card.

Charley continued on without appearing to notice my attention wandering. "Well, Anise might not be having the party anyway."

I glanced up. "Why's that?"

He shrugged. "I don't know. A leak or something flooded their basement, which is where all the booze is. Just ask Mr. Devort."

"Oh well. I guess that solves that little dilemma."

Scrubbing at his ever-present two-day growth, Charley raised his eyebrow. "Actually, Anise asked me if she could use the Inn for the party."

"That's not a bad idea. Maybe she is a thinker after all. What'd you tell her?"

"You know Anise. I tried to tell her no, but she made me promise to think about it and get back to her."

Charley's family had owned the Baylor Inn for a couple of generations, and it had passed to him after his mom died three years ago. He kept it open because it was the only place for out-of-towners to stay the night. I knew he'd rather shut it down and live there in peace, but the town needed an inn, and Charley felt the weight of that responsibility.

I suspected if he'd dared to close it anyway, he would have been run out of town.

"You really think I should do it? What about my customers at the Inn?"

"Tell Anise to invite them too." I turned my attention to my computer, hoping he'd take the hint. "If she really wants to have the party there, she'll agree."

He gave me one of his thoughtful looks.

"What?" I asked.

"I'll say yes if you'll go too."

That wasn't a hard decision. It might be funny to see Charley scowling at former schoolmates for an evening. "If I can get someone for Dad."

He handed me his cell. "Call the agency."

"I have my own phone." I grabbed my phone and wiggled it in front of him. Then I punched in the buttons and made arrangements for the Saturday after Thanksgiving.

Amazed at how relieved I felt, I stood up and gave Charley a hug. "Thanks. I'm looking forward to it." He pulled me tight. Awkwardly so.

There I was, pressed against Charley, when someone opened the door across the foyer and came in. I stared, certain I was imagining things as a face from the past entered my line of sight.

Those familiar gray eyes clouded. "Oh, hey. Sorry. Am I interrupting?"

"Billy?" I pushed away from Charley, wishing for all I was worth that I had a paper bag to breathe into.

Charley gave a short laugh. "Oh! That's the other reason I came by." He slung his ape arm over my shoulder, and it was all I could do to keep from jamming my elbow into his side. "Billy Fuller's back in town. I told him to stop by and say hi."

"Hi, Billy," I said, feeling utterly foolish.

"Hi yourself." His eyes never left mine. Like something out of a Lifetime movie.

"I better go," Charley-the-traitor said. "I have some Inn stuff to do."

He left, and neither Billy nor I said anything for a minute. Finally, he broke the silence. "So, you're running the auction house."

"I am."

"I heard about your dad's condition. I'm truly sorry."

I hadn't seen Billy since graduation. Right after he'd kissed me for the first and last time and then left town the next day without saying a word. I'd had a major secret crush on the preacher's kid my entire life, but he didn't seem to notice until that night.

I walked behind my chair and stood, feeling better with a barrier between us. Billy leaned against the frame that separated the living room from the foyer. He looked way too good in a pinstriped button-down shirt and a pair of semifaded jeans and flip-flops, which really were inappropriate for autumn in the Ozarks.

"So," he said, shoving his thumb through the air toward the direction of the door. "You and Baylor?"

"Friends." I took a deep breath. "You home for a visit or to stay?"

"For a while." He shifted between feet. "My plans are tentative."

I nodded.

"Well," he said, "I'll let you get back to work. It was nice seeing you. We'll have to have coffee sometime and catch up."

"Sure. Maybe sometime. I'm pretty busy."

He smiled and looked into my soul. "Maybe when you're not too busy."

"Yeah, maybe."

He turned to leave and then turned back, and I thought he might say something else. Instead, he stared for a long second, gave me a sort-of-smile, and lifted his hand. "Good to see you, Lars."

My heart leaped into my throat, disabling my ability to respond. I stood clutching my chair until I heard the front door click shut.

CHAPTER THREE

I learned to bake a cake by reading the back of the box of mix. I normally marked my dad's birthday by crafting a ridiculous hand-made card, and, if feeling adventurous, I'd wash his car as a gift. But I was growing up, and by the time I was ten I learned to think about his feelings a little. I rushed to the grocery store after school, then home, and when he came home around eight that night, a very lopsided, poorly frosted mess of a cake sat on the dining room table. He came in bellowing at me because I'd left my bike in the driveway.

His face changed and his bellowing stopped when he saw the cake. And me grinning next to the table.

"Happy birthday, Dad."

He grabbed me and hugged me so tight there was almost nothing left of me. "I don't know what I'd ever do without you," he whispered against my hair.

She hardly slept, but when she did, she dreamed of Markus. Her eyes filled with tears. He had loved her once. She didn't know why he had stopped loving her. One day he had walked away.

She was alone. But she had been alone long before the madman had thrown her into this pit.

⟨ornament⟩

I had trouble concentrating on my investigation of an antique mantel clock and a figurine I was almost sure went back almost two hundred years because I couldn't get Billy off my mind.

His sudden "Hi, I'm back in town, ready to break your heart all over again" appearance seemed surreal six hours later when I finally gave up, saved my work, and shut down my computer.

I closed up the crates, made sure all the curtains were shut so no one snooping around would see inside, and grabbed my bag. I did a walk-through to make sure all the lights were out.

I was just leaving the kitchen when a thump caught my attention. I tiptoed backward and grabbed the biggest butcher knife I could find, then headed toward the noise, knife wielded like a sword.

A sliding noise coming from the living room angered me. Someone was messing with the items I was cataloging.

"Lauryn!" someone called. I jumped, dropping the knife. I bent to pick it up just as a pair of beat-up Converse high tops came into view. "What's with the knife?"

I stood up, coming face to face with Miranda James, the crazy Internet reporter who didn't know when to leave well enough alone. "Miranda!" I shook my head. "What are you doing in here? How did you even get in? It's all locked up."

She rolled her massive green eyes. "You're telling me. I had to jimmy the lock to get in." She smiled. "But I knew you were here, so I didn't figure you'd mind. I knocked first. Kind of."

"What's kind of?" I couldn't believe her audacity. She had been unbearable after the murders, but I thought she'd settled down some. The woman had to be at least my age, and I was guessing maybe a couple of years older. The college-age goofiness was getting old, in my opinion.

"Well, okay, I didn't knock. I knew you wouldn't let me in if I did."

"I almost stabbed you." I didn't try to be polite. The day had just been too hard.

"Yes, but you didn't, so we can be thankful for that." She put her hands on her hips and looked around. "So, what'd you find today? Anything good? Anything that proves Markus Chisom was a vampire?"

I couldn't stand one more word from that husky voice that always sounded strained. Charley called it sexy. It drove me nuts. Almost as nuts as she already was. "Okay, look. I know you have this theory that certain places attract the supernatural."

"Yes." She nodded, and I saw a blur of frizzy red hair slide past my vision as I walked by her. She followed, speaking so fast I couldn't get to my point. "And Abbey Hills is one of those places."

"You've watched way too much *Buffy*."

"You know, you shouldn't discount movies and books as total fiction. There is some basis of truth in everything. The subconscious knows that, which is why authors can come up with such seemingly outlandish tales of darkness and demons." She paused. "And vampires."

I ushered her toward the door. "Markus Chisom was a good man and an upstanding member of this community."

"Vampires work their way into society. It makes it easier to keep their true identity secret." She shook her head. "Which proves my point that they shouldn't have to live in the shadows."

"Doesn't the light kill them?" I couldn't believe I was even playing her game.

"Old wives' tale."

I rolled my eyes, opened the door, and nudged her out in front of me.

On the porch, I locked the door and faced Miranda. "Look, don't let me catch you breaking into this house again, is that clear? And for the record, I'm going to speak to Jill about it."

"It's not like I'm going to steal anything. It's just an investigation, and if you didn't have anything to hide, you'd let me in."

"Miranda. Your mind just doesn't quit, does it?" I shook my head. "We aren't letting anyone in, and it isn't about hiding anything. It's about security."

Her cell phone started playing the Barney song. Her eyes grew even bigger. "Oh, shoot, it's Barney's. I'm late for my shift. Would you mind dropping me off?"

"Fine. Get in the Jeep."

I half listened to her chatter on and on about vampires and ghosts and witches and the evil that is supposedly drawn to places like Abbey Hills. "They can't help it," she said. "I mean, it's like the universe wills it and somehow they all come." As she got out of the Jeep, she captured my gaze and I could not look away. "I'm not crazy. I know what I know. The sheriff and the highway patrol are hiding something about the killings."

"They might be hiding something." I had never been satisfied with their watered-down answers. "But that doesn't mean they're hiding vampires. You're wasting your life on that Web site."

Her eyes narrowed. "You'll see. When I prove I'm right."

"Just stay out of the Chisom house. Capiche? Next time I'll call the sheriff and have you arrested for trespassing."

"If you catch me." She grinned and waved. "Thanks for the lift."

What a fruitcake.

Just before driving away, I glanced through the café window and into familiar gray eyes for the second time that day. I caught my breath as he gave a small wave. His mother and father sat across from him, and in the seat next to him, a little girl. My stomach dropped. I lifted my gaze back to Billy, and I knew the child belonged to him.

The Lincoln Town Car stopped in front of a sprawling two-story farmhouse behind a sign that read Baylor Inn. The folks in town had recommended the place with high praise. But Amede couldn't see much to endear this run-down inn to anyone. Unfortunately, it was the only place in town to stay, so she had little choice.

"This is really quaint." Juliette smiled as she looked through the car window. "I like it."

"It's ridiculous. Go inside and check us into our rooms, please. And send the bellboy for our bags."

"Will do."

Amede pressed her fingers to her throbbing temple. She tried to overlook Juliette's immaturity. As Roma was wont to remind her, the girl was only twenty-two years old. But Amede dreaded the end of Roma's time as her companion and servant. Resented very much having to let go of another friend. Right now, she looked closer in age to Juliette, as she had Roma forty years ago. Being perpetually thirty years old might be some women's dream, but for Amede, Roma's lined face spoke of nothing less than beauty, grace, loyalty, and wisdom, and she would have loved nothing more than to become old gossipy dowagers together. But that wasn't to be.

She imagined what another generation would look like, imagined watching Juliette grow old, have children and grandchildren, and train them to serve in the Dastillion household, as generations of Morioux had.

Roma reminded Amede that she had resented her as well, had thought her the stupidest of girls and her mother, Stella, before her and Emily before her. "Face it," she'd said to Amede just before Amede and Juliette left on the two-day trip from New Orleans to Abbey Hills. "You hate change. You've been stuck in the same rut decade after decade in this stuffy old house. Getting out of town will do you good. You haven't been out since the last time you went looking for her and that was, when? In the sixties? Yes, it was because you loved the Beatles."

"No, I *drove* a Beetle."

"Ah, yes." Roma laughed. "With flowers painted on it."

Amede smiled at the memory, just as Juliette returned. "I'll help you to your room, Miss Amede. Then I'll come back for our bags."

Amede frowned. "You? I told you to send the bellboy."

"They don't have one."

"What sort of...oh, never mind." She waved the girl aside and exited the car. "I can get my own bags."

"Miss Amede, I...well...that wouldn't be right."

"Nonsense." She lowered her voice and leaned in to Juliette. The girl grew stock still, tense as though afraid Amede might take a bite. "For heaven's sake, I just want to tell you something."

"Yes ma'am."

"I'm stronger than you could ever be, so carrying my own bags into the inn is not something I find completely objectionable."

"Oh. Yeah, I guess that's true."

The girl's scent lingered as she walked to the back of the car to retrieve the bags. Amede closed her eyes and tried to center herself before Juliette returned. Juliette smelled of fresh air and salty flesh. Humanity. Amede hadn't felt this strong an urge to feed in many years. The force of it set her off guard.

She would need to feed soon.

I trudged up the walk to the one-story ranch-style house I shared with my dad. As much as I had always wished for one of the historic homes—and there were plenty of them in Abbey Hills—we'd always lived in a modest section of town. I still loved the old homes, but I had finally developed an appreciation for what it meant to be a homeowner, since Dad had turned everything over to me as soon as his diagnosis was confirmed by three doctors.

I loved walking through the door and immediately feeling the presence of my mom. Dad hadn't had the heart to change the eighties décor after Mom's death. From the country blue and ducks in the kitchen to the burgundy and forest green in the living room, I wouldn't have had it any other way.

"I'm home!" I sat on the entryway bench and tugged off my cowboy boots. So glad to be home.

"I'll be there in a sec!" Cokie called from down the hallway. Probably Dad's room, where he spent most of his time in his recliner watching TV.

The smell of dinner cooking seduced me and I followed my hunger into the kitchen, where the aroma of onions and garlic combined with some kind of meat to make my mouth water. Unable to resist, I opened the oven door. Inside, a roast was browning.

I grabbed the teakettle from the stove and filled it with water, then set it back on the burner as Cokie entered the room.

"How's Dad?"

She gathered her breath. "It's been a challenging day."

My heart went out to her. "What happened?"

"A little bit of everything." She sighed. "Let's see. He got lost once on the way back from the kitchen. He had a couple of accidents. And while he was talking to the photograph of your mom, he started yelling at her for leaving him. Making all kinds of accusations."

"That's new." I'd never witnessed him yelling at Mom before. "Isn't it?"

"It's the first time I've seen it."

"What was he accusing her of?"

She shook her head. "It's not worth mentioning. He wasn't in his right mind, and no sense upsetting you."

"Do you think I should take the pictures out of there? What if Mom's photos are making him agitated?"

"Every case is different, Lauryn, but I wouldn't." She smiled with kind eyes and again I thought she looked tired, sick. "Let your dad hang on to the few memories he still has for as long as they will stay."

"What would we do without you, Cokie?"

"Let's hope we never have to find out." She went to the counter and picked up the potato peeler.

"Let me do that. You don't look too great." I peered closer and noticed her face had drained of color. "What's going on?"

"Just a little sick." She turned on the water faucet and grabbed a glass from the cupboard. When she finished she looked at me. "If you don't mind, I'm going to call it a day."

"Of course. Do you want me to drive you?"

She usually walked or rode a bike until the weather got bad.

Cokie nodded. "I think you'd better."

I gathered up my dad and turned off the teakettle.

"Tell me about your day," she said.

"I didn't get as much done as I wanted to, but I looked through some crates today, and let's just say proceeds from the items I found today alone could pay for the high school upgrades."

"The school board'll be happy to hear that."

"Yes, but do you really think we need a new gym floor? It seems like a waste of money to me when the old floor is fine."

"You might feel differently if you had kids." She chuckled. "My daughter goes to that school, and believe me, it's about more than the gym. We're getting new computers and a new cafeteria too."

"Is Cara home?"

"Yes, and waiting for her mama to make her some supper, I'm sure."

"I swear, Cokie, I don't get how you work as hard as you do and still raise such a great kid all alone."

She smiled. "Only the grace of God."

I wanted to tell her that she gave God a lot more credit than He deserved considering how much she had struggled her whole life, but I knew she would find a way to offer an answer that somehow still affirmed her faith. I chose to keep quiet instead.

"What else happened today?"

I told her about Charley, omitted the part about Billy, and finished up with Miranda. "She's convinced we have an epidemic of the supernatural right here in Abbey Hills. And that we should let them all come out of the coffin."

We pulled up in front of the tiny house she shared with her daughter. "Well, you never know." She closed her eyes, as though summoning strength before she opened the door.

"Get some rest tonight, okay?" I said. "And if you need me to call the agency and have them send over a temp tomorrow, just let me know."

"I'm sure I'll be okay after a good night's sleep."

I waited for her to get inside before pulling away. I couldn't shake the feeling that something was terribly wrong.

I drove home with Dad in the backseat talking to a hallucination about the hell of living under a tax-and-spend government. I thought he was talking about the current administration, which he had voted for, until he insisted that, by God, he was voting for Reagan. My dad was the bluest Democrat I'd ever known. Suddenly he's voting for Reagan? That was definitely the Alzheimer's talking.

I felt too hollowed out to find the humor in that. I just wanted this day to be over.

CHAPTER FOUR

Billy's family invited me to go see Jingle All the Way with them in Springfield, followed by a trip to the mall and dinner at the Olive Garden. Billy and I talked about it all week. On Saturday morning I woke up to Dad tickling my toes. "Get up, sleepyhead. Time's a wastin'."

I couldn't stop smiling, just thinking about the day's adventure.

"Get up and eat your breakfast so we can go." Dad seemed excited.

I was confused. "Are you going too?"

"Well, yeah! The big Modranski auction. This one is going to pay for our trip to Disney this summer. I thought you wanted to help. Remember? Work together, play at Disney together."

The joy drained out of me. How could an eleven-year-old remember dates for auctions? It had seemed like a great idea at the time. I guess Dad forgot too when he'd offhandedly told me I could go with Billy's folks.

Dad left the room, whistling. I knew I couldn't let him down. We had a plan. Work together today, play together at Disney this summer.

I called Billy and explained that I had work to do.

That Disney trip? Something—I can't remember what—
came up, and we never went.

———

Terror came in many forms.

Scary creatures of the night meant nothing to her. As far back as she could remember, she had been the one feared. Monsters and demons didn't frighten her in the least. But day upon terrifying day of loneliness had become more than she could bear.

When he'd first visited her, he had demanded answers. How had she become the creature she was today? How was it even possible that such abominations existed? She'd been in her own hell. The agony of burnt flesh.

Back then she believed she would eventually overpower him. But many days without nourishment had taken their toll and she had finally surrendered to the inevitable. She felt her mind slipping into the past as she tried to keep a grasp on reality. His words replayed like a recording, even after he had gone.

The early memories began like a far-off dream. Happy days playing with the other children in the Vieux Carré, the section of New Orleans now referred to as the French Quarter. How different her life was than those of the slaves—even those in her very own father's house.

A child of privilege growing up on St. Ann Street, she was the daughter of a beautiful free woman of color and the wealthy son of affluent shipping mogul Henry Dastillion Sr.

Even as a little girl, Eden had understood how special her mama was. If she entered a room, whispers became buzz and the men flocked to her. Her perfect olive skin glistened and exuded a scent that no man could resist. But

Mama's startling green eyes flashed only toward Eden's papa. The first moment Eden's mother saw him at the quadroon ball, she knew he would be hers. He was enchanted. Within a few months, Henry had purchased her a home on St. Ann Street. He was infatuated and completely unaware that Mama had bespelled him.

I awoke to the sound of ice pinging my window. It made me happy to know winter was coming. Granted, it was an early icing, five days before Thanksgiving, but I liked it just the same. I could smell something cooking in the kitchen and I smiled. Cokie must have felt well enough to come to work today. She'd been off the last few, and Dad hadn't been happy with her rotating replacements. I stretched and then reality hit. That wasn't a nice Cokie-cooked smell. Even if it wasn't Saturday, Cokie's usual day off.

I caught a whiff of acrid smoke. Something was really, really burning.

I threw back the quilt and bounded from my bed. I sprinted down the hall. Smoke billowed from the kitchen. "Dad!" I called out, praying he would answer. My imagination threw him on the kitchen floor, badly burned or passed out from smoke inhalation.

My lungs burned and the coughing began as I stepped in the kitchen. The smoke was coming from the oven. Covering my face with a dishtowel, I twisted the knob to the off position. I opened the window and the cold air blasted in. "Dad!" I called, coughing from deep in my chest. "Dad!"

"Good grief, Shar," he said, coming into the kitchen, calling me by my mother's name. "What did you do?"

I released a sigh. "It's me, Dad, Lauryn. And I'm pretty sure I'm not the one who did this."

The only times I corrected my dad's memory lapses were when he called me by my mom's name. It was just too heartbreaking, too weird. Sometimes it snapped him out of it; sometimes it didn't. This time it worked. "Lauryn? I'm so sorry, honey. I guess I forgot the biscuits."

"It's okay, Dad." But my mind was playing the "what if" game. What if I hadn't woken up? What if he had turned on the gas but the pilot light didn't work? I'd have never known until it was too late. *Oh, Dad. What am I going to do?* I took his shoulders and steered him toward the hall. "I'll tell you what. I'll get dressed and we can go to Barney's for breakfast. You always love his chocolate chip pancakes."

He stared blankly at me for a second. Then he nodded and patted my cheek. "Are you trying to get out of going to school?"

Truthfully, Dad had gotten me out of more school than I tried to skip on my own. Anytime an impromptu fishing trip came up or he wanted to take a road trip, it didn't matter that I had a test in history or art. Dad was cool that way. Those days were our times to talk about anything that might be weighing on my mind…or on his. I knew about his dates, our finances, the clients and their money problems. He knew about my crushes, my grades, my worry about what he would do when I went away to college.

I gave myself a second to collect my composure. Then I smiled and spoke with patience. "It's Saturday. School's out."

"In that case we'll go eat at Barney's."

I walked my dad back to his bedroom and settled him in his recliner while I hurried to my room and slipped on my favorite fat jeans, an MSU hoodie, and my cowboy boots. I glanced in the mirror and stuck out my tongue. My hair was impossible, so why bother? Short, curly, unruly no matter what I tried. At least I could have been given a pretty color. Even kooky Miranda had a neat shade of red to complement her impossible do. But no.

Mine was not only impossible; it was dishwater blond—the ugliest hair color known to humankind.

Rather than fight a losing battle, I grabbed a stocking cap with earflaps and shoved it down on my head. And only because there was practically a one hundred percent chance of running into someone I knew, I used a bit of mascara and a mineral-based powder foundation and toner. I stopped short of lip gloss. It just didn't feel like a lip gloss kind of day. I packed my ChapStick instead.

I walked across the hall, collected Dad, and left the smoky house, hoping the smell would be gone by the time we got home.

Amede stood on the balcony of her second-floor room and looked out over the river behind the house. Even through the icy mix falling from the sky, her eyes took in more than the average pair of eyes, and half a mile away she spotted a cave in the cliff above the river, tucked behind a wall of trees. She wondered what animals were hiding in there.

Though the ice was an annoyance she had rarely experienced in New Orleans, she was relieved that there would be no sunlight to cause her eyes to ache.

Her gaze followed the movements of a deer grazing in the field behind the house. Her heart pumped in her ears. She gripped the icy railing, barely noticing the cold as she fought to maintain discipline. She must remember where she was. Who these people were.

A knock at the door brought her to her senses. She moved back through the open french doors and across the room.

Juliette stood at the door, holding a tray that she looked about to drop. "Here, give it to me," Amede said.

"Thank you." She hesitated. "Is there anything you'll need from me today, Miss Amede?"

"I don't think so. Do you have plans?"

"Not unless it clears up," she said. "I just wanted to check with you in case it does. I'd like to go see the town and check out the barbeque place. Charley raves over it."

It had never occurred to Amede that Juliette might wish to explore the town during their stay. Roma never would have left her in a strange place, but Juliette wasn't Roma. And she had given her friend her promise not to be too hard on the girl.

Amede waved her away. "I can make do without you for one day."

A smile slid across Juliette's face, and Amede couldn't help but notice the similarity between the girl and Roma.

Amede took her tea to the settee. She untied the ribbon around her bundled letters, lifted the first, and began to read.

1870

Dearest,

Your absence from Dastillion Court is almost more than I can bear. Father grows weaker daily but remains determined that he shall not do what is necessary to gain his strength. I know his firm stance on the matter has become one point of contention between the two of you and I have to say, I understand his point. After all, how can we continue to live in society if people are dying around us? Regardless of my understanding of his point of view, I have no sympathy for him after the way he cast you out even while I pleaded with bitter tears for him to relent.

But know this, dear one, he is not long for this earth, and when your oppressor is gone, I shall welcome you back with open arms regardless of our differences.

Until then, I beg of you to think of me often.

Yours,

Amede

The next two letters read much the same as the first. Words of love, loneliness, longing. Amede wasn't sure when she started crying, but tears dropped onto the letters. She quickly dabbed them away with her handkerchief.

After all the years of searching, to no avail, she finally had a solid lead. She sipped her tea, her glance falling upon the large envelope.

Lauryn McBride.

This was where her search would begin.

CHAPTER FIVE

I never considered Billy a crush until our seventh grade year, and I would have died before I told him. But Dad figured it out. He noticed during a career day, where the parents came and talked about work and ate lunch with the students. Dad noticed us talking, and apparently I watched Billy walk away with a "sappy" look on my face.

I denied it, of course, but Dad insisted and finally I admitted it.

To Dad, there was no one as great as me, so he convinced me to invite Billy to the Sadie Hawkins dance. Dad sat by the phone while I called.

"Hey, Billy, it's Lauryn."

"Hey, Lars," he said, using the nickname I didn't put up with from anyone but him. "What's up?"

"I was wondering if you're going to the dance Friday." I gulped. "The one where the girls ask the boys."

"No, I—"

I grinned at Dad, relieved I'd gotten to Billy first.

"Do you want to go with me?"

"I . . . um . . . I'm waiting for . . ." He hesitated. I filled with

dread. Billy didn't like me that way. He had to be waiting for Anise or someone else really pretty to ask him.

"Hey, don't worry about it," I said. "I didn't want you to go with me anyway. I only asked because someone dared me to."

I hung up and burst into tears.

Dad held me, reassuring me that I would always be his first choice.

The memories kept her sane. At first she had resisted going back. Now she lived almost exclusively in the past. It was more bearable than the present. If only she knew Mama's spells. Mama had been powerful to the end. She would have been so disappointed in Eden.

Eden reached up and touched her face. The scars were trails of disgrace. Thank God no one could see her. Death would have been better. She never should have run from the burning house. If only she'd have allowed herself to die that day. But fire had always terrified her. The servants whispered of her and her mama burning in a fiery pit called hell where one never died but burned forever. She'd thought about this and had been terrified that the fire would burn forever and she wouldn't escape, and somehow she'd summoned the strength to run from the house.

Reality had been terrifying. The past was much safer, so she went there often in her mind, thankful that there were many, many years for her mind to wander.

Mama couldn't marry papa. It was against the law because she was a quadroon and he a white man. But that didn't stop them from living together despite the moral outrage from the good Christian folk in New Orleans society. The men could certainly buy beautiful slave women for their beds. Their sons could attend the quadroon balls and find mistresses, buy their houses, father their bastards, and abandon them when they married a woman accepted by society. But God forbid they should openly love a woman of color, free or otherwise.

Eden's father had been the exception, in that he fell in love with Eden's mother. Yes, he had married a proper white woman from a proper family in order to provide an heir for the Dastillion name. But he never stopped coming to see Eden and her mama.

For years he remained kind and devoted to his wife as she lost child after child, finally carrying a pregnancy to term. She wept when Amede, and not a son, was born, but Papa delighted in his second daughter. The doctor warned that his wife must not become pregnant again or she would die. And since his wife failed to provide a son, Henry poured his love and attention onto his daughter. Amede would inherit Dastillion Court.

And, though Eden would want for nothing all of her days, she would never be a legal, legitimate heir. The law simply wouldn't allow for it. She would inherit the home on St. Ann Street where he had kept her mother. She would wear beautiful gowns and everyone would know Henry Dastillion was her father, but she could not bear his name, nor would she be his heir.

Even now, Eden felt this stigma. And she hated Amede for being the one her father loved.

B arney's was packed, as I had known it would be. A little ice storm wouldn't keep the old-timers away. There were way too many world problems to solve. Plus the Chiefs were playing on Sunday, so that would need to be discussed as well.

Janine—Charley's Janine—a willowy, dark-haired, overly made-up waitress seated us right away, despite the line. She led us to a seat near the back of the room, a secluded little table. "Thank you," I whispered, knowing she seated us ahead of at least three other couples waiting in line. "I don't want anyone giving you a hard time on my account."

"It's okay. Most of them understand." She winked, setting a menu in front of each of us. "And to heck with those who don't. You starting off with coffee?"

I nodded. She knew the drill. Regular for me, decaf for Dad.

She hovered over our table, and I could tell she wanted to ask about Charley. I realized that was probably the reason she seated us. But whatever the reason, Dad hadn't been forced to stand shoulder to shoulder with people he couldn't remember, so I was grateful.

"You seen Charley lately?" she finally asked.

My heart went out to her because I knew how much she loved him. Charley was all kinds of idiot to walk away from this woman. "Yesterday at the Chisom house. He said Anise talked him into having the reunion party at the Inn."

She snorted. "There's no way Anise could have talked Charley into that." She peered closer, and I felt myself blushing.

"Okay," I admitted. "She asked him and he said no until I told him he ought to do it. A party is probably exactly what he needs to throw, don't you think?"

She ignored my attempt to bring her into Charley's psyche. "You'd tell me if you and..."

"Come on, Janine. Charley is a friend. Apart from you, I'm about the only one in town who puts up with him."

"I know, but...is that because you have feelings for him? I mean, all these years I've had him pretty well exclusively. Now that we're broken up, do you think you two would ever..."

"Okay, Janine, look into my eyes and repeat after me: 'Charley and Lauryn are friends. Nothing more. I have nothing to worry about.'"

Relief covered her face, but I still saw doubt in her eyes. She looked as though she wanted to say something else, but Barney hollered from the kitchen. "I'll be back to get your order. I sure hope Miranda shows up. Barney's going to pop his cork if she's late again."

"Think he'll fire her?"

She shook her head. "He ought to, but she entertains him too much with her weirdness."

"Too bad. Maybe if he'd fire her, she'd go away and stop with the vampire nonsense."

"I don't know," she said, starting to walk away. "Some of it's pretty interesting. You ever been to her Web site?"

I nodded, ashamed to admit such a thing.

She gave me a knowing grin and headed toward the window.

I was perusing the menu, although I already knew I was ordering chocolate chip pancakes, when I sensed a figure next to the table. I glanced up to find Billy standing there.

"Hi," he said.

"Hi." I looked from him to the little girl next to him, who was holding his hand.

"I wanted to introduce you to someone."

But before he could, Janine rushed to the table, setting down our cups.

"Hey, Billy. You guys teaming up?" She said his name but was looking at me. "It would be a huge help if you'd say yes. We're swamped and running out of tables, and people are waiting."

I could almost hear her inner voice reminding me that she'd just done me a favor by not making me wait. I owed her.

I felt everyone's eyes on me. I directed my gaze to the kid. "Wanna sit here?"

She shrugged. "If Daddy says so."

He sent me a look of apology.

"It's okay," I said. "Were you going to introduce me to someone?" I smiled at the little girl and she smiled back.

Billy cleared his throat. I could tell he was nervous about the introduction. But the expression on his face when he looked at the little girl was anything but shame. "Lauryn McBride, I'd like you to meet my daughter, Peach."

My stomach felt weak. Billy Fuller was a father. And it appeared, for all intents and purposes, he was a pretty good one. I was dying to ask him about Peach's mother, but I held back. I was sure answers would come soon enough.

I could feel Billy's eyes on me as I stared at his daughter, willing me to say something. "Hi, Peach. That's a really nice name." She was biracial and beautiful, and her gray eyes matched Billy's.

"Thank you," she said. "So is yours." She smiled, showing off an all-I-want-for-Christmas-is-my-two-front-teeth smile.

"Take off your coat," Billy instructed the child, "and have a seat next to Miss Lauryn."

She slipped out of a pretty red coat and laid it over the back of her seat. She scooted onto the seat in that funny little way children have of climbing up. She looked expectantly at me.

I had no idea what I was expected to do. "Yes?"

"Will you please push in my chair so that I don't get food on my sweater, Miss Lauryn?"

"Of course."

She offered me that smile again. Her gaze darted to my dad. "Who's that?" she whispered.

'Dad." He hadn't looked up from his menu since Billy and Peach arrived at our table. But as soon as I spoke directly to him, he did, his expression one of surprise as though this were the first he'd noticed we weren't alone at the table. He turned to Billy and frowned. I could see he was trying to remember. "Look, Dad. Billy Fuller has come home."

Billy held out his hand. "Nice to see you again, Mr. McBride."

Dad nodded, but his eyes remained vague. "Billy, I haven't seen you at the house in a while. Lauryn misses you when you stay away. Mopes around all day." He grinned. "Don't you, honey?"

"Sure, Dad. I spend all day moping over Billy Fuller."

I stared pointedly at Billy. He looked away.

"Sorry, Mr. McBride," he said. "I promise to do better from now on."

"Good! How's football season coming along? You going to kick Branson's butt this year?"

Billy grinned. "Definitely."

"Dad," I broke in. "Billy's a preacher now like his father. He's been in Haiti, is it? For the last few years."

Billy nodded. "Yes. Haiti and the Dominican Republic."

His eyebrows lifted. "He is? Well, that's nice. I'm not much of one for religion. But I say more power to you. That's why we live in a free country. Supposed to be free anyway."

Alarm bells sounded in my head. Dad was infamous for his heated political debates. Embarrassingly blue in a practically all-red state. Of course, in view of his disturbingly heated debate with himself the other night when he vowed to vote for Reagan, I was no longer sure what would come out of his mouth. Normally, I would have let him rant because his doing so reminded me of the old days. But his blood pressure had been high lately, despite his blood pressure meds, and I figured a debate was the last thing we needed.

"Dad, this is Billy's daughter, Peach. Peach, my dad, Ted McBride."

His gaze shifted to the little girl and he forgot all about the fact that the Republicans were nothing more than rich guys with tax breaks and a right-winged agenda. Or that the Democrats were nothing more than bleeding-heart liberals out to tax and spend the country to death. Whatever way he was leaning that day.

She grinned. "Hello, Mr. McBride."

Lucidity returned to my dad as quickly as it left earlier and he grinned back at the little girl, although I wasn't sure he was actually with us in the twenty-first century. "Call me Mr. Teddy. That's what all the kids call me. Have you ever had chocolate chip pancakes?"

"No, Mr. Teddy."

"Well, you're about to, little sister."

Peach frowned, which caused my dad to do the same.

"What's the matter?" he asked. "You don't like chocolate chips?"

"I like chocolate chip cookies." Her eyes went wide. "A lot."

"Well, see? The pancakes are even better."

"Grandmother told my daddy I shouldn't eat sugar for breakfast. She said it makes me hyper and hungry for the rest of the day."

Dad's expression darkened and he turned to Billy. I tensed, wondering if a brawl might commence over chocolate chip pancakes. "This child has never had a chocolate chip pancake? Barney is famous for them. Are we going to insult the man over a little sugar?"

I laughed. How would Billy say no to such reasoning?

He winked at his daughter. "Grandma didn't realize we would be having breakfast with Mr. McBride. And besides, chocolate chip pancakes aren't the same as chocolate chip cookies."

"That's right," I said, unable to hide my amusement. "You get to put a bunch of sugary syrup on the pancakes."

The sarcasm was lost on the child, but Billy gave me that crooked grin he'd been sending my way since kindergarten. My heart fluttered a little, but I commanded it to behave. I had to look away from his eyes for it to obey, and when I did, I caught sight of the sheriff in an apron. Janine showed up, finally ready to take our orders. I made a motion toward the sheriff. "What's Jill doing?"

Janine followed my gaze and rolled her eyes. "Pinch-hitting for Miranda until she gets here. She called. Said she had to finish her blog first."

"She must be some entertainment for Barney to put up with her," I said.

Janine gave me a knowing look. "You know how Barney is about strays and eccentricity. She's both rolled into one ball. Anyway, you ready to order?"

We did. And she walked away. Billy glanced thoughtfully after her. "Did she ever get together with Charley Baylor?"

"They lived together from the time he came back from the police academy until last year."

"They broke up?"

"He left her. No one really knows why. Even Charley doesn't know why." I wanted to say, "Just like I don't know why you left me." But I didn't.

Before I could say anything else, Jill approached the table. She and Barney had married a few weeks earlier, so she was Sheriff Jenkins but also the first lady of barbeque. I could see by the somber expression on her face that this wasn't about chocolate chip pancakes. She was definitely in sheriff mode.

"Good morning, Sheriff," Billy said, standing. Gentlemanly.

She waved him back to his seat. "Good to see you again, Billy," she said, and the offhand way she'd spoken set off warning bells in my brain.

"Is something wrong?"

She nodded. "Someone broke into the Chisom house."

Billy spoke right away. "Was it thieves or vandals?"

All I could hear was Miranda's voice saying, "If you catch me." Surely she wasn't stupid enough to go back to the house after she'd been caught breaking in on Monday.

"I just got the call from Charley," Jill said. "He's over there checking things out now. The front door was jimmied but not broken." She turned to me. "Would you be willing to head over a little later and see if you notice anything missing?"

Try to keep me away. I started to get up, but she shook her head and put a hand on my shoulder. "Not yet. Let us dust for fingerprints first. No sense adding more to sort through."

"Well, you're going to find mine there anyway."

She nodded. "Of course. But let's keep it as simple as possible for now."

"Okay, when?"

"Can you be available this afternoon?"

All those hours to wait. Dread seized me as I thought of the wonderful works of art, the antiques. Worth a fortune.

"I'll be there just after noon," I said. That was the latest I was willing to hold.

"I'm headed over there now. I'll let Charley know."

She pressed her hand to her temple.

"Do you have a headache, Jill? I have some ibuprofen in my purse." I started to reach for it, but she shook her head.

"Just tired. We've been up all night working."

"We?"

"Charley and me. I can't really talk about it right now."

I nodded, curious. "Okay. No problem."

"I better go. Charley will be going through the house with you. That's not a problem, is it?"

I frowned. "Why would it be?"

Realization lit her eyes. "I forgot the two of you are friends. He rubs most people the wrong way."

"I can handle Charley." I smiled.

"Okay. Take it easy." She included us all in a good-bye wave.

I watched her pause at the door, lift her hand, and wave at her husband, who was watching through the window. His face softened as she smiled and he lifted his massive hand. The silent language of love.

When I turned back to the table, my gaze locked into Billy's, jolting me to the reality that no matter where he had been for the past seven years, we had unfinished business.

CHAPTER SIX

After the debacle with Billy and the Sadie Hawkins dance, I stopped hanging out with him at school, games, functions. I definitely never went to church or VBS with him again. He tried to talk to me. He actually explained through a note that his parents wouldn't let him go to the dance because there was a revival at church that night and as the son of the preacher, he had to be there. But by then, my pride was too wounded. I was too embarrassed, and as I look back now, I have to admit I was just too spoiled to conceive of the idea that I couldn't have exactly what, or whom, I wanted.

Since Billy was pretty much my only friend, I became a loner. The next year I started spending time with Amanda Baylor. She was cool and smoked cigarettes without coughing. I didn't smoke with her that year, but when she got caught, I was sitting with her behind the building and for some dumb reason fessed up.

Dad gave me a talking-to and then laughed and told me not to smoke anymore. It was gross and would stain my teeth, and I'd be talking like a biker by the time I was thirty.

And that was that...until the next time when I really was smoking.

She shrank back against the wall, her legs drawn to her chest. Her eyes followed him, on guard, wary, as he paced the six-by-six room like a caged animal.

She tried to understand his accusation, but he made no sense.

"How? How did you get out of here?"

But she hadn't left the room. Did he really think if she could get out that she'd ever return to this hellhole?

"I can't let you kill again. I can't. I won't." He shook his head as though a madman possessed his soul. She shivered. She'd seen this sort of thing before. Unholy and frightening and uncontrollable. He whipped around and shoved a trembling finger toward her. "How? How did you do this?"

She hadn't done anything. How could she when she was locked up inside this room day in and day out?

He ranted, his voice becoming breathless as he grew more frenzied. "I saw it. The deer. Drained just like before." He made a slashing motion across his neck and down his breastbone. In the shape of a cross.

She understood enough to realize the animals were being killed again in the manner her father had taught her to kill. Ritualistic slayings pointed to religious cults, not vampires. A clever deception.

Her jaw tingled with the memory of warm liquid rushing down her throat.

Hope lifted her spirits. Even as the back of his hand fell like a brick across her face, she wondered if perhaps the new animal killings meant someone was looking for her.

With each blow, she imagined the day she could exact her revenge—the day she would kneel over him and rip open his throat.

Laughter began deep inside of her and refused to stop even though the blows grew harder the more she laughed. Finally, blessed blackness came and she no longer felt the pain.

J uliette sat alone among the lunch crowd at Barney's, glad to be away from the dried-up chain around her neck. She pulled out her laptop and connected to Wi-Fi.

The waitress came to her table just as her e-mail popped up.

"Oh, cool, a MacBook," the server said.

Juliette nodded, taken aback by the sight of the young woman. Her crazy red hair seemed to spring out from every possible opening of her bandana. She wore a pair of shorts over rainbow-striped tights. Her eyelids were slathered with a shade of teal eye shadow that Juliette had rarely seen outside of Mardi Gras.

"I'm Miranda. I'll be your server. Duh." She gave a laugh. "Have you ever wondered why servers say, 'I'll be your server'? Isn't it obvious? I think I'll talk to Barney about that."

"I guess I see your point," she murmured.

"So you should check out my Web site. Things That Go Bump in the Night dot com."

"I'll do that." She smiled. Another wannabe writer with a boring blog about topics only she and twenty-five of her closest friends cared anything about. "So, what's good here?"

She shrugged. "I'm a vegetarian so I wouldn't know. A lot of people eat the barbeque. Personally I gag every time I see it."

"Are you for real?" Juliette couldn't believe she'd just said that out loud. But since she had, she committed to the thought. "Maybe customer service isn't your gift."

"It really isn't. I'm only working here until my Web site starts turning a profit. I'm really close."

How could anyone stay irritated at someone so blatantly self-aware? "I'll have the catfish and fries. And sweet tea."

Bemused, she watched the woman walk away. Juliette had never been one to judge on appearance, but Miranda had a look all her own. Her red hair, which was pulled up into a poorly executed ponytail, had an almost nappy look to it, but the girl was pale as a lily. Perhaps most striking were her large green eyes that seemed translucent.

Curiosity got the better of Juliette before she clicked on her first e-mail, and she went to the girl's Web site. She rolled her eyes. Witches, ghosts, and vampires. If she only knew.

Juliette clicked back to her e-mail. Every now and then she caught a glimpse of a red blur and looked up to find Miranda bopping from table to table. Clearly the locals put up with her as though she were a mascot or something.

She clicked back to the Bump in the Night Web site.

During my time in Abbey Hills I've learned several things. 1. People of the Ozarks have an affinity for barbeque, which I personally believe is revolting. 2. Small-town law officials really do pull cats out of trees and help the elderly carry in groceries. 3. The people don't judge appearance—very important when you have bright red hair and a figure like Olive Oyl. And 4. There is an energy here that draws weirdness. I guess that opens me up for all kinds of jokes, so bring

them. I don't care. I will keep repeating myself until I prove my
theory. The cops aren't telling the whole truth about the death of
Markus Chisom and, more importantly, Eden, the woman supposedly killed in the fire. They say it's not important that her bones were
never discovered.

What? Since when? Even in the hottest fire, there will be some
bone fragments, but only those of Markus Chisom were discovered.
Where is Eden?

There was a picture of the beautiful African American woman beneath
a caption that read, *"Have you seen this woman?"*

"Beautiful, isn't she?"

Juliette jumped. "Warn a person."

"Sorry." Miranda set Juliette's tea and condiments for her meal on the
table.

"No. I'm sorry to be so jumpy." She offered a smile that the red-headed
girl quickly accepted. "I got so interested in your writing I didn't notice you
coming."

"So you like it?"

"It's very entertaining."

A cloud settled over Miranda's face. "It's not supposed to be entertainment. It's supposed to be informative."

Barney called from the kitchen, and Miranda walked away without
another word.

Juliette knew she must tread lightly. This girl could be a danger to
Amede. And whether Juliette liked it or not, she was bound to protect Amede
at all costs. The two families were tied together by a blood vow that only the
death of the last Dastillion would break.

To protect themselves, the Dastillions had insisted upon a proviso that if the death should come at the hand of a Morioux, every generation thereafter would be cursed.

No one had ever had the courage to test the oath's power. At least as far as she knew.

As Juliette imagined her life play out before her, watched herself grow old caring more for Amede than her own eventual family, she pressed her lips together and tried to convince herself that she might be the Morioux with enough conviction to stand up and test the theory.

But who was she kidding? She would never have that sort of courage. The most she could hope for was that Amede would die at someone else's hand.

Then she would be free.

After an excruciating four-hour wait, I finally pulled up to the Chisom house. I'd had no choice but to bring Dad along for the ride because there was no one to look after him.

Determining whether or not anything was missing would be problematic since I'd been working in the house for only a week.

There were dozens of crates and trunks in the attic and basement. Not to mention all the pieces in each room. Each item had to be cleaned, photographed, cataloged, and assessed. If I didn't have the appraisal value of an item, I'd have to do exhaustive research. It took me four hours to authenticate a single painting. I hadn't even begun to go through the rooms. Luckily, I had photographed each room extensively, so I would at least have an idea of what I was dealing with.

"Let's go, Dad," I said, reaching across to unhook his seat belt.

He grabbed my wrist. "What do you think you're doing?" His grip was like iron, digging in with bruising strength.

I forced myself to remain calm as he grew more and more agitated. "We're going to go inside the Chisom house."

"You're lying. You're trying to leave me here."

"Dad, I'm not. I promise. We're auctioning off the house."

"What do you mean? Why haven't I heard anything about this?"

His grip was as firm as ever, and I could feel my skin pull and burn. In his right mind, my dad wouldn't hurt an ant, let alone me. He'd be heartbroken if he discovered he had caused me pain. "I wanted to surprise you."

His face changed and his grip loosened. I fought back tears and covered my wrist with my hand. He peered closer at the home. "These old houses usually need a lot of work."

"This one has been impeccably preserved." I got out and went around to open his door. He kept his eyes on the home as we stepped forward, the interest in his face growing. I had a feeling it might have been a good thing that I had no one to leave him with today.

A truck pulled into the driveway. Billy opened the door and got out.

"What are you doing here, Billy?" I asked, trying to sound nonchalant.

"Jill asked me to fix the door. Someone hacked away at the lock."

"So it wasn't a professional job?"

He shook his head. "Apparently not. And from the looks of things, the thief was either searching for something in particular or didn't know the value of the antiques and artwork inside."

"Thank goodness for that." My mind played back Miranda's flip answer that I would have to catch her breaking in. Was the girl that brazen?

Inside, Charley sat on one of the crates I'd had him bring upstairs last Monday, sipping on a can of Dr Pepper.

I cringed on both accounts, but he stood as we entered, so I only had to mention the second. "Hey, Charley, don't spill that on anything."

"I won't." He pretended to trip. "Oops." He gave a teasing laugh. "Sorry, couldn't resist."

"You're just the life of the party, aren't you? Honestly, Charley, you'd think a guy who owns a Victorian inn would know better than to drink a soda around priceless antiques." But I smiled to take the bite out of the words.

"Okay, fine." He walked into the kitchen and returned empty-handed. "Happy?"

"Relieved. Thank you."

His eyes settled on my dad and he scowled. I widened my eyes at him. Thankfully, his face relaxed. He gave me a "Keep an eye on him" look and I nodded, glad he didn't say anything to hurt Dad's feelings.

Dad moved his fingers over the wood carvings along the staircase. "Beautiful," he said. "Oak. But this isn't the original staircase."

I had suspected the same and loved the fact that my dad was having this moment. "It's more Georgian, isn't it, Dad?"

His hand trembled as it did from time to time. Reverently he continued to trace the ornately carved newel. "I'm not sure. I've never seen carvings like this."

I followed the trail of his fingers. I hadn't noticed before, but the markings were disturbing. Demonic. The stuff of nightmares.

I had forgotten about Billy until he stepped up. "It's almost like the craftsman is telling a story of ghosts and demons fighting against humanity."

"Looks like hell," Charley said, and I glanced up curiously. "As in the real hell. You know, the devil?"

"Dante's *Inferno*," I murmured.

"I'd love to see the rest of the woodwork in this place." Dad's eyes were alight with admiration for the craftsmanship. Something I hadn't seen in so long. I turned to Billy. "Would you mind showing my dad around while I talk with Charley?"

"Sure." He nodded to my dad. "You should see the mantel in the study."

I shot Billy a grateful smile and my heart soared when he smiled back.

"Well, look who still has a crush." Charley snickered like a sophomore.

"I'm not talking about that with you, Charles."

His face clouded. "Don't ever call me Charles."

Surprised by his sudden reaction, I raised my eyebrows. "Well, how was I to know that? No need to bite my head off."

"Well, just don't call me that, okay? I'm sorry I got snarly. It's been a long day."

"Fine. I won't call you Charles. But don't tease me about Billy."

We settled our little argument with a moment of silence. He walked into the kitchen, presumably to have a sip of his Dr Pepper, and I set my bag on the steps. Then I remembered that Amanda had always called him Charles. She'd been the only one.

I reached into my bag and retrieved the photographs of the rooms. I had organized them room by room in order, starting in the foyer. Nothing seemed to be missing at first glance, but there wasn't much in here. I had already removed the art from the walls.

"It's the darnedest thing," Charley said, coming back into the room.

"What is?"

"The jewelry box in the master bedroom was open, but it was still full of jewels. You know, necklaces and stuff."

"Jewels? Charley! You could have said something." I headed toward the master bedroom with the deputy close behind.

"Yeah, they left a lot of expensive stuff."

"Are you a jewelry appraiser all of a sudden, Charley?" I tossed back over my shoulder. "How would you know if the pieces are costume or real?"

"Point taken." He followed close behind. "Your dad seems better today. That has to be a relief."

"Yeah. Especially since he practically burned the house down this morning."

"What happened?"

"He tried to cook breakfast, then forgot what he was doing." I sighed. "My own fault. I have to be more careful."

"I think you're too hard on yourself."

I didn't answer but couldn't help feeling a little better just knowing someone understood.

I headed to the dresser, finding the jewelry box as Charley described it. While I gently, almost reverently, rummaged through the jewelry, I told him about my morning.

"I don't know how you do it." Admiration edged his tone and I smiled.

"We have good days and bad days. But mostly a combination of both. I think you were right about the jewelry, Charley." The necklaces, bracelets, and earrings that hung out of the box were beautiful, and I couldn't help but think, as Charley had, that they looked authentic. The jewelry box itself was nineteenth-century, two-tiered mahogany with a phoenix carved on top. Why a man would have a jewelry box in his bedroom was curious, but who was I to judge?

The box alone would bring as much as two grand at the auction. We were dealing with either one dumb thief or, more likely, someone on a mission for a particular item. I wasn't sure what to think about that. And how could we possibly determine whether the thief had found what he—or she, if I was right about Miranda—was looking for? So little had been cataloged.

I spent the next hour carefully going through the items that had already been logged. Charley followed me around, irritating me with his hovering. Charley's a toe tapper—one of those ADHD sorts that can't sit still. But I didn't want to hurt his feelings, so I bit my tongue and concentrated on finishing up quickly. "It looks like everything is here."

He nodded. "Good to know."

"But as I said before, Charley, I haven't cataloged most of the stuff. Something might have been stolen from the things I hadn't gotten to yet."

"Guess we'll never know."

Good to know he was watching over the town. "There are always the fingerprints, right? You guys dusted the place."

He shrugged and shook his head. "Fifty-fifty chance. If the perp had brains, he was wearing gloves anyway."

I sighed and slipped off my own gloves. "Well, I have to get my dad home."

"We still on for Anise's party?"

"Yeah. If you kept your end of the deal, I'll go. The nurse's aid is booked to stay with my dad, so I'm looking forward to it."

"Well, I kept my end, so I guess it's a date."

It wasn't anything close to a date, but I saw no reason to mention it. I was pretty sure Charley was only interested in me as a friend. "What did Anise say when you told her she could have it at the Inn?"

"She said she got Janine's RSVP that day, and she wasn't bringing a date."

"Poor Janine."

"I can't help it if I stopped having feelings for her."

"Look, Charley. When you live in a town the size of ours, you can't date a girl forever, plan to marry her, and then just dump her for no reason. It's not right. You're humiliating Janine. At least tell her why."

His gaze narrowed and I could see he wasn't a bit remorseful. "Life's too short to play by all the rules." And with that he snapped around on his black squared-off boots and headed clickety-clack across the floor.

I wasn't sure how I felt about one of Abbey Hills' three law enforcement officials not wanting to play by the rules.

I wandered through the house until I found Billy and Dad in the kitchen sitting at the incredibly old and beautifully preserved wooden table. My heart leaped into my throat at the sound of my dad's laughter.

"Hey, guys. What's so funny?"

"We're talking about old times." Billy gave me a slight shake of his head, so I knew Dad wasn't exactly in the twenty-first century. But that was okay. He was smiling, he was laughing, and I was happy with that.

Billy helped with Dad's coat. Gently, but not in a way that Dad might have gotten defensive about, like he so often did when I helped him. Billy walked us out to the Jeep. Ice had started falling again and the roads were coated.

Billy and I flanked Dad, ready to grab him if he slipped on the ice. After Dad was in his seat, safely buckled in, Billy held my elbow as if to steady me, and we walked around to the driver's side. "Be careful," he said softly. "The roads are slick. The salt trucks can't keep up with it."

"I'll go slow." Despite the weather, I was suddenly warm. Billy stood close, his arm resting over my opened door, blocking the icy wind with his broad chest. He didn't have any idea how badly he was wrecking my heart in that moment.

"The sun's about down, so watch out for black ice."

"I will." I slid into the seat and turned the key. The engine roared to life.

"You still leave your keys in the car?"

I shrugged. "I didn't mean to. I forget now and then that Abbey Hills isn't the same town we grew up in."

People used to leave their houses unlocked, windows open. It was a safe, secure town until the murders. Because I was too busy to allow those things to affect my routine, I sometimes forgot to lock doors or take keys from the ignition.

Billy's face had taken on a look of disappointment. "It's a shame. I really wanted that sort of environment for Peach."

The mention of Peach splashed me with cold, stinging more than the falling icy pellets. Not because of her. I couldn't help but like the child.

"I better get Dad home."

"Lauryn…I want to explain about Peach."

"Billy, you don't owe me an explanation."

"Yes, I do. After the way I left things graduation night."

So he did remember. My emotions couldn't quite catch up with my mind, and I held up my hand. "Not now, Billy. I need to get my dad home before this weather gets any worse."

His expression fell. "You're right. Be careful on the ice."

I pulled away from the curb. *"Be careful,"* he'd said. Even sliding on the ice, I felt safer away from Billy than the crazy hot and cold I felt when he was anywhere near me.

I jumped as "Bad Boys" blared from my phone. My ringtone for Jill. "Hey, Sheriff."

"Bad time?"

"No, well, I'm driving and it's pretty icy. I'm using the earpiece though, so if you can't hear me, that's why."

"Should you hang up and concentrate on driving?"

"I'm okay for now. Everything all right?"

"I just wondered if you were able to pinpoint anything missing from the house."

"Not that I can tell." I was approaching a stop sign soon, so I slowed the Jeep, and we started to slide a little. It wasn't too difficult to regain control.

"That's a relief."

"Too bad Mr. Chisom stayed to himself so much. If he'd had any close friends or a girlfriend who might have been in his bedroom. Someone—"

I suddenly remembered seeing Markus with a woman. I gave a little gasp as I realized who she was. "Jill! Have you talked to your sister about any of this? Didn't she hang out with him when she came back last spring?"

"No way, Lauryn." She hesitated. I knew she realized it was the best lead we were likely to come up with. "I can't put her through that."

"Well, I can."

"You don't understand what happened between them, Lauryn."

"I don't want to dredge up a bad love affair. Believe me, I am dealing with my own issues in that department, but, Jill. . ."

She released a breath. "It wasn't exactly a love affair."

"What then?"

"It's not my story to tell. But I seriously doubt Nina is going to remember anything from that house. The only thing she ever mentioned was an antique car in the garage."

Jill was obviously struggling between her loyalty to Nina and knowledge that her sister might be the only person in Abbey Hills who had spent time inside the Chisom home while Markus was still alive.

"What if I promise not to mention anything personal? All I care about are the items in the house and what she might remember from the photographs I've taken."

"We'll see."

"Okay, listen, I better pay attention to driving in this garbage. And, FYI, you might talk to the mayor about using some of my hard-earned tax money to salt the roads in ice storms."

She chuckled and I heard relief behind the levity. "I'll get on that. Talk to you later. Drive safe."

I clicked off the headset and turned my Jeep toward Cokie's house, praying the nurse's aid was home and willing to let my dad hang out with her for a while.

A few minutes later, after dropping Dad off, I headed out to the reserve, where Nina's veterinary office was located. I rationalized that I could speak with Nina alone and not involve Jill, who clearly thought her sister might have issues. But this wasn't about anyone's personal life or romance or whatever Nina's relationship might have been with Markus. Rather, I wanted to know about the actual contents of the house. I was just trying to do my job. And I had no intention of asking about their relationship.

The storm grew fierce as I drove. I squinted to see the road through the deluge. I kept the Jeep at a near crawl, suddenly feeling very stupid for risking my safety on a whim.

Through the storm, something appeared in the road ahead of me. Instinctively, I swerved. A scream pushed from my throat as the world upended.

My head slammed hard against the top of the Jeep. My dad's face flashed in my mind. "Dad!" I called out, almost expecting him to come to my rescue. Like the Superman he'd always been. Always there to come to the rescue. He'd get me out of this. Just before darkness folded over me, I realized he wasn't coming. He would never come to my rescue again. One last thought hammered in my mind: who would come to his rescue?

Ice was falling again. Amede closed her eyes, struggling against the urge to throw back her head and let out a scream. After agonizing moments, the inward volcano spilled over and she sprang to her feet, grabbed a sweater, and headed for the door. She hurried down the steps into the foyer, eyes focused on reaching the door and getting out of the house.

Through the sitting room doorway, she spotted Juliette sitting sideways in a chair next to the bay window, her legs draped over one of the arms, a book in her lap. A strand of her long black hair curled around a long, slender finger. The expression on her face was reflective and peaceful. The image caught Amede by surprise. She had never thought of Juliette as the sort to enjoy a book in front of a fire. The girl rose in Amede's estimation. Then she noticed another figure in the room. A young man carrying two mugs walked through the opposite door that led to the kitchen. Juliette looked up and color rose in her cheeks. She took one of the mugs, and her lashes swept downward, shyly. Irritation rose in Amede. She was in no mood for human mating rituals.

She spun toward the front door, and Juliette jumped. The book in her lap crashed to the floor with a thud as she set the mug on the table, stood up, and started toward the foyer. "Do you need something, Miss Amede?"

Amede waved her away. "No. I am going out for a while."

Juliette touched her fingertips to her throat. "Out? What do you... Do you need me to drive you somewhere?"

"I mean out for a walk. Alone. Do not let me interrupt you and your... friend."

The young man smiled. "Caleb Stowe."

"Caleb just checked in a few hours ago."

Amede nodded. "Then I am sure we'll run into each other sooner or later. If you'll excuse me."

But he had already walked through the room and into the foyer, hand extended. She did the polite thing and shook his hand. "Did the ice storm force you to stay at the Inn?"

"No ma'am." His gaze lingered on her face, and Amede felt like screaming. She had to get out of this house. She barely heard as he continued. "I'm on a cross-country trip to check out America's small towns. Abbey Hills seemed like an interesting one."

"Yes, well. Perhaps you'll think so. Please excuse me."

"You're going out?" Caleb glanced toward the window. "It's brutal out there."

A frenzy of need threatening to overtake manners and good sense rushed through Amede. "Yes, thank you. I enjoy inclement weather."

Juliette turned to Caleb. "Will you excuse us for a second? I need to talk to Miss Amede before she leaves."

"Sure," he said with a shrug. "Nice to meet you, ma'am."

"Yes, you too. Good evening."

To Amede's relief, he walked back into the sitting room.

"Thank God," she said to Juliette. "I thought I'd have to feed on him to get rid of him."

Juliette's eyes widened and even Amede was surprised she'd uttered the words.

"I didn't mean that, of course." She shook her head. "I'm not sure what's wrong with me. I feel like I have to feed again."

"You fed yesterday. Grandmere said every three days at the most."

"Don't you think I know that?" Amede snapped, then forced herself calm. "I apologize. I am not myself."

"If you go out, will you be able to control where you feed?"

"What do you... Oh." She wanted to be insulted but knew it was a fair question. "I'll be fine."

"Do you need the car?"

Amede shook her head. "I'm going to run."

"I'll wait up for you in case you need something when you get back."

Amede nodded. "I have to go now." She opened the door and stepped out onto the porch.

Amede headed directly for the field behind the house where she'd witnessed deer, rabbit, and squirrels roaming for the past few days.

She had been so intent upon escaping the house that she failed to notice a young woman getting out of an SUV. She wore a restaurant uniform of some sort. Amede's keen senses reeled with the stench of grease, barbeque, and fruit pies. Offensive smells. Amede stepped back as the girl sashayed forward, grinning, showing big white teeth and deep dimples in either cheek. "Hi!" she said, her ponytail bouncing as she walked. "I'm looking for Charley. Seen him around?"

"I'm afraid I do not know anyone by that name." Amede's head ached from hunger. The vein in the girl's neck pulsed, driving her to distraction.

"Seriously? Charley owns the Inn."

"Oh. Of course."

"Yeah. He was supposed to meet me after my shift at work, and I was afraid he might have been in a wreck in this stuff." She waved toward the sky at the falling ice. "He drives way too fast. But there's no one in the ditch between here and town. So I assumed he was here."

"If I see him, I will mention your visit."

"Oh, there's no need. I'll just wait for a while." She stepped toward the Inn and stopped. "Are you coming? It's pretty nasty out for a walk around the grounds."

The door jerked open and Juliette walked onto the porch. "Oh, hi.

Didn't I see you at Barney's earlier? Better get inside before you freeze." She looked past the young woman to Amede. "Everything okay, Miss Amede?"

"Yes, just getting something from the car."

Carefully controlling the frenzy growing inside of her, Amede presented a chilly smile. She couldn't leave the property on foot while the girl watched, and going for a drive made no sense on such a night. The one thing she had learned in all of her years was never give anyone a reason to suspect you. She turned back to the house. "I believe I left it in my room, come to think of it."

Juliette carefully ushered the waitress away from Amede as she walked back inside. A smart girl, that Juliette.

Amede forced herself to walk calmly and gracefully up the steps. Once in her room, she locked the door and headed for the balcony. She jumped, floated to the ground, and landed on her feet. Then she raced toward the field. She hadn't felt hunger like this in years, had forgotten how strong the compulsion could be.

Her mind raced back to the vein on the waitress's neck. Pulsing. She shook away the image as eyes glowed at her in the dark. A slow smile tipped her lips as she began the hunt.

CHAPTER SEVEN

I got my act together for a little while during eighth grade. Ms. Davis, the new history teacher, arrived in Abbey Hills. She was youngish, the "carpe diem" sort of teacher Robin Williams was in Dead Poets Society. I loved her right away, and with my penchant for the old days, she took a special interest in me. I was thrilled when she attended an auction my dad conducted. I loved introducing my two favorite people to each other. I was not prepared for the sparks between them. The day of their first date was the last day I could stand Ms. Davis. It was also my last decent grade in her class. I wasn't about to give her the satisfaction. Clearly, she had used me to meet the town's most eligible bachelor.

Hunger burned so deeply she felt if she looked down she would find a large gaping hole where her stomach should have been. She moved from side to side, trying to ease the ache, but nothing helped. Reaching up, she grabbed at her hair.

She sensed that she wasn't alone.

"Who's there?" she whispered. She hadn't heard him come down.

"Who is it? Answer me." Fear gripped her in the dark silence.

"Please, someone. Answer me."

M y head ached and I felt the cold down to my bones as I came to consciousness, not quite sure of my surroundings. I opened my eyes and discovered I was lying on the steering wheel. Then it came rushing back to me. The thing in the road, then sliding into the ditch.

I reached forward, wincing at the pain in my shoulder, and switched on the ignition. The Jeep sputtered but refused to start.

So stupid. Why did I think it was a good idea to drive to the veterinary clinic in such horrible weather? I should have waited until tomorrow after the salt crews did their job and cleared the roads. I was impulsive and stupid.

Relief rendered me weak as I saw headlights coming down the highway. My headlights were still on, so I clicked the high beam on and off a few times. Hopefully whoever was coming would see the flicker even from the ditch.

The slow-moving vehicle slid to a stop. In a matter of minutes the glow of a flashlight shone in my face. "Lauryn? Is that you?" It was Charley's voice.

"Yes, it's me." Who else would it be?

"Are you okay? I called in the wreck. The ambulance is on the way."

"Oh, Charley, you dummy. I don't need an ambulance. I just hit my head on the steering wheel. I'll be fine. But my Jeep won't start."

He opened the door and pushed something to my head. I pulled back. It was a cloth. He pressed it back against my head. "Don't be stubborn. You have to get checked out. You have a big gash on your head. What happened anyway?"

"There was something in the road and I slammed on the brakes."

"Looks like you hit a deer."

"I didn't hit anything. I saw it in the road and slammed on the brakes. It was already down."

"Here, take the bandana and keep pressure exactly where I have it. I'll be right back."

Charley was gone for a few minutes. When he returned, he seemed shaken.

"What is it?" I asked.

"A deer, the second one in two days."

"And I didn't hit it, right?"

"You didn't."

"What was it doing in the road?"

He released a frustrated breath. "You can't let this get out."

"What?"

"Last night the General found a dead deer on Nina's doorstep."

"Nina? I don't get the connection. How did a deer end up dead—"

"I can't tell you everything. But it has to do with those killings last spring. Or, at least it was the same sort of killing."

Those killings. When his sister was murdered. He wasn't acting very emotional about it, and that worried me more than if he'd been freaking out. I reached out and took his hand. "Are you okay?"

His eyes widened in surprise. "Why wouldn't I be?"

"Charley? Don't be a tough guy, okay? Talk to me if you need to."

"It's fine. I'm over Mandy's death. This is a new investigation. But don't mention it. We don't need a bunch of reporters back here or people starting to panic."

"That's certainly true. Especially when we're trying to have a good auction." My head throbbed and my fingers were stuck to the now-soaked bandana. "I feel a little dizzy."

"Lean your head back, but don't fall asleep. I'm going to call and see what's keeping Jeremy." Jeremy was the local first responder. As soon as the ambulance was called, he should have come and assessed the situation until the ambulance arrived. Especially since he lived along this highway.

I heard the ambulance siren. And then the next thing I knew, I was in a gurney and they were carrying me. My stomach started to churn.

"Charley!" I called out.

"He's gone."

"Can you hand me a cell phone? My dad has Alzheimer's. I need to call his caregiver."

Someone handed me a phone and, in a fog, I punched in Cokie's number. She assured me everything was fine and instructed me to take care of myself. She would take him home and stay there with him so he wouldn't be disoriented.

I settled back in the ambulance and braced myself for the forty-five-minute drive that I was certain would stretch to at least two hours on these icy roads.

I dozed, dreaming of ritual sacrifices and people in black hoods with chalices filled with blood.

I woke with a jolt and realized the gurney was moving. The blue and red lights of the hospital drew closer, and then the nurses took over.

Two hours later, I lay in a hospital bed with ten stitches and a concussion. I fussed, but the doctor insisted I stay overnight so they could make sure I wasn't hurt worse than they imagined.

Reluctantly I called Cokie with the news. I promised to compensate her for spending the night, listened to her become indignant at the very suggestion, and then teared up when she said she loved me.

Jill picked me up from the hospital the next day. My headache gave me a constant reminder that I had a concussion, but otherwise I was fine.

The roads had cleared overnight, and by the time Jill and I were driving back to Abbey Hills, it seemed unbelievable they were the same roads I'd skated across the night before.

"Charley confessed to telling you about the deer last night."

I nodded. "And the one the night before."

Jill was suddenly serious. "Okay, the deer in the road was killed the same way the animals were killed last spring. You remember how that was?"

"Yes. And Charley told me that too."

"Listen, Lauryn, I can't give you all the details, but this is serious, and I'm afraid Abbey Hills may be in danger of more killings. I don't mean just animals. Not that animal killings aren't horrible enough. But I think it's just a matter of time before this escalates like last spring."

My body went hot and cold all at once as her words took me back to the way the town had panicked over the murders of Amanda and Carrie. Back then I was so focused on rounding up small auctions to oversee and writing articles for magazines that I hadn't given myself the luxury of mourning. Not even for Amanda, my one-time school chum.

The expedient thing had been taking care of my dad during the most startling days of his decline. I had heard about the murders. But I somehow checked out and didn't allow myself to take it personally. I refused to believe the murders were going to affect me. And they hadn't. Not really. Maybe this was my punishment for being so self-absorbed before. This time the universe would make sure I paid close attention to what was going on.

"So, throat cut, blood drained..." I swallowed hard.

"Exactly the same. The reason I insisted on picking you up when Billy offered was because I think it's important for you to be protected. I'm afraid going through Markus Chisom's things has stirred something up. I don't know how we can move forward with that. I don't want to take a chance on more people getting killed."

Pressing past the offhand comment that Billy had offered to get me from the hospital, I voiced my worry. "Do you think the deer are a warning to stop the auction?" The thought sickened me. I had gambled everything on this sale. I'd even taken out a mortgage on the house to hold us over until the estate sale.

Jill sighed. "I think so. I'd stop the thing if it were up to me, but the mayor says no."

I tried not to show how relieved I was. "We'll have to get some security."

Jill nodded. "There are a couple of security companies in Springfield. I'm getting some bids. We'll install an alarm system."

"Good."

"And I don't want you working over there alone. Especially after dark."

I opened my mouth to protest, but she held up her hand. "Even the mayor agrees with me on that point."

"Jill, you're a cop, for Pete's sake. Are you going to coordinate your duty schedule with a big strong man too?"

"That's different. I'm a police officer. I'm trained to deal with this sort of thing."

"I have a black belt in karate." Okay, yellow. Still, I could yell and flip someone over my shoulder if he came at me from behind, and I could kick him in the groin if he came at me from the front. What more did a girl need to protect herself? I had mace too.

Jill gave me a dubious raise of her brow.

I acquiesced. "Well, I didn't get quite to black, but I do carry a gun. You know that. I went through your concealed carry training."

"You barely passed."

"They moved the targets on me."

That look again. I scowled. Who was I kidding? I would be lucky to defend myself against an aggressive dog much less a maniacal ritualistic serial killer.

"Fine, I'll leave the house before it gets dark."

She gave me a satisfied smile and nodded.

"Another thing. My sister's willing to talk to you about Markus and the house. I assume you were headed out there when you rolled the Jeep?"

"Yeah."

"Dumb, but it did prove to Nina how important it is that we fill you in on everything."

"Great. When?"

"She'll be out of town until next week. Going to have Thanksgiving with her ex-husband and their children."

"That's chummy of them to stay so friendly."

"They're engaged again."

"I don't suppose you want to fill me in? On the Markus thing, not the reengagement."

She shook her head. "Like I said, it's her story to tell. I just pray it all ends with the deer. I'm not sure what will happen to Abbey Hills if we lose another person in our community to murder."

I knew the weight of responsibility was on her since she was the local law sworn to protect and serve. I reached out to take her hand. "Let's not borrow trouble."

She nodded. "You're right. But the thought of it starting all over again. Why is God allowing it to happen here?"

I squeezed her hand and let go. "I don't really know, Jill." I didn't know why God did most of the things He did. But if I could have a face-to-face with Him, I'd sure as heck ask a lot of questions. First about taking my mom and second about why He had to take my dad too. Did He just think it was funny messing with my life, or was He really so detached from humanity that He didn't realize what was going on?

The pain meds kicked in by the time Jill pulled into my driveway, and I barely made it to my bed before passing out. When I woke up, the sky had brightened and the distinct smell of breakfast wafted to my room. I smiled, grateful I had at least one thing I could count on—Cokie's unfailing love and support. I had no idea what I'd have done without her.

Juliette could barely enjoy the rising sun as she stood on the porch, cell phone in hand, listening. Grandmere's voice made her all the more homesick for New Orleans. She hated every second of her time in Abbey Hills.

"Grandmere, I have no idea when Amede plans to come home. The woman she came to see hasn't been available so far."

"Have patience, hon. It won't last forever."

"It seems like it's already been forever."

"I hope you're hiding this attitude from Amede. You know your duty."

She kicked at the wooden porch. "Yes, Grandmere," she replied impatiently. "How could I not know? You've been drumming it into my brain since my mother died."

"You're the only one. There's nothing to be done about it." Her voice was firm but held a hint of sympathy that was just enough for Juliette to recognize. Grandmere must have suffered her own resentment from time to time.

"I know you're right," she said. "I'll try not to complain."

"Good girl. Now, what is happening that has you so troubled, besides the obvious?"

Juliette caught her breath. "How did you know?"

"I know you are troubled and it has nothing to do with being so inconvenienced. This is about fear. I can feel it."

Sometimes Juliette forgot her grandmere's origins in voodoo. Juliette had never embraced the religion, choosing instead to be neutral about all religions. But Grandmere and most of the Morioux women dating back as far as Eden's mother had embraced the arts. Some were given to black magic, but Grandmere had never used her gifts for harm, at least that Juliette knew of. And if she had, Juliette didn't want to know.

"Well?" Grandmere asked.

"Amede had an episode."

"What sort of episode?"

Choosing her words carefully, Juliette cleared her throat before trying to explain. "It was like uncontrollable hunger. It was a little scary. I thought she was going to attack a girl who came to the inn."

"Well, I've told you she can't go more than three days without blood. She will get aggressive, argumentative. It's like going through withdrawal from a drug."

"I know, Grandmere." Juliette realized her tone sounded impatient, but she had been so nervous about Amede harming a human that she wasn't sleeping well.

"Perhaps you'd better tell me exactly what is happening."

Juliette relayed the events of the other night. "Last night, she went out again. Grandmere, I'm worried about her. She paces her room. She's agitated almost as though she's claustrophobic."

"Juliette," Grandmere said cautiously. "I want you to listen carefully."

"Yes?"

"You mustn't leave Amede alone. She won't hurt you because of the oath. No matter how she threatens, you do not need to be afraid. Is that clear?"

"You're freaking me out a little bit, Grandmere. What am I supposed to do?"

"Just be sure you don't leave her. She only reacts this way when another vampire is close. It's like the way dogs get a little crazy when wolves are near. Only worse."

Juliette felt her heart jump into her throat. Another vampire wouldn't be bound by the oath. "Are you telling me she's going primal?"

"In a manner of speaking, yes, and mainly because she doesn't drink human blood. Vampires who drink human blood are more bestial. That animalistic quality draws her. She must be made aware of what is happening and she will do her best to control herself." She drew a breath, but Juliette could hear her voice shaking. "I will overnight an herb potion. It will help calm her."

Relief washed over Juliette.

"Will she recognize the other vampire?"

"Most definitely. I've seen Amede around many vampires who drink human blood, but the only one she's ever had a strong reaction to was Eden."

Juliette felt her stomach turn over. "Eden? Do you think she's here?"

"I would almost bet on it. I have to go. Grandpapa needs me."

"Give him my love."

"I will. Remember, don't leave her alone. Call me if anything else occurs."

Juliette promised, and they ended the call.

She hated the idea of being at Amede's beck and call twenty-four seven. It was bad enough when she didn't need constant supervision.

She turned to go inside but stopped short as she found Caleb sitting on the wicker porch swing, staring at her. "How long have you been there?" she asked, her stomach twisting at the fear he might have heard her conversation. She was not allowed to give away Amede's secret for any reason.

"I took a stroll around the house. There's a pretty nice trail back there." He jammed his thumb toward the side of the house. "I came up from the side steps." He smiled. "I'm sorry for interrupting your solitude."

Relieved, she returned his smile. "You didn't really. I was heading back inside."

"How about a walk? We could try out the trail together."

She wanted to say yes, but her grandmere's warning burned in her ears. "I wish I could, but I have to go check and make sure Miss Dastillion has everything she needs."

"She keeps you hopping."

Juliette felt a sudden, surprising resentment. She didn't care how good-looking, tall, dark, and mysterious he was, what did he know about her responsibility to Amede Dastillion? "Yes, she does. But I'm her assistant. It's my job to look after her."

"True. Well, enjoy your day, little assistant." He sent her a wink and flashed white, straight teeth. "Hopefully we'll have some time to talk later."

Suddenly shy, Juliette averted her gaze and nodded. "I'd like that. But I have to go now."

She hurried inside, breathless and wishing it were later so she could join Caleb in the sitting room and have a few minutes to enjoy herself, away from the craziness of looking after a primal vampire.

She knocked on Amede's door and got no answer. Knocked again; still no answer. She pulled out her phone and dialed her number. The line went straight to voice mail.

"Hey, if you're looking for the lady staying in that room, she left earlier."

The man two doors down lugged his suitcase out the door.

Juliette peered at the man. She hadn't ever really paid attention to him thus far. "You saw her?"

He nodded. "Yeah, I came in from the fitness room when she was leaving."

"Did you notice whether she walked or drove?"

He nodded his head. "Drove a black Town Car."

"Oh my…"

"Everything okay?"

"No. I mean, yes. I mean, thank you for the information." She ran down the stairs and rushed outside. The car was gone. How could she have not noticed?

"Change your mind?" Caleb still sat where he'd been five minutes earlier.

She shook her head. "Caleb, I need a favor. My boss is missing. I think she went into town."

"What can I do for you?"

"I have to find her. She…she forgot her medicine and could hurt herself if she doesn't have it."

He stood and gave her a lazy grin. "Sure. My pleasure. Amede is lucky to have such a dedicated assistant. Come on. We'll find her."

Juliette slid into his black Mustang. The car smelled of new leather and cologne. If only she weren't on a mission she might have relaxed and enjoyed the few moments with a hot guy.

But her mind conjured up the image of Amede tearing up Abbey Hills, leaving one dead body after another.

If Amede harmed anyone, it would be on Juliette's hands.

CHAPTER EIGHT

Ms. Davis caught on to my temper tantrum sooner than Dad did. She detained me after school one day about three months after she started seeing my dad. I could tell she was hurt but also determined as she sat me down and tried to have a heart-to-heart. Poor lady didn't know who she was dealing with. I'd been biding my time, waiting for the right moment, and that day, luck was with me.

"I know you're not happy that I'm dating your dad."

"I don't know what you're talking about, Ms. Davis." I smacked my gum and she closed her eyes for a moment.

"Then maybe we should schedule some tutoring sessions. Otherwise you're not going to pass this class. And you know you have to pass or take summer school."

The threat wasn't idle and I knew she wasn't being mean, but I used it to my advantage just the same. At home that night, I talked to Dad about it.

"Ms. Davis said if I didn't chill out about your relationship with her I wasn't going to pass history."

Dad put down his paper and stared at me. "I'm sure you misunderstood."

I shrugged. "Yeah, probably." I kissed him good night and started to leave the living room.

"Wait, kid." He patted the footstool and I walked back and sank down at his feet. "Tell me everything."

Inwardly, I smiled. I repeated the entire conversation—my version, at least. In the end, they had a huge fight and I got my dad back.

She had never seen things in shades of gray. She'd always followed her heart and never regretted anything she'd done. Her survival, her happiness mattered most. She was what she was. How could she apologize for obeying her natural instincts? How could anyone even ask her to? Did man ask a lion to apologize for stalking its prey?

During those whirlwind days before the war, before the harbors were closed, when New Orleans was the port for King Cotton and French silks, Amede's world and Eden's were much different. Three years younger than Eden's fifteen years, Amede enjoyed a life consisting of music lessons, art lessons, tutors, and preparation for running a home. Eden's life, though Papa tried to interest her in those things, was much different. Her interest diverted from lessons to her mother's lifestyle.

Eventually, her mother gave in and began to teach her the black arts. Night after night she attended the rituals, assisted her mother in the incantations and spells. The voodoo rituals, the beating drums, the slaughtered animals and wild dancing filled Eden's dreams, and she awoke craving the spilled blood. When she finally gave in and consumed the blood of a sacrificed chicken, her mama hadn't been surprised, hadn't seemed concerned. Instead, Mama took her to Papa and he told her the truth.

"You'll be strong and young and you won't age past the appearance of thirty, as long as you consume blood." He didn't speak to Eden of human blood, but she instinctively knew the strength she gained from animals was much less than she would receive from humans.

Nearly a year later, by chance, she observed him returning home close to dawn. Blood stained his clothing. After that, she hid and watched as he slipped out of the house in the dead of night a couple of times a week. And she knew…

A few weeks later, she begged him to take her hunting. Finally he agreed, and together they ravaged the docks where the weak and homeless lived. The drunkards and prostitutes. She never felt remorse, though she could feel Papa's. He admonished her not to harm the innocent, especially children.

"There are angels for children. Angels that go before God and intercede on their behalf. Stick to murderers, drunkards, liars—those who are already an abomination to God—and perhaps there will be absolution for your sins."

He took her to a priest, but her confession had the cowardly man shaking in his boots. She had never been afraid of God since. Until now. What would she face when death finally came?

I popped the Tylenol 3 while I waited for Charley to pick me up and drive me to the Chisom house.

"I think you should stay in bed today," Cokie scolded. She poured me a cup of coffee and set it down catty-corner from her own cup. "Lauryn, you know the doctor didn't mean for you to go back to work so soon."

"He said as I felt like it." I had to admit I would rather stay in bed and sleep, but with Thanksgiving this week, Cokie would be off Thursday and there was no way I could take Dad to the Chisom house for a day of research and cataloging sale items. So as much as my head ached, I had no choice but to make the most of the available time.

"What if the sheriff's right, Lauryn?" Cokie's worry-lined eyes searched my face.

"About the killings?" I shrugged, not because I didn't care, but because there was nothing I could do about it.

"I just don't think you should be at that house alone."

"I'll keep the doors locked, and sometime this week the security people will be installing an alarm. I'll be safe. Besides, Charley will be in and out and so will Jill."

At the sound of Charley's name Cokie frowned.

"What's that about?" I asked.

She looked up with innocent eyes.

"You know, the look you get when I mention Charley?"

She shrugged and grimaced. "Well, I just think he's a little strange, that's all."

"You would be too if you'd lost your sister the way he lost his. It was brutal."

"It was a terrible thing to happen." She sipped her coffee and set it down. "But Charley was already odd. Don't you think? The murder just made him worse."

Cokie was usually such a good judge of character that I couldn't get over her uneasiness about Charley. But he was my friend; he had been good to me.

"Maybe I know him a little better than you do," I said. "We've known each other since we were pretty young."

"He hasn't always lived in Abbey Hills?"

I shook my head. "His father grew up here, but he went away to college, married Charley's mother, and they had a family. I don't remember them visiting. But after Charley's grandmother passed away, the Inn fell to his father. The family moved here and has run the Inn ever since."

"How old was Charley?"

"Ten I think." I frowned, trying to remember Charley's first day of school. "Fifth grade."

Charley knocked and I started to get up, but Cokie waved me back into my seat. "Finish your coffee and eat that bagel. He can wait a few minutes."

Charley didn't seem to mind. He helped himself to a bagel and allowed Cokie to bring him a cup of coffee. "Hello, Mr. McBride," he said to Dad. As usual, Dad pretended to know who Charley was. Charley went along with it, which made me smile, and even Cokie seemed to soften to him for a little while.

"How is your fiancée, Charley? I haven't seen much of her these days."

Charley tensed. "We broke up awhile back."

Cokie's eyebrows went up and she looked at me. I'd get an earful later for not filling her in. But the whole town knew. The only reason Cokie didn't was because she refused to go out to eat. I admired her frugal ways, but you can't keep up with the town gossip if you don't go where the town gossip lives and breathes.

"Anyway," I said, sipping the last of my coffee. "Ready to go, Charley?"

He had grown uncomfortable and nodded eagerly, shoveling down the rest of his bagel.

I kissed Dad good-bye, suffered a short homework lecture, and then Charley and I walked to his truck.

"Trent on duty at the station today?"

He nodded. "And Jill. She wants two of us on at a time, so we'll be rotating double shifts for a while."

"I guess that's a good idea."

He helped me climb in. "How's your head?"

"It's okay for now."

"Soon as I drop you off, Billy and I are going to get your truck."

My heart leaped at the sound of Billy's name. "I appreciate it. I just hope it won't take much to get it running again."

"I'm going to take my tow chain and see what we can figure out."

"Thanks, Charley."

"So, what's the deal with Billy Fuller? I figured he'd be coming around more." Charley turned the key in the ignition and the truck purred. Charley wasn't an old truck kind of guy. He liked new and shiny.

"He's only been back a few days."

Charley shrugged. "I'd have already asked you out by now."

"Well, Billy and I never dated, Charley, so why would he?" I gave a short laugh.

"Want me to ask him?"

"Uh, no, what are we, in high school?" My heart raced because I knew Charley, and he just might have done something crazy like that. "I don't have time for drama in my life. My dad takes all my focus."

He reached over and put his hand on my shoulder. It was warm and reassuring. "Your dad seems to be holding his own."

"His mind is going away. I don't even feel comfortable taking a nap when Cokie isn't there to keep an eye on him."

"What the—" Charley's cry took me aback until I followed his gaze and realized he wasn't responding to my comment. "Stay in the truck," he commanded. A crowd milled around the parking lot of Barney's Café. Jill's patrol car was there, lights flashing, and Trent tried to back people away.

I started to get out of the truck, but before my foot hit the pavement, Miranda jumped in front of me. "What happened?"

"I don't know. I was just going over there when you gave me a heart attack."

A frown creased her brow. "I didn't mean over there. I already know there's some dead guy in a truck. I meant your head."

My stomach rolled over at her easy words. "I had an accident Saturday night. What guy? Do you know?"

She shook her head. "Want me to go find out for you?"

"No thanks." I scowled at her. I didn't enjoy being irritated so early in the morning. But she didn't have to go far to get on my nerves. "I'll find out for myself."

She followed me as I walked through the crowd. "Do you know who it is?" I asked as I reached the General, a grizzled old-timer who was a fixture in Abbey Hills. He glanced at my head and nodded. "Jeremy, the first responder who lives out my way."

I cringed, remembering how upset Charley got when Jeremy didn't show up to my accident.

"I guess now we know why he didn't respond to Charley's 9-1-1 call."

I didn't even bother to ask the General how he knew about that. The General knew just about everything that happened in Abbey Hills pretty much the minute it happened.

Charley scanned the crowd, arms raised. "Okay, folks, head back into the café or drive away, but don't stay here loitering in Barney's parking lot unless you want me to start writing tickets."

"Big bad deputy," Miranda whispered. "You know the dead guy died the same way as the animals."

The delight in her voice chilled my blood.

"I wish I could get a photo of it for my Web site."

"Miranda!" I turned on her, anger burning in me. "That man is some-one's husband, son, and brother. He was three weeks away from becoming a father for the first time. This isn't something to gloat over."

"All right. Sheesh." She averted her gaze. "Don't get yourself worked up. I'm sorry, okay? It's just. . .interesting."

Charley's face had gone ashen. He had no business directing the traffic here. Especially since no one was paying any attention anyway. I made my way to Jill. She looked at me, her face as white as Charley's. "Believe me now?"

"Look, I need to get Charley out of here, but he's not going to leave until the crowd is under control. Do you think you can do something?"

Her eyebrows rose as if she had just noticed Charley was even there. "Yeah. We definitely need to get him away from here."

She got her bullhorn and went to work dispelling the crowd. Ten min-utes later, Charley sat shaking in the driver's seat of his truck.

"Want me to drive?" I asked.

He shook his head. "Give me a second. I'll be okay."

"Listen, Charley. Do you think you should take a leave of absence until things get solved?"

Ignoring the question, he started the engine and carefully pulled out. Miranda's red hair flashed through the window at Barney's and I thought back to her callous statement. "Did Jill question her about the break-in?"

He nodded. "She has an alibi. Was nowhere near the place and there are plenty of witnesses to prove it."

"I find that hard to believe."

"It is what it is. Ever think someone might have been framing her? Using her words against her?"

"Like who, for instance?" I asked. "I was the only person who heard her say she jimmied the lock and they'd have to catch her doing it in order to arrest her."

He shrugged, clearly much less interested in a break-in than he would have been an hour ago.

When he pulled up to the curb in front of the Chisom house, I didn't get out. Charley looked awful and I hated to leave him to drive off alone given the horrible thing he'd just witnessed.

"Hey, are you going to be okay?"

Turning to face me, Charley let down his guard and his eyes filled with tears. "No matter what I do, I can't save anyone."

"Charley, you can't take the responsibility all on yourself." I searched for words to say, but anything I thought of seemed so trite. "I feel safe knowing you're looking out for me."

"What good did I do Amanda or Jeremy?" He slammed his fists against the steering wheel.

I jumped at his sudden movement and he turned, sorrow clouding his eyes. "I'm sorry, Lauryn. I'm just frustrated. All the killing. It's just...I don't know, we have to find a way to make it stop before more people die." He opened his door. "Come on, I'm going to walk you inside and make sure everything is secure before I drive over to get Billy."

"Why are you going to pick up Billy?"

"I told you, we're going to get your Jeep out of the ditch." He shook his head. "Listen much?"

"Charley, you don't need to do that now. Maybe you should just—"

"Let me decide what's best for me, Lauryn."

I held up my palms. "Sorry."

We barely talked while he searched the house from top to bottom, the protective friend and brother figure I'd missed since my dad stopped being sound enough to play the part.

When he headed to the door I followed and wrapped my arms around him. "I appreciate your friendship, Charley."

He grabbed on to me, holding me tight. "Same here, Lauryn. I'm sorry I snapped at you. This is tougher than I want to admit." He kept holding on, long past the natural place to end the embrace. "Helping you helps me feel better. Okay? So let me."

"Okay." I pulled back and smiled at him.

He walked outside and waited.

I stared at him.

"I'm not leaving the porch until you lock the door."

"Take care, Charley." I closed the door and twisted the lock, and he walked away, the sound of his boots thumping on the sidewalk.

The hunger finally settled by the time Amede received her tea. She hadn't left the café during the uproar outside. Experience had taught her that it was always best not to become part of the crowd. Particularly if photographs were being taken.

As the patrons were filtering back in, her server finally brought the tea she had requested twenty minutes ago. The girl looked familiar and seemed to have recognized Amede. "Oh, you were at the Inn the other night, weren't you?"

The pulsing vein. Now she remembered.

"Yes, I thought I recognized you." Amede smiled. "Did you find Deputy Baylor?"

The girl's face turned pink and she shook her head. "I waited but he never showed up. I found out he was tending an accident."

"I see."

"Can I bring you something besides tea? Breakfast?"

"I would love a fruit plate if you have one."

The girl gave a gentle smile. "I'm sure we can put one together for you."

"Thank you." Amede should have felt guilty, but all she wanted to do was sink her fangs into that plump, rolling vein.

She pulled out her laptop as the girl walked away. Since the ice storm the Inn's wireless hadn't been functional, and the manager didn't seem to have the authority to fix anything without Charley's approval.

Before she could click on her e-mail, a breathless Juliette slid into the booth across from her. "Miss Amede, what have you done?"

Her eyebrow rose at the insolent tone. One thing she wouldn't abide was arrogance from her servants. "I've ordered a cup of tea and a fruit plate. Do you not approve, Juliette?"

"You know what I mean."

Amede frowned, then realized the silly girl thought she had killed that poor man in the parking lot. "You know better than that." She smiled and shook her head, thinking that Roma would have a good laugh over her granddaughter's foolishness.

"We need to talk."

"Actually, I need to have my breakfast and my tea in peace." Amede narrowed her gaze and spoke with a tone that left no room for doubt. "If you are going to insist upon speaking to me in that manner, you may find another place to sit."

Juliette lowered her gaze respectfully. "I'm sorry, Miss Amede."

"That's better. Now, what's wrong?"

She cast a furtive glance around the room. "I think it best to wait until we're alone."

"Fine, then if you don't mind, I'd like to check my e-mail. I see I have one from your grandmother."

Juliette's eyes grew big. "From Grandmere?"

"Yes, and the subject line is 'Eden.'" Amede smiled. She glanced up at Juliette. "Somehow, she always knows."

"Knows what?"

Amede lowered her voice. "When I'm sensing Eden is close."

She opened the e-mail.

Amede,

Juliette is concerned at the way you've been behaving. Now, don't be upset with my granddaughter for noticing. But you've been hungrier, more agitated, fierce even. You know those symptoms. I have a calming potion made from swamp root and herbs. It's on the way to you overnight and should arrive tomorrow. I have made offering for the potion and if you drink it in a tea, it will soothe you. In the meantime, be careful and allow Juliette to care for you.

Roma

She glanced up from the e-mail. Stood suddenly, closed her laptop. "Let's go."

She tossed cash for her uneaten meal and a generous tip on the table.

The server stopped short, carrying a plate of fruit. "I am sorry," Amede said. "We must go. Something has come up suddenly."

"Do you want me to put it in a to-go—"

The door closing behind them cut off her words. Amede didn't speak until they reached the car. She handed Juliette the keys and climbed into the backseat without waiting for Juliette to open her door.

Juliette got into the driver's seat and slid the key into the ignition, bringing the car to life. "I'm sorry, Miss Amede. I only mean to protect you."

"If I am so obvious, I'd better close myself in my room until tomorrow when Roma's tea arrives."

"You're not angry, then?"

"You called your grandmother when you noticed changes in my demeanor?"

Juliette nodded.

"That was the right thing to do. It shows good sense that you would call for help from someone who knows best. You will serve me well." Amede wondered at the look on the girl's face. She didn't seem pleased. "Have I offended you, Juliette?"

"No ma'am. I'm concerned with getting you back home. That's all. I... I thank you for your confidence in me."

"Good. Now, today you must call Miss McBride and set up a meeting with her for sometime after tomorrow."

"After tomorrow?"

"Well, I best not meet her until I have given the tea time to get into my system."

"But Thursday is Thanksgiving, Miss Amede."

"Yes?" Amede frowned as Juliette stared at her in the rearview mirror and the car swerved over the centerline.

"I take it we are to spend Thanksgiving in Abbey Hills?"

"Well, I hadn't really thought that far ahead, but, yes, I suppose."

"All right then, I'll make arrangements for the holiday here."

Amede glanced up just as Juliette looked into the mirror again. Her eyes flashed dark. And for a moment, Amede could have sworn she looked exactly like Eden.

CHAPTER NINE

The summer after tenth grade, I got a job as a lifeguard at the public pool. I loved the red Baywatch uniform and felt pretty hot as the guys checked me out and teased me about pretending to drown, which they did regularly.

Billy spent almost every day at the pool, and we finally made up from the seventh grade dance misunderstanding that I never admitted was due to my own stubbornness. One day after a long afternoon in the sun, I stood outside talking, laughing, and goofing off with Billy when Dad pulled up to take me home.

"Hey, Lars," Billy called.

"Yeah?"

"Can I call you later?"

I shrugged. "It's supposed to be a free country." I repeated what my dad always said.

"So is that a yes or a no?"

I gave him a cryptic, hopefully sexy smile. "You figure it out."

Dad was frowning when I got in the car and buckled up. "Who's that?"

"Billy Fuller."

"Preacher's kid?"

I nodded.

"You going all Holy Roller on me now?"

Embarrassment warmed my cheeks. "No way!"

"Well, you watch out for preachers' boys. They're so repressed they only want one thing."

"Okay, Dad."

When Billy called that night, Dad was sitting there, pretending not to listen, so I blew Billy off with a lame excuse about needing to do laundry.

He didn't call again or come back to the pool the rest of the summer.

Eden grabbed her stomach, listening closely for the sound of his boots on the ground above. She knew he would come today. She could feel the gnawing hunger and knew Amede was near. Excitement settled over her. Amede would find her, and when she did, he would be sorry for everything he'd done. She smiled as she heard him coming. Amede was a secret she would keep from him. No matter how much he hurt her.

Cokie and her daughter, Cara, came to our house for Thanksgiving dinner. Cokie did most of the cooking, but I peeled potatoes and Cara baked pumpkin pie, so we were all feeling pretty darned proud of ourselves by the time we sat down to a turkey with all the trimmings.

After the week we'd had, between the animal killings and Jeremy's murder and my accident, I desperately needed a good day, and I was so glad Cokie had decided to stay in Abbey Hills and spend the day with us.

She normally spent holidays with her family in St. Louis. But this year, she just didn't feel up to a five-hour drive twice in four days. So of course she insisted on coming over and cooking. In return, I insisted on buying the turkey and all the trimmings. Normally, Dad and I would drive to Branson for seafood on Thanksgiving and Christmas. I wasn't a bad cook, but we had never been into such a big meal just for two.

Cokie and Cara's presence made the day special. It was an opportunity to pretend my family was more than just Dad and me. By two in the afternoon, we were all stuffed and lazy. Dad went to his bedroom for a nap, and I settled Cokie in front of the television and made her put her feet up while Cara and I cleaned up the dining room and kitchen.

An old 1940s Christmas movie was playing when I came into the living room. I stretched out on the couch to watch and quickly dozed.

I awakened to shuffling, thumping, and grunts from Dad. Panic ignited in my gut, but then I remembered Cokie was there. If Dad was up and around, so was she. I sat up slowly. My head still felt sluggish from the Tylenol I took after dinner.

I found Cokie, Cara, and Dad on the other side of the couch in the middle of a clutter of boxes and tubs marked "Christmas decorations." It took me a minute to orient myself, and then I realized what was happening. Dad always started decorating for Christmas the day after Thanksgiving. His nap must have fooled him into thinking a day had passed.

Cokie looked up and rolled her eyes. "He insisted we get started now. Sorry we woke you."

I shrugged and glanced at the clock. "A two-hour nap is long enough for anyone."

"It's about time you woke up, sleepyhead." Dad's voice was edged with excitement, almost giddy. He stood over the biggest box, the one that held our artificial tree.

I used to envy Billy Fuller because his parents made a tradition of waiting until the first snow after Thanksgiving or the first Saturday in December (whichever came first) and driving out to the two hundred acres owned by the Fuller family. They would cut down their tree, take it home, have hot chocolate and banana bread, and then decorate. It wasn't until a few years into adulthood that I realized it wasn't the tree or the tradition that made me covet Billy's ceremony. It was his mom. He had one to fill up the space only a mother can fill, and I didn't. My dad could have made hot chocolate and banana bread—although he never did—but a child dreams of that slender hand reaching forward with a warm slice of bread, then stirring in extra milk to cool down a steaming cup of hot chocolate. There was a mom hole inside of me. And no way to fill it.

And now, with each passing day, a dad hole was growing larger and larger. Who knew if this might be my last tree to decorate with him? I joined in the festivities with gusto.

The four of us spent the next two hours putting branches in peg holes, stringing lights, and hanging the same ornaments we'd been hanging on our tree my whole life. The tree was a little sparse because at least two or three ornaments got broken every year and we never thought to replace them. "Hey, Dad, maybe I'll grab a box of silver and gold ball ornaments next time I make a trip to Wal-Mart. What do you think?"

"I don't know…"

I looked into his cloudy eyes and my heart sank as I realized he was fading.

"Your mother likes the ones..." He frowned, glancing around the room, his hand slipping through his thin hair. "The..." He looked at me, his eyes so full of innocence and question. "What am I doing?"

"You were just going back to your room to watch the History Channel, Dad."

"Oh, yeah. Th-that's right."

I slipped my arm around shoulders that were becoming more frail every day. Dad came along without complaint, without a struggle. Compliant and helpless as a child.

I settled him into his recliner and pressed a kiss to his forehead. He patted my face, and our eyes met. "You're a good girl, kid."

My eyes filled with tears. Dad used the title "kid" as a term of endearment. It had been his name for me as long as I could remember. I missed it. "Thanks," I whispered. "You're not so bad yourself." His eyes turned toward the television, like a toddler waiting for *Sesame Street* to begin.

In the kitchen, Cokie had brewed green tea, which I loved and she hated, and warmed up a pumpkin muffin for me. I sat at the table, my chin resting in my hand.

"He's going away," I said, picking at the muffin.

She nodded. "He is that. More every day."

I scowled at Cokie. "You're no encouragement."

She shrugged. "Do I get points for lying or something? It's always best to face the truth and prepare for it, hon."

"I don't want to face the truth." My voice quaked and tears were just below the surface. How was I supposed to care about Thanksgiving and

Christmas after this year? By next year he probably wouldn't know me at all. I could barely breathe at the thought of him leaving me alone. We were the two musketeers. The two peas in a pod, the dynamic duo. How could I be expected to be the one left? The thought left me weak.

The doorbell rang and I frowned. It was nearing seven o'clock, and I couldn't imagine who might be coming by.

"I'll get it," I said, but Cokie placed her hand on my shoulder as she walked by on her way to answer the door.

"Just sit there and finish your tea and muffin."

I stared out the window into the darkness, remembering back to other day-after-Thanksgiving decorating. I couldn't remember decorating with my mom, but I'm sure I must have. Dad had always been there, tickling my toes to wake me up the morning after Thanksgiving. I'd walk into the living room to find lights strung wall to wall where we got them out the night before to do a light check.

"Look who I found at the door." Cokie's singsong voice entered the kitchen ahead of her two-hundred-pound frame, drawing my attention from the window.

Billy and Peach entered the room behind Cokie. Billy's mouth curved into a smile.

"Hi, you two," I said. "What brings you out on Thanksgiving night?"

"We wanted to stop by and see how your head is feeling."

"Much better, thanks." After I started Monday with such gusto, I'd had to take off the next two days because the prescription for my headache had really knocked me out. But today I had awakened much stronger and without the piercing headache.

Peach was carrying a pie and I focused my attention on the little girl. "What's that?"

"Grandma sent a pumpkin pie."

"Wow. That was nice." I raised my eyes to Billy. "Be sure to thank her for me."

"How about you sit down and have some of that pie with us?" Cokie suggested.

"Or at least a cup of coffee?" I asked.

Billy searched my face and nodded. We sat around the kitchen table, laughing and enjoying the pie and coffee. One by one people drifted out of the room until Billy and I found ourselves alone.

"Well, I suppose it's them, not us," I said.

He laughed, and the sound washed over me like something warm and familiar. "I'm surprised Charley isn't here."

"Charley?"

"Seems like the two of you are together a lot." I smiled at him and he blushed. "I guess I'm a little jealous."

"Charley's a friend. And he worked during the day today. He's having his dinner for the guests at the Inn tonight."

Billy nodded. "I forgot his parents used to do that. How's he holding up with everything?"

I didn't want to betray Charley's unflappable facade, but I didn't think he would mind if Billy knew a little. "He's starting to feel the pressure now that the killings are beginning again. With Amanda dying this same way, I'm worried about him."

Billy shook his head. "It's so unbelievable that Abbey Hills could have a killer on its hands. First Amanda last spring and then Jeremy a few days ago. It's scary. People are skittish and barely out past dark since Jeremy was found."

I realized the news hadn't broken about the animals. I assumed Charley would have told Billy when they picked up my Jeep on Monday, but apparently he hadn't. And Jill wanted it quiet until she was ready to make it public.

"A lot has changed since you left, Billy. And most of it not so good."

He nodded and we fell silent for a moment. He took a breath and let it out. "I changed a lot too while I was gone." He reached out and took my hand. "I want to tell you about Peach. Can I?"

"Oh, Billy." I sighed and pulled my hand away, cradling my mug in both hands. "Does it matter seven years later?"

"It does to me."

And as I stared into his eyes, I realized it mattered to me as well. And so I listened.

"The night you admitted your feelings for me, I was twelve hours away from boarding a flight for Haiti." He shook his head. "I had my calling and you seemed like a distraction."

His words stung more than a little. "Ouch. And my dad always said you were the one I had to watch out for. I wonder what he'd think if he heard you now."

Billy smiled. "Let me rephrase that. As much as I wanted to stay and see where the night would lead us, I knew there was no way I'd leave you if I started holding you."

"Better."

"I met Stephanie, Peach's mother, the very first day. She was two years older and had been in Haiti for two years already. She even had a gang leader out for her blood because she wouldn't stop rescuing children from the street and throwing away the drugs they were selling for the drug lords.

"I fell hard for her. She was so brave and beautiful and everything I wasn't. We were married within three months, and she got pregnant almost immediately. She refused to slow down, kept rescuing kids off the street.

She delivered Peach and got back out there within a month. It didn't matter what I said to her; she was stubborn and not about to fail in her calling. One night she didn't come back. They found her body in a filthy back alley, stabbed."

"I'm so sorry." I didn't know what else to say. Anything I could think of sounded trite and not nearly enough. Reaching across the table, I took his hand.

He squeezed it. "It's been six years. Her death strengthened who I am as a minister, a missionary."

"And you stayed in Haiti after your wife was murdered?" I shook my head trying to get a grip on the idea of it, but it just didn't make sense. "I'd have left that day."

"I know that seemed the logical thing to do. But her death lit a fire under me, and I knew I had a calling. I couldn't go."

I nodded. "Who cared for Peach?"

"She had many mothers from all nationalities between the missionaries and the Haitian women who lived at the mission."

"So what made you decide to come home?"

He shrugged and expelled a long breath. "It was just time."

I waited for him to elaborate, but he didn't. "Well, it's good to have you back. Even if it's just for a little while."

"Thanks." He grew serious. "I know your life is pretty hectic with your dad and the business, and I don't want to pressure you, but if you're going to Anise's party Saturday, how about going with me?"

I swallowed hard, wishing like crazy I was free to accept the invitation. "Sorry, Billy. I promised Charley I'd hang out with him. He's nervous because it's the first real event he's ever hosted other than the Thanksgiving meal he does every year to keep up tradition."

The smile washed from his face. "Oh. Well, I'll see you there, anyway. You said you and Charley are just friends, right?"

I grinned. "Just friends."

He nodded. "I guess I could always ask Janine."

I laughed. "That might get Charley's attention."

We talked about old times for the rest of the evening, and as nervous as I'd been when he first arrived, I had to admit that it was beginning to feel easy, as though he'd never been gone. Of course Peach was a beautiful and sweet little reminder that Billy hadn't thought about me the way I'd thought about him all this time, but I was optimistic just the same.

I walked him to the door well past midnight. Peach slept peacefully with her cheek against his shoulder. "I'm glad you came over," I said, suddenly shy. "Tell your mom thanks for the pie."

"I will. Let's do this again soon. After the party maybe?"

My heart could barely contain my excitement as I agreed to coffee after the party. I watched him go, cradling Peach in his arms. I had no idea where this could possibly lead, but I couldn't wait until Saturday night.

Amede could remember when Mr. Lincoln declared Thanksgiving a national holiday. It had taken three decades and much persuasion before Papa decided to begin observing the day with turkey and trimmings. Throughout the Depression, the Dastillion name had been synonymous with benevolence. But the practice had slowly faded with Papa's death.

She had been alone for so many years that she'd long ago stopped celebrating the day. What had she to be thankful for anyway? To stuff and cook a turkey, bake a pie, and sit down to eat at her long dining room table all alone would be pointless. A preposterous pretense.

The deputy had insisted they join him for dinner in the leaf- and gourd-decorated dining room, along with three other guests.

The guests sat in their finery, faces aglow with thankfulness. Something Amede had never understood. And when everyone bowed their heads in reverence and a hush spread over the room, something welled up inside, pulling up a scream. The heartbeat that proved she was alive pumped in her ears, and a knot in her chest cut off the flow of air to her lungs. All of this before anyone uttered a word.

"Heavenly Father," prayed the deputy, "we thank You for Your many blessings on this day that we gather to give thanks..."

Amede clenched her hands in her lap. Her nails dug into her palms as she fought primal urges. She imagined herself leaping onto the table, eyes wide, teeth bared, fangs out and ready to sink into the nearest neck. She had been the epitome of control for so many years that the thought startled her, terrified her. More and more violent thoughts had crept into her mind the past few days, despite the potion from Roma.

Just as she was about to fling back her chair and run out of the room, the deputy said, "Amen."

As chatter around the room flittered into a buzz, she felt the tightness in her chest ease. She glanced about the table, assessing the guests she had kept away from for the most part. Juliette seemed to know them all well.

Juliette was seated next to Caleb Stowe, who still hadn't left Abbey Hills. Amede could only assume Juliette was a large part of his reason for remaining. Handsome, olive skinned. Probably French. Amede observed the dynamic between them.

She had never really noticed before, but Juliette was quite an attractive young woman.

The two spoke softly, but Amede's keen ears allowed her to pick up the conversation.

"Are you getting bored in this little town?" the young man asked. His voice held a tinge of the South, but not Louisiana. Georgia, perhaps? That would never do for Juliette. She must marry someone from New Orleans. Someone who understood their ways. The marriage of voodoo and Catholicism, the fine line between evil and good.

Juliette's cheeks turned pink and she shook her head. "I do miss New Orleans, though."

"New Orleans. Were you and your family in New Orleans during Katrina?"

"Yes, but we were safe."

That was because Roma brought her family and half her friends to Amede's home to wait out the days while the water receded until they were able to return to their damaged homes. Amede paid for Roma's home to be repaired. The Dastillions had always taken care of their people.

"I'm glad," he said softly. He lifted his wine glass and waited for Juliette to raise hers. She did and shyly drank to his toast. Their eyes never left each other. Amede felt a twinge of worry. She didn't want to have to hurt Juliette. Perhaps Roma hadn't spoken with her yet about suitable companions. She would have to speak to Roma about it soon. And from the looks of things, the sooner the better.

Vaguely, she realized the deputy was speaking. She turned and stared. "I apologize, Deputy Baylor," she said, smiling. "What was it you said?"

"It's okay. Wine makes my mind start to wander too." He gave her an indulgent smile. "I asked if you'd like to share what you're thankful for this year."

Everyone's attention was on her. She gathered in a breath, finding it difficult to stay in the room as her stomach clenched and the smell of humanity beckoned. But she allowed her smile to take in each person at the table. "Well, I am thankful to be welcomed to such a warm and charming town as Abbey Hills."

There were smiles, amens, hear-hears all around the table. Only Caleb Stowe remained still, unmoved, one dark eyebrow arched. A chill crawled up Amede's spine as the young man stared at her over the rim of his wineglass. The deep red liquid flowed through his lips, and for the barest of an instant, he smiled.

CHAPTER TEN

*My junior year I graduated from smoking cigarettes with Amanda
Baylor to smoking pot. I liked it. And I liked the feeling that I
didn't care what anyone thought of me. Anyone but Billy.
Amanda and I sat in our usual spot on the side of the building.
Who knew why the teachers didn't do something about us. I
guess people see what they want to see. Billy saw. He came and
sat with us one day. Tried to invite us to a church thing. Concert
or something. "Yeah, no thanks, Billy," I said. "I'm not into that
stuff."*

"What? Good music?" he said.

*Amanda laughed. "Christian rock music. Oh my gosh. Can
you even picture it?"*

*I laughed with her, and Billy gave me a sad smile. "Okay. Call
me if you change your mind."*

"Like that's going to happen," Amanda called after him.

*I said nothing. I watched him go and felt like I was dying
inside.*

Would she ever stop hurting from the latest beating? Without blood, her wounds didn't heal as quickly as they had when she was nourished and strong. Slowly, painfully, she grabbed on to the fetid cot, caked with dirt and crawling with God only knew what. She pulled herself up and tried not to cry out as the pain nearly sent her unconscious onto the equally filthy floor.

Papa must have felt like this after he decided to step onto the straight and narrow. He had starved the part of him that made him strong. Amede nursed him, begged him to at least take animal blood, but he had refused. "You shall abstain from anything strangled and from blood."

It had taken him a year and a half to die.

How long, she wondered, until death rescued her from this living hell?

A mede got out of the Town Car in front of Markus Chisom's house, grateful she would finally be meeting with Lauryn McBride.

She had Charley Baylor to thank for the opportunity. He had set up the meeting and met her at the door.

"You found the house." He smiled. "Lauryn is at her desk. She's expecting you."

Amede's skin crawled as she walked through the house. She sensed Eden here. Or maybe that Eden had been here at one time. The sensation slammed into her stomach. "I didn't realize you would be here, Deputy." She offered a tight smile.

He nodded as he led her through the foyer. "Yeah. Security. We had to tighten things because of—"

"Miss Dastillion," Lauryn McBride said, standing suddenly. "It's good to see you."

"Amede, please."

She smiled and motioned to a wooden chair. Amede sat and placed her hands in her lap. "Amede, then. What can I do for you?"

"First, I wanted to thank you in person for your thoughtfulness. The letters meant a great deal to me."

"It was my pleasure." The young woman seemed to scrutinize her, but not in the suspicious way Amede had grown accustomed to, as though she were an oddity. "But I should tell you I made copies of them for the house estate. They probably won't sell, but their presence lends an authenticity to the desk. Details like that will help bring a better price."

Amede's smile froze. Her privacy had been violated. Those letters belonged to her. No one but Eden had the right to read them. They spoke of her love and longing for her sister. Her anguish at her father's death. Her loneliness, lost love. The woman had no right!

Amede leveled her gaze at Lauryn, looking at her with earnest appeal. "May I convince you to simply keep one letter on the desk for show and allow me to take the others?"

Lauryn's brow furrowed. Not in challenge so much as confusion. "Is there a particular reason you want the copies? I doubt anyone will actually read the letters. You know how people are."

"Then there should be no real reason to have them there. Correct?"

Lauryn's cell phone rang. "Excuse me. It's my father's caregiver. I need to take it."

"By all means," Amede said.

"Cokie? Is everything all right?" Pause. "Oh, shoot, I forgot. I'll pick it up on the way home."

She disconnected the call and looked up. "Sorry about that. My dad just took his last pill."

Amede waved away the apology. "Is your father ill?"

"Alzheimer's."

Amede could afford to be sympathetic. A girl's father meant everything. "I'm so sorry. My father suffered something very similar. It was difficult to watch his decline."

Lauryn nodded and offered a grateful smile. "It's not easy, is it?"

The bond of sisterhood that occurs when women understand each other's struggles was formed in an instant. And it was exactly the moment Amede needed. Lauryn's expression softened. "The copies of your letters are in the study. I'll get them."

"Thank you."

"It's no problem. I understand the letters might contain important family matters, even if they are a hundred years old. But I will need to see legal ID before I can hand them over."

"Of course."

She returned a moment later carrying a manila folder. Amede showed her a copy of her driver's license and Lauryn handed it over.

"Thank you again." She fought the urge to hug the folder.

"Also, Charley mentioned a missing ring? To be honest I haven't gotten far in the cataloging process, but I'd be more than happy to go over the list of catalogued items and see what I can find. If nothing else I can keep the list handy as I go through the rest of the house. That way if I find anything I can set it aside and we can figure out how to go about returning it to you."

"Figure out how?"

"Through certificates of authenticity or receipts from your family documents? Even photographs of ancestors wearing the ring can help. We'll give you first option of purchasing it after appraisal."

"That sounds reasonable. I'll see what I can find."

A frown creased Amede's brow. If only she could ask about Eden. But she couldn't risk revealing her identity until she knew they would be safe. It took only one person who knew who and what Eden was to put them at risk.

"Is there something else, Miss Dastillion?"

Swallowing her queries about Eden, Amede shook her head, then stopped. "Actually. There is one other item. It would be extremely valuable, so of course I would be willing to pay the appraised price."

"What is it?"

"A book." She cleared her throat. She couldn't very well tell this woman her father had given it to her. "A first edition of Wuthering Heights."

"I see..." but Amede could tell she didn't.

"The book was brought from England and is a first edition. There should be an inscription to another Amede from her father." She smiled. "I am her namesake, of course."

Lauryn nodded. "I'll see what I can do. And I'm sure no one would object to your paying full appraisal value to keep it out of the auction."

"This is very kind of you." She stood and offered Lauryn her hand. "I'll have my assistant do some research to see if there are certificates of authenticity or photographs in our possession at Dastillion Court." She smiled. "Thank you for your time."

Lauryn walked her to the door, where Charley had been posted. He opened the door for Amede. "If you're staying in town, then I'll see you tomorrow night at the party."

"Party?" Amede tilted her head.

Charley nodded. "I forgot to post it. There's a party at the Inn and all the guests are invited."

Amede struggled to hide her dread at the news. "I'm sure it will be an entertaining evening."

She walked out to the car, clenching her fists. This had not gone as she intended. Other than retrieving the copies of her letters, she knew nothing more than she had before the meeting.

"Eden," she whispered. "Where are you?"

Juliette slid the gloss over her lips and smiled at her reflection in the mirror. The thought of a party lifted her spirits. Each day that dragged on without finding Eden was one more day Juliette realized she wasn't just filling in for Grandmere. With Grandpapa's illness, Grandmere would be caring for him until he no longer needed her or passed away. Even then, Juliette was certain Grandmere would not return to the Dastillion home.

Juliette's fate was sealed. Unless she unsealed it. It wasn't fair that she be held to a blood oath made over a hundred years before she was even born.

Billy pulled up to the Inn just after I did. Already, a pretty good crowd had arrived, which I took as a good sign for Anise. I was happy for her.

Anise had hired some teenage boys to valet the event, so I handed over the keys to my slightly dented Jeep that for all it had been through wasn't much worse for wear.

Billy grinned and took two steps to my one to catch me before I went inside. "I'm a little nervous," he said, jerking his thumb toward the teen who had just slid behind the wheel of his car.

"Oh, it'll be fine."

"That's easy for you to say. Yours is already smashed."

I smacked his arm and laughed. "Hey! Have a little respect for my poor Jeep's plight."

"Whatever." His hand moved to my back and he guided me over the doorstep into the Inn. I tried not to allow his touch to affect me but failed. I was way too conscious of the warmth of his palm. As we became the objects of greetings, he stepped closer, as though staking his claim.

I smiled as I looked around Charley's inn. Anise had most definitely made the place more festive than I had ever seen it.

"Nice," Billy said.

"There's Charley."

"Who is the woman? One of his guests?"

Charley walked toward me with Amede Dastillion at his side. "Yes, she's from New Orleans."

Amede's mouth tipped in amusement when they reached us. "I think the deputy is hoping for as many friends as possible to keep that Anise woman away from him. She is very demanding."

Charley's face bloomed but he nodded. "Anise is driving me crazy. I wish I'd never let you talk me into this."

I laughed. "Well, I'm glad I talked you into it. And it looks like she did a bang-up job. Besides, I thought you said I needed to get out. Don't take all the joy out of it for me just because you have to put up with a little bossing around from Anise."

Amede looked from me to Charley and I could see the question in her eyes. "We're sort of each other's support group." I didn't want to bring up Amanda or my dad, so I just left it at that.

Charley nodded. "I insisted she come tonight. I was afraid she might spontaneously combust if she didn't get out of the house for a little fun."

"Yeah, he's a real knight in shining armor." I rolled my eyes.

Billy glanced around. "It's good to see so many old friends."

Anise walked into the conversation at that moment. "Old? Sweet Billy, we are not old. Just seasoned, that's all." She slid her bare arm around his neck and brought him in for a lingering embrace. My claws began to unsheathe, but I caught Amede's eye and she gave me a knowing look. One that said, "Are you going to let her get away with that?" But I wasn't about to give anyone the impression I was jealous. Because I wasn't. I shrugged as if to reply, "He's a free man."

"I'm so glad you could make it, Lauryn." Anise's smile didn't quite reach her eyes, and her tone always sounded just a little phony. "Do you know you're the talk of the party?"

"Oh?"

"Of course." She smiled that capped smile. "Everyone is dying to get a peek at all the antiques inside the Chisom house." Her gaze landed on the bandage still covering my stitched forehead. "Oh, goodness. I forgot you were in an accident. How are you feeling?"

"Much better. Almost as good as new."

"I'm glad." She smiled and I couldn't tell if she was looking for more information or not.

"Is it true the deer was killed the same way those poor animals were last year?"

Charley's posture shifted and I took the hint that he'd like to answer this one.

"What are your thoughts on that, Deputy?" I asked. The rest of the room had quieted and everyone tuned in to Charley.

"It's true that we haven't caught the person or persons responsible for the deer killing. But, folks, don't forget, this is deer season, so it might have been an accident. It's possible the animal fell off of someone's truck and they didn't notice. Don't go making this more than it is."

"Is Jeremy's death related?"

Charley's face went emotionless. "The coroner's report isn't in yet."

Anise shuddered. "Well, I sure hope it's not starting up again like before."

"Now, listen," Charley said. "I still need everyone to use caution. Don't go out alone, be careful of strangers." Charley suddenly turned to Amede. "I don't mean you," he reassured. "You're not a stranger. We know what you're doing in Abbey Hills."

"Well, that's a relief." Her fingers touched the tip of her collar in a matronly way.

I wasn't sure what to think about this woman. Her soft Creole accent fell like a whisper on the ears and her smile was difficult to resist, but I wondered why she would come so far and stay for more than a week just to retrieve a ring. I would gladly have sent it to her.

Charley slid his arm around Amede's waist, resting his palm on the curve of her back. She stiffened, as though someone had dropped an ice cube down her dress, but I doubted he noticed as he turned her. "I'm going to introduce Amede around to some other people."

I couldn't believe the liberty Charley took until the front door slammed open and Janine blasted into the room, eyes blazing. Even from where I was sitting I could see her entire body shaking.

"Uh-oh," Billy said. "Charley must not have told her he was bringing another woman to the party."

"And he must have seen her coming through the picture window. That's a little harsh. Do you think you should——" I was going to say "go try to calm her down." But it was too late. Janine spotted Charley, his hand still at Amede's back.

He turned, and like in a movie, their gazes met across a crowded room, only this was no romantic moment.

He scowled, and that expression was clearly all Janine could take. "Charley Baylor," she screamed, "I'm sick of you humiliating me in front of this whole town."

I watched the scene unfold with some sort of sick fascination. I had never seen Janine so out of control. Her eyes were wild, her breathing labored as she stood there in her uniform from Barney's, her coat only half covering one of her arms. I reached out and took Billy's hand, and he laced his fingers through mine. The warmth of palm to palm eased my tension, though I still dreaded the coming confrontation. There was no way things could end well for both Janine and Charley. And as much as Charley and I had become friends, I couldn't help but believe Janine had been wronged in this situation.

No one made a sound as Charley left Amede's side and took long purposeful strides across the wooden floor. Part of me wished he would slip on the rug and fall. Not enough to hurt him. Just to ease the tension and maybe even the playing field before he confronted poor Janine.

But he stayed steady on his feet as he gripped her arm and leaned in close. He spoke quietly, but the room was so silent it was easy to pick out his words. And we all listened.

"What do you think you're doing? You're humiliating yourself."

She jerked her arm away.

"I'm humiliating myself?" She stepped back, tears beginning to show in the tremble of her lips. "You're the one humiliating me. I've given you my whole life, Charley. Every day since I was five years old I've dreamed of marrying you. You said you loved me. You said you wanted to marry me. And then you just dropped me. For no reason. And now I find you here, with this...piece of trash." She pointed a shaking finger at Amede.

Amede's eyes narrowed and flashed, but she stayed deadly still.

"Janine, let's go somewhere private and we'll discuss this civilly."

"Civil?" Janine spewed out a bitter laugh and shook her head. She ripped the engagement ring from her finger. "Here. You want it back? I'm finished, Charley. I'm done crying my eyes out. I'm done turning down dates with other men who aren't so emotionally unavailable. Do you hear me? I am so over you."

"I think everyone in Abbey Hills hears you."

Her lip curled into a sneer and she flung the ring at him. Charley ducked, but not in time to keep the token from catching him squarely in the cheek. I noticed a scratch immediately.

Charley clapped a hand over the wound and hurled a profanity at the woman he had loved his whole life. Or used to love, anyway. He bent and retrieved the ring.

Janine spun around and stormed out of the house as quickly as she had arrived. Charley stood unmoving and stared at the closed door.

I hurried to Charley. "Are you okay?"

He shrugged and scowled. "Well, I guess that's that."

"It doesn't have to be. Go after her. She loves you; that's why she's so angry."

He stared at me, shaking his head. "It's finally over."

Slowly, talking resumed around the room. And more than a few whispers. Charley turned and walked away without even saying good-bye. He ignored Amede, walked to the bar, poured himself a drink, downed it, and poured another. Poor Charley. I wondered if he was exhibiting signs of posttraumatic stress disorder brought on by Amanda's death. What else could it be?

Amede went to him. Her face had gone a little ashen when she saw the blood on his face. She handed him a napkin and spoke softly. He scowled and pressed it against the trickle of blood flowing from his cut.

He walked away, presumably heading to the bathroom to wash his cheek. Amede met my gaze. She lifted her hand and, to my surprise, walked across the room to the door and left the same way Janine did. Her eyes were dark, her gaze narrow and almost frightening.

I sensed Billy's presence and turned as he took me gently by the arm. "What's going on?"

I shrugged. "Looks like Charley's getting ditched. I wonder why she didn't just go upstairs to her room."

"Maybe she needed some air."

"Who needs subzero air?"

"I don't know. Her, I guess." Billy's thumb moved along my wrist. "Poor Janine. I never knew Charley was such a jerk."

"I don't think he's really a jerk. He's been trying to pull away gently for months, but Janine refused to let him go. She insisted he was just depressed over Amanda's death and that he'd come to his senses. That's why she hadn't given him back the ring."

It felt a little odd to be standing up for Charley, considering what just happened. But in all fairness to him, and rotten personality aside, he really had tried to be gentle in the beginning. What else can you do when someone won't accept that a relationship is over? I stared at my hand, still clasped in Billy's.

"Do you want to go?" he asked.

I turned to him. "Yeah. Do you?"

"Are you kidding? I'd be glad to get out of here. How about going to Barney's for ice cream?" He grinned.

"In subzero weather?"

"It's never too cold for ice cream."

Suddenly everyone wanted to catch up with Billy or talk about my harrowing deer incident. Charley came back into the room, discovered Amede had left the party, and walked to us. "Hey, I have to get out of here for a while." He looked at me. "You won't be mad if I don't stick around, will you?"

"Why would I, Charley?"

He shrugged. "I talked you into coming."

"It's okay. Go walk it off or whatever you have to do. Do you want to call me tomorrow?"

"Yeah." He bent down and pulled me in for a hug.

I was aware of every curious gaze in the house. But I didn't care. Charley was rough edges and sharp corners, but he had his good surface too, if a person cared enough to look.

"I wonder where he'll go?" I asked.

"Probably a bar to wait out the party so he can have some peace and quiet," Billy mused.

I hated to think about him drowning his sorrows in a beer, but I knew Charley drank on the sly.

"You're probably right." I shoved aside the mental images and focused on Billy. "Want me to ride with you or meet you there?"

"What do you think?" His eyes moved to mine. I caught my breath. I hadn't felt this way in so long I'd forgotten the sensations that could sweep through me looking into his eyes.

Billy showed the "valet" his ticket, and in a minute the kid drove up and opened my door for me.

As we drove down the gravel road toward the highway, we saw Charley's squad car parked behind Janine's ten-year-old Ford Escort. I tried not to stare as we passed, but I couldn't help but notice Janine cradling the steering wheel. The driver's door was open, as if she was waiting for him. Charley turned and our eyes met. I waved a good luck.

"I wonder how that's going to end," Billy said, pulling my attention back to him.

"I don't know. At least Charley seems to be showing some sensitivity. He could have just passed her up like she's not even there. It may sound odd, but I kind of hope they'll get back together," I said.

"You're a romantic."

I shrugged, staring out as a soft snow started falling. "I'm more of a cynic. But I'd like to believe that some people can love their whole lives and actually stay in love."

He flipped on the wipers and stared thoughtfully out the windshield. "Sometimes love isn't enough."

"I guess."

He reached out and pulled me over to him. "Are we talking about Charley and Janine or us?"

"There never really was an us, was there?"

He glanced at me. "There almost was."

I nodded.

"Do you think there could be a maybe?"

Laying my head against his shoulder, I sighed. "Maybe, Billy."

CHAPTER ELEVEN

I wanted to get an after-school job to save for a car. All the kids were getting cars and I wanted one too.

"Why?" Dad asked. "You have the Jeep."

His Jeep. We'd had it for as long as I could remember.

"I know, but it's old and the clutch keeps sticking."

And it was his, as he always reminded me when I wanted to drive somewhere he didn't want me to go. Like to the mall in Springfield, by myself. Or anywhere without his protective eye.

"Okay, if you want to get a job, why not work for me after school? There's always cataloging and making phone calls."

"I'd rather work in the mall. I heard a couple of the restaurants in the food court are hiring."

"Then you'd have to drive back and forth." He shook his head. "I don't like that idea. It could be dangerous."

So I worked for Dad, saved my money, and never bought a car. Eventually I inherited the Jeep for free, so I used my savings for clothes, gas (the Jeep guzzled it up), and whatever kids blew money on.

Papa had never encouraged his daughters to be close, but nothing could stop it. Not once the blood tie was made. As different as the two of them were, as much as Eden resented her sister, there was an undeniable need to be close.

If only Amede could have thrown off the constraints of Papa and Dastillion Court the way she had. Amede didn't know why Eden left Dastillion Court that first time. She had known Papa forced her to leave, but not the reason.

Mama had been the cause, though her intent was only to keep Eden close. Once Papa realized that the blood tie between the Morioux and Dastillion families had been performed without his knowledge or consent, and once he understood the bond it created, he banished Eden and her mama to St. Ann Street, where her mother had spent most of her adult life as a mistress.

But the tie had already been made between the Morioux family and the Dastillion family in a ritual using Mama's, Amede's, and Eden's blood. Eden was the only person with Morioux and Dastillion blood. Her blood connected the two families.

After the ritual, even Papa had only to be near Eden before his own hunger for blood grew uncontrollable. Amede never understood because Eden's mama kept her sedated with potions and incantations. It was the only way Papa would forgive her.

Eden could feel that tie pulled upon more every day. Amede would find her soon. And when she did, Eden would feed on the blood of her captor. She would keep him alive long enough for him to feel the agony he had inflicted upon her.

If she closed her eyes, she could picture the bloody, wonderful scene. Soon. Soon Amede would find her, and her suffering would end.

I sat up with a start, my throat burning. Something definitely wasn't right. I shoved back the covers and rushed across the hall to Dad's room. I pressed my palm to my chest as relief flooded over me. He was sound asleep in his bed.

I backed quietly out of his room and pulled his door closed. As I turned, a hand clasped my mouth from behind.

Fight or flight kicked in and I began to struggle as another hand grabbed me around the waist, lifted me, and carried me into the living room. The intruder held me tight against him and spoke into my ear. "Lauryn, calm down. It's Charley."

I went limp as the hand slowly came away from my mouth. "Charley?" I turned and saw him. "What are you doing, you idiot?" I hit him on the chest with the flat of my hand. "Lord, Charley."

I reached for the lamp, but he stopped me. "Don't turn it on. I'm in trouble."

"What kind of trouble?"

"Jill is after me."

"Sheriff Jenkins? What does she want, and why are you running? Will you just tell me what's going on?"

He walked to the living room window and looked out, then turned to face me.

"Janine's dead."

I gasped. "Oh my gosh. What happened? Did you—"

"No, I didn't do it." His voice sounded offended and angry. "But I doubt anyone's going to believe that."

"Why wouldn't they? I do."

"The argument, she left, then I left, and several people drove by when I was pulling up behind her down past the Inn."

"Well, let's just go tell Jill you were trying to make things right with Janine." I folded my arms across my chest against a sudden chill in the room. "What happened between you two?"

"She was dead when I walked up on her. I never got to apologize."

I leaned hard against the back of the couch, thinking about Janine draped over the steering wheel. If what Charley said was true, that meant she was already dead when Billy and I drove by. How could I not have recognized something like that?

"What are you going to do, Charley?" I stared at him in the dark.

"I don't know. I saw her dead and I just took off."

"That looks really bad, Charley!" I shook my head.

"Don't you think I know that?" Charley scraped his fingers through his hair. "The stupidest thing I could have done was run away. And that's exactly what I did."

"Jill will believe you. She'll give you the benefit of the doubt. She should know after what happened to Amanda that you would never kill someone, let alone a woman." I stood and walked into the kitchen. "Come on, Charley. Sit down while I call Jill."

He wouldn't fight me. Charley knew when he came over to my house that I'd listen to him and then I'd make him do the right thing.

As I dialed the number my mind recapped the last few days. The body count in Abbey Hills was rising and I couldn't help but wonder when it would end.

Snow blanketed the field below the Inn, giving it a Currier & Ives beauty. Amede could appreciate that. And that was precisely what she was doing, standing on the balcony outside her room with a warm cup of calming root tea when a knock on her door interrupted her hour of reflection.

Barely concealing her irritation, she opened the door to find a very common-looking woman dressed in a man's uniform.

"May I help you?"

"I'm Sheriff Jenkins. I need a few minutes of your time."

Amede stiffened. Surely this wasn't in reference to the slain deer. Amede had been careful with the animal remains. She hadn't left them lying in the middle of the road. "May I ask for what purpose? Have I broken a rule in your town?"

Sherriff Jenkins smiled. "No ma'am."

"Miss," she corrected. "Miss Dastillion. If you'll permit me a few minutes to dress, I'll meet you in the sitting room. Say, fifteen minutes?"

The sheriff's lips pursed, but she nodded in acquiescence. "As quickly as possible, please."

"Certainly. I hope nothing is amiss."

"I'll wait for you downstairs."

Amede dressed as quickly as possible. Her stomach churned as she wondered what the sheriff was going to ask. It was never good when soldiers or officers or vigilante groups requested a few moments of her time. She knew this from years of experience. She and Eden hadn't been very discreet in the early days when ruled by a youthful lack of discipline rather than intelligence.

She applied her cosmetics carefully and brushed her dark hair back into a ponytail. When dealing with women in authority, Amede knew there was generally a better outcome when she appeared more average than someone a husband might find attractive.

The sheriff was sipping a cup of coffee when Amede arrived downstairs a few minutes later.

"I hope I haven't kept you waiting too long."

"Not too long." She set her cup on the coaster lying on the coffee table in front of her. "If you don't mind having a seat, we can get started. I have several others to interview."

"Interview? May I ask what this is all about?"

She slid a photograph across the coffee table. "Do you recognize this woman?"

Amede's jaw clenched. "Yes. She was at the party last night."

"I understand you were Deputy Baylor's date."

Amede smiled at the term. "I wouldn't exactly call that a date. The party was here. I simply had a conversation with him. He introduced me around and was kind to me, and that's as far as it went."

"Were you witness to the encounter Deputy Baylor had with this woman?" She gestured to the photograph.

Her lips curled at the memory of the other woman's insults. "How could I not be? She wasn't very discreet."

"Can you describe what you witnessed?"

Amede pretended to think, although every movement, every word was etched in her memory. "Let's see...she threw her engagement ring at Charley and cut his cheek. And then he called her a couple of profane names."

Looking down at her notepad, the sheriff nodded. "Okay, what happened after the incident?"

"The woman left and Charley went to the bar. But he was bleeding so I suggested he go to the rest room to clean up." She shuddered at the memory of forcing herself to move away from the blood. Her urges were growing and the tea wasn't helping much. She would call Roma later. There had to be something stronger.

The sheriff lifted her eyebrows. "And what happened then?"

"I told him it was very clear that the two of them had unresolved feelings and perhaps he should give her back the ring."

"What did Charley say to that?"

Amede smiled. "In an unpleasant manner he suggested perhaps I should mind my own business. He went to the rest room and I gathered my things and left the party."

"You went upstairs to your room?"

"No, I went outside for a breath of fresh air."

"Is there anyone who can corroborate your story?"

"Juliette and Caleb were outside on the porch."

"Who are they?" The sheriff's eyebrows went up in question.

"Juliette is my assistant and Caleb is a guest at the Inn. They met a few days ago and have taken a liking to each other."

Amede still didn't know how she was going to explain to Juliette why Caleb wouldn't be an appropriate partner.

"I'll need to speak to your assistant and the young man."

"They're out for a walk right now. Sheriff, has something happened?"

"Janine was found murdered."

"Murdered? Mercy." Amede frowned. Why would the sheriff be here if she weren't a suspect? "You think I had something to do with the woman's death?"

Sheriff Jenkins shook her head. "No more than anyone else. I'm questioning everyone from the party last night."

Standard procedure, the sheriff assured her, but Amede wasn't so sure. She was a stranger in a town where strange things were happening. That was enough to place a bull's-eye on her back. Her status as Charley's so-called date made things even worse, although technically Lauryn McBride was supposed to have held that honor. What a mess.

"One more thing, Miss Dastillion. Why exactly have you come to Abbey Hills? According to the Inn's registry you've been here, roughly, two weeks. About the only reason for visiting Abbey Hills other than to see family is to be close to Branson. Doesn't seem to me you're all that interested in Branson. So why are you here?"

Amede crossed her ankles and observed the sheriff. "Are you sure I am not being accused of a crime?"

"Like I said, you're no more a suspect than everyone else from the party, but a crime has been committed and you were there."

"Do I need to call a lawyer?"

Standing, the sheriff shook her head. "We're just asking questions, Miss Dastillion. As I said, standard procedure."

Amede followed the sheriff's lead and stood as well. She was at least four or five inches taller than the petite woman and enjoyed looking down. "Well, in answer to your question, a kind woman who is overseeing the auction of a lovely home in this town sent me some letters belonging to my family estate in New Orleans. I traveled here to thank her in person."

"Lauryn?"

"Yes."

"Those must have been some important letters."

She nodded. "They are. And in the spirit of full disclosure, I will tell you I've also come to search for a couple of missing items from our estate. Since the letters were here, I am hopeful the other items might be also."

"Have you spoken with Lauryn about these other items?"

"I have," Amede said. "My assistant is putting in a search for the proper documentation so that I will be given first chance to purchase them."

"What, may I ask, are you looking for?"

Amede stiffened. She didn't want to disclose anything until she had the opportunity to search herself. But the sheriff would not be easily put off. "A book. And more importantly, a ring that was passed to my father from his father and his father before him. It is valuable, but the greatest value is senti-mental, not monetary. The ring has been missing from our family estate for eighty years. It's time to return it to its rightful place."

Jill tipped her head. "Eighty years. . .but your father received it from his father?" She smiled incredulously. "You look way too young to have a dad so old."

Struggling not to show her emotion, Amede clenched her hands until her nails bit into her palms. How could she have been so foolish? "I came as a surprise to my parents, and my father was much older than my mother."

"Okay. Well, I hope you find what you're looking for and that we are able to come up with an acceptable solution to returning your property."

"As do I." Amede pulled in a breath. "May I see you to the door?"

"I think that's all I need for now, so yes, thank you." As the sheriff stepped into the cold air, she turned back to Amede. "How long do you plan to be in town?"

"At least one or two more days."

"I'd like to ask you to stay until we've completed our investigation."

Amede touched the top of her collar. "So you do think I killed her?"

The sheriff sighed. "Look, you were there, you were insulted and you were with the dead woman's fiancé. You put two and two together. Don't you think it's logical that you are at least a person of interest?"

"I had no idea he was betrothed. And we truly weren't there together. Charley invited Lauryn McBride as his guest. But she clearly preferred Billy's company, and Charley gravitated toward me. We were simply passing time. That's all."

"Well, either way, we'll need to ask you to stay in town for a few more days."

She had no intention of leaving this place until she found Eden. "That will be fine, Sheriff. And please don't hesitate to ask if there is anything else you need."

"When your assistant and the young man return, please ask them to come to the police station so I can get their statements."

"I'll do that."

Amede watched the sheriff slide into the squad car and drive away from the inn.

She had to find Eden soon and take her away from this place. She couldn't figure out if Eden was being locked away against her will, if she'd been harmed and couldn't move, or if she was just a few miles away and didn't want to reveal herself. But Amede knew that if she could feel Eden so strongly, Eden could feel her as well.

"Interesting development, isn't it?" Amede recognized Caleb's voice behind her. She forced an amiable expression before turning to face him.

"I'm sure it will all be cleared up in a timely manner."

"I'm sure it will," he said dryly.

Amede narrowed her gaze and stared into Caleb's almost-too-blue eyes. "Just what is your reason for visiting Abbey Hills, Mr. Stowe?"

"Remember, I'm doing a tour of small-town America. You can't get much smaller than Abbey Hills. Or, as it turns out, more interesting." He stuffed his hands into the front pockets of his Levi's.

"If you consider murder interesting."

"Don't you?"

Amede released a breath. "When did you and Juliette return from your walk? The sheriff wants to speak to you both."

"Just came in through the back door."

He grinned as Juliette entered the room and walked to his side. "Are you ready for breakfast?" she asked. "The cook is serving in the dining room. It looks like stuffed french toast and bacon."

Amede's spine steeled as Caleb draped his arm about Juliette's shoulders and escorted her from the room.

She would not suffer the relationship much longer. Juliette must soon be told that the young man would not do. Amede only hoped the girl wouldn't take long to accept the situation for what it was. Morioux descendants served Dastillion descendants, and that was just the way things were. An entire line of ancestors had accepted their lot in life, and Juliette must do the same.

PART TWO

*No man is an island, entire of itself...any man's death
diminishes me, because I am involved in mankind; and
therefore never send to know for whom the bell tolls; it
tolls for thee.*

—JOHN DONNE

CHAPTER TWELVE

My senior year, Billy went on a crusade—schoolwide. He made no secret of the fact that he was going to heaven and was determined to take us all with him. And somehow it worked for him. He was still quarterback, still popular, still kind, and still every girl's dream date. Especially mine, although I would have died before I admitted it.

I didn't have Amanda to smoke with anymore so I gave it up. In the spring, Billy invited me to a weekend Mega Youth Rally. I decided to go and got all caught up in the "Jesus is my friend" atmosphere. I felt different when I got home and told Dad I was going to start going to church.

Dad tried to be supportive but I could tell he wasn't crazy about the idea. Finally I got him to fess up. "God is all well and good if you need a crutch." He patted me. "But He didn't keep your mom from running off, did He?"

"Mom didn't exactly leave on purpose."

He hesitated and his eyes seemed to stare through me.

Something churned in my gut. "What...Dad?"

His lips turned up into a smile. "Nothing, baby. If you want to go to church, then you should go. Just don't lose yourself in the process."

I never went to church with Billy. When he questioned me about it, I told him I didn't need a crutch.

"God isn't a crutch, Lars, He's an anchor."

"Whatever." But his words stayed with me.

For a long time I regretted my decision.

Eden was seventeen years old, ready to become a mistress to a wealthy white landowner as her mother had before her. Since Eden's first quadroon ball, her mother had received many offers, but Mama spurned each with disdain. The men offered houses on St. Ann Street, jewels, a monthly allowance, and a promise never to raise a hand to Eden. All she had to give in return was herself.

Her papa despised the idea and tried to convince her mother she should marry one of the prominent free men of color in the city, but her mother flatly refused. There was no future, no happiness for a woman who married a colored man, free or otherwise. Better to bed a man who would worship her and to bear his children outside the bounds of matrimony than to live with a man who had no power.

Eden chose a man named Gilbert Fontaine. While Amede attended her first ball, dancing with a dozen beaux, Eden was becoming the mistress she was born to be.

By the next morning, the media had learned of Janine's murder, and with Jeremy's death the week before, local camera crews were camping out in Abbey Hills. Morning news showed the scene outside of Barney's. The frenzy reminded me of last spring after news of the fire got out. Two deaths in the old home following the other two murders had caused a media invasion that lasted for weeks.

Cokie arrived at her usual time, eight o'clock, and before I was even out of the shower, the table was set and wonderful aromas filled the kitchen and beyond.

"You know, Cokie, I've told you a hundred times you don't have to cook breakfast."

"Just sit down and eat." She carried a platter of pancakes to the table, where Dad was already seated with his newspaper. He could barely read it anymore, but Cokie was determined he should stay with his routine until it was absolutely impossible for him to carry on.

"Morning, Dad," I said, sliding into my chair at the table.

"Morning, kid." He set down the paper and looked me over. "Where do you think you're going?"

"Work. I'm cataloging and researching at the Chisom house today. I have to meet the security company at nine." I grabbed the milk jug and poured myself half a glass of one percent.

"What security company?" Dad asked. I knew he wasn't in the moment, but I pretended we were carrying on the same conversation.

"Jill contracted one from Springfield to put in a system at the house. You remember the yellow Victorian on Jackson Street? It's next to the sheriff's house. We were there the other day and you admired the carvings in the stairs."

He frowned, trying so hard to remember, and my heart went out to him. It was usually easier if I controlled the conversation. Asked questions but answered them myself. "I'm so excited to get back to cataloging the antiques."

I had questioned Jill about the wisdom of going back to work at the house with Janine's death so recent, but she'd asked me to meet with the security company because she was too busy with the media and the investigation. She'd placed Charley on paid administrative leave for now, but so far he hadn't been held.

Details about Janine's death hadn't been released, so no one really knew how she died except for the law officials and medical personnel. I was sure the sordid details would soon make their way onto one newscast or the other, especially since Jeremy's death mirrored hers.

My cell phone rang just as I was about to walk out to the Jeep. Billy's deep voice came over the line. "Are you on your way to the Chisom house yet?" he asked.

"Just walking out the door."

"Prepare yourself for a fight."

"Why?"

"Have you checked out Miranda's Things That Go Bump in the Night lately?"

"No."

"It's all kinds of wild speculation about Markus Chisom's and Eden's deaths."

"What kind of wild speculation? They died in a fire."

"Together."

"So?" I didn't have time for crazy Miranda today. I needed to get through this cataloging and hold the auction. My dad's symptoms were getting progressively worse, and I desperately needed the commission from this auction so I could start thinking about maybe a live-in nurse for him. Or possibly a live-in facility.

"I'm going to meet you at the Chisom house. You're gonna need my help to get in."

It wasn't that I didn't want to see him. Of course my heart sped up at the thought, but how crazy was it out there if Billy didn't think I could get inside alone? "Is it that bad?"

"The yard is covered with reporters."

I let out a sigh. "How am I supposed to get any work done?"

"I'd plan on bringing earplugs and be glad the security guy is coming today."

"How did you know about that?" I said as I opened the front door and stepped onto my front porch.

"Jill told me when she asked me to keep an eye on you."

"Lauryn!" A hiss from the side of the garage caught my attention.

"Billy, I'll see you over there," I said, curiosity getting the better of me.

I walked around the Jeep. A mop of red hair appeared. I shook my head and rolled my eyes. "Miranda, what are you doing?"

"I need somewhere to hide out." She glanced down the street like she was waiting for the paparazzi.

"Little girl, you have no idea how much trouble you're in. Do you know what you've done, stirring up speculation with those ridiculous lies about Abbey Hills being overrun with vampires? Vampires! Are you crazy? I mean seriously?"

She thrust her chin out in defiance and climbed into my Jeep without my permission. "I report the facts the way I see them. Just because no one else has the vision to see things from my perspective doesn't mean I'm the one who's wrong."

I set my bag in the back of the Jeep and got in the driver's side. "Then what do you need my protection from?"

"Everyone has been reading my site. I've had ten thousand hits since yesterday." She grinned.

"Clearly you're all broken up about it."

"Well, it's nice to be finally getting some recognition, but that's not the point. Everyone wants an interview. But I'm saving my story for the highest bidder. I mean, if they want me they have to pay for it, right?"

"I would definitely think so." I rolled my eyes and cranked the motor.

"Why do you always have to mock?"

"Because you think there are vampires in Abbey Hills. And because I need the comic relief. I have too much stress in my life."

"You're mean."

"Where do you want me to let you off?"

"I was hoping you would let me come to Markus Chisom's house with you. It's like the only place the sheriff has forbid the media from entering. They can't even go on the lawn since it's city property."

"You're not coming in with me, so you can forget it."

"Come on, Lauryn. I won't touch anything. I promise."

The front of the Chisom house was completely blocked by news media, so I was forced to park behind Billy's truck in the driveway. I cast a long side glance at Miranda. "See what your handiwork has done?"

"I stand by my stories."

"Miranda, can't you understand that Jeremy's family can barely mourn with all the calls they keep getting and the news crews outside their door? The same with Janine's parents. It's tragic."

Her expression dropped. "I guess I can see why they are upset."

"And here you are, too much of a coward to face the people you brought here with your outlandish accusations."

Her eyes narrowed. Then she stared out at the sea of reporters. "You're right. I'm a coward. Please, please help me."

"Oh, for the love of Pete." I grabbed a cap from my backseat and tossed it to her. "Put this on. You're not going to get past anyone with that hair."

"Thank you so much. I promise I'll make it up to you."

"The only way you can do that is to stop with the crazy accusations on your crazy Web site."

"Um. . .anything except that, I swear I'll do for you."

"Girl, you're a mess." I jerked my door open. "Make a run for it. Billy's inside waiting to help me get in."

Juliette leaned against Caleb's shoulder, sleepily happy to be sitting with him on the porch and not caring that it was freezing outside. They snuggled under a quilt and enjoyed heat from the fire pit.

"Tell me about your life in New Orleans."

"Would you be shocked to learn that my grandmother is a voodoo priestess?"

Caleb inhaled a sudden breath. Juliette angled her head to gaze up at him. The smile lifting his lips made her realize the gasp was a tease, not shock. "Are you?" he asked.

"A voodoo priestess?" She shook her head. "No, I have no religion."

He chuckled.

Juliette frowned and sat up. She looked at him. "It's not something to laugh about. Voodoo is magic, and it's dangerous if the person performing it isn't a good person."

"And is your grandmother good?"

Juliette frowned again. "She is."

"You don't sound too convinced."

Juliette settled back down against Caleb's shoulder. She wouldn't discuss the one time she had seen her grandmere summon blackness with her art.

Grandmere was good; she just had to be. Caleb seemed to sense she didn't want to talk about this anymore. He pulled her close and she relaxed again. "Are you happy serving Amede?"

"I haven't been doing it long. Grandmere has been serving her family for fifty years. Mother was supposed to take over, but she died young. When my grandpapa got sick, Grandmere asked me to come along on this trip. Nothing has been said about me taking over for Grandmere once we get back, but I have a feeling I can kiss school good-bye."

"You don't want to serve?" He spoke almost in a whisper. "Then don't serve."

"You don't understand. It's a family duty. Our family serves their family." She drew a quick breath. "Don't get me wrong. We are well compensated. Very, very well compensated. It's something I will always do."

They got lost in the quiet of the afternoon and the glow of the fire. Caleb reached over and drew her closer. Juliette trembled as he tilted his head and captured her lips in a soft first kiss.

Amede shook violently as she stared at the red-headed girl's Web site. She recognized the girl. She was the other waitress at the café.

Things That Go Bump in the Night

Something about these recent murders in the little town of Abbey

Hills, MO, has given me a moment of pause. Yes, pause because two

families are mourning the loss of their loved one, pause because a

town is mourning the loss of two members of their community.

But another pause, one that is for reflection. For YOU to reflect.

Last spring the police implied that the murders were done by a

woman known simply as Eden. She was the yoga instructor/new-

comer and something of an earth mother.

The murders stopped after the fire, but Eden's bones were never

found. Now, over half a later, identical killings of animals and two

humans have occurred. And yes, even though the cops haven't released

the cause of death publicly, my sources confirm the throats were cut

and blood drained.

Folks, wake up and smell the coffee! How many people have to

die before we admit that there are vampires living in and around

Abbey Hills?

Amede wasn't sure what to make of the Web site. The girl made sense.
Of course Eden wasn't dead. Amede felt her presence every day. But apparently the town believed her to be. Amede's heart beat fast at the thought that
a year ago, Eden walked these streets, spoke with some of these people. She
knew this town and they knew her.

Urgency burned inside of her. She needed to discover what had happened.

She scrolled back to links from April and clicked the first.

Abbey Hills, a quaint little Missouri town in the heart of the Ozarks.

Let me introduce you to the peaceful, gentle living. The town is old-fashioned with one stoplight, a barbeque café, and a female sheriff. There's one church, a community church. Abbey Hills is just about the perfect place to grow old. Except for one thing: if you live in Abbey Hills, chances are you won't grow old...

Amede read page after page, and when she reached the page that described the fire, she wept.

"Eden," she whispered, "where are you? Call to me. Let me know where you are so I can find you and take you home."

CHAPTER THIRTEEN

Predictably, Billy was valedictorian of our senior class. The Abbey Hills tradition dictated a graduation party at the river. There was beer, brats, and hot dogs. No one really got drunk. We were too nostalgic; mostly we sat around and talked about our future. I planned one last summer as a lifeguard before college. Billy's plans surprised me, devastated me, knocked the breath out of my body.

"I'm leaving for Haiti in the morning."

I think we were all stunned. No one said anything for a good thirty seconds. Then the questions started. Billy's eyes stayed focused on mine, and a minimovie of our entire relationship replayed. Childhood friendship, teenage missteps, what might have been. Tears threatened behind my eyes and I couldn't bear the thought that someone might see. I got up, grabbed a beer from the ice chest, and walked down by the riverbank alone.

I heard footsteps behind me a minute later and knew who it was. Billy sat next to me and slipped his arm about my shoulders. Silently, he pulled me closer and I laid my head on his shoulder.

"Don't go, Billy," I whispered.

He sighed.

"I mean it." I sat up and took his hand. "Stay with me. I don't want you to go."

He lifted my hand and pressed it to his lips. "It's not about what we want, Lars. This is my destiny. I have to go."

"I love you." I pressed myself close to him and our lips met. I had no idea what I was doing. I'd never been seduced. Never tried to seduce anyone. All I knew was that I would give myself to Billy if he'd only stay. Billy was right there with me, matching me kiss for kiss, caress for caress, and then suddenly he was on his feet, shaking, breathing hard, gaining composure. He bent over and handed me my shirt.

"What's wrong?" I asked, knowing full well I had crossed a line.

"I love you too, Lars." He turned and walked away from me, branches crackling beneath his feet.

―

He was calm today and she huddled against the wall. When he was calm he was contemplating. He wanted to talk. He wanted her to tell him about being a vampire. How many people had she killed? She didn't reveal to him how many. Instead, she answered, "Fewer than the other vampires I knew. I couldn't bear to take human life." She lied. Killing didn't bother her. Had never bothered her. She'd chosen those who deserved death as much as possible, but when she had slipped and killed decent people, she'd never lost sleep over it. She accepted who she was.

Her answer angered him. "Then why? Why didn't you keep yourself to only animals? You could do that, couldn't you?"

Because the cost was great. "I couldn't do it."

He became enraged. "You'd rather kill humans."

Yes, yes she would. As a matter of fact, if she could get to him right now, she would sink her teeth into his neck. But she didn't say that. He was enraged enough. He had begun to pace, so she braced herself for the beating that was sure to come.

I slammed on my brakes and rushed up to the house fifteen minutes late. In all the craziness with Miranda and the press, I'd forgotten Cokie had an appointment and needed me home at two thirty. The news reporters were beginning to thin out, except for the few still looking for Miranda, but an hour or two ago she'd snuck out the back of the house and they had no idea she'd gone.

Cokie came to the front porch and waved. She was carrying her coat and purse and didn't wait for me as she hurried to the car. She was late because of me, and I felt terrible.

I knocked on Cokie's window and waited just a second while she rolled it down. Her smile was tight, her expression tense. "Sorry, no time to talk, hon."

"I understand. Sorry I was late." She returned my smile and I knew she didn't hold a grudge. "I'll see you later when you pick up Cara. She's still coming over after school, right?"

Cokie started the Honda Civic and looked in the rearview mirror. She seemed distracted. "Okay, I'll see you. Oh, your dad's a little antsy today, so I kept him away from the carbs. I set out some tilapia and salad for your supper. The omega-3s in the fish can't hurt his brain, if you know what I mean."

"Okay, thanks, Cokie. See you after your appointment."

I finished my walk to the house, sat on the bench, and slipped off my boots. "Hi, Dad, I'm home."

"Hey, kid," he called back, and I smiled. He didn't really seem all that antsy to me, but that could've been because Cokie cut back on his carbs.

I stared at the fish on the counter and wrinkled my nose. "I don't think so." I'd rather give Dad an extra omega-3 pill. I slid the plate into the refrigerator and snatched up the teakettle. I filled it, set it on the stove, and switched the burner on high. Leaning back against the counter I closed my eyes and gathered in a deep breath. I took a few minutes to gather my thoughts. When the kettle whistled, I opened my eyes to find my dad standing in the doorway. "Hey, Dad. How was your day?" I headed to the stove to turn off the burner. "Cokie set out fish, but it looked gross. I think we'll order pizza. Any objections?"

Dad's hoarse, fearful voice stopped me cold. "Who are you?" he asked. "This is my house. Why are you handling my Shar's things?"

"It's okay, Dad. It's me, Lauryn."

"You better get out of here before I call the police."

It wasn't until then that I noticed he was carrying a golf club. He slowly raised it. "I won't let you steal from me."

Tears sprang to my eyes as real fear clenched the pit of my stomach. "Dad. It's me, Lauryn. Your daughter."

"I mean it! You get out of here!" Just when I was trying to decide how to respond, he rushed me. My dad rushed me with a golf club. I sidestepped him easily, but he overshot, sent the kettle sailing, and hit the stove, his forearm landing squarely on the hot burner. His skin sizzled. He cried out in pain, dropped the club, and jerked back from the stove, then stumbled and crashed to the floor.

"Dad!" I rushed forward, kicking the golf club out of the way as I reached him. The burn looked bad, at least six inches long and already beginning to blister around the edges. Dad's skin was paper thin. The damage was horrifying. "Come on, Dad. Let's get you up so we can go to the hospital."

Dad stared up at me with childlike eyes as though begging me to take away the pain.

"It's going to be okay, Dad. I promise."

Tears welled in his faded eyes. "It hurts."

"I know. Shh. I'm going to make it better soon." More and more since this nightmare called Alzheimer's began, he was the child and I the parent. And clearly not doing a very good job of it.

I tried to lift him, but a scream tore at his throat. "It hurts!"

"Hang on, Dad. I'm calling an ambulance."

I placed the 9-1-1 call and sat on the floor next to him until the paramedics arrived. By the time they got him onto the gurney, he'd passed out from the pain. I didn't even think to follow behind in my Jeep so I'd have a way home. Instead, I rode with him to Skaggs Regional Medical Center in Branson.

Halfway to the hospital, his blood pressure dropped. "Shock," one of the guys said as they worked on him and got it steadied.

I couldn't believe I'd allowed this to happen. I sat near his head. It was the best place to stay out of the way.

The ride to the hospital took about half an hour, but it felt like hours and hours. My stomach churned from the dip and sway of the Ozarks highway, and my head felt like a migraine was coming on. The staff had been apprised of our ETA, and nurses were waiting to assess his injury.

"You'll have to wait outside," one said, glaring at me suspiciously.

"Don't you want to know what happened?"

The nurse scanned her chart. "Says here he was disoriented and burned his arm on the stove and then stumbled and fell." The fifty-something nurse looked at me over the top of reading glasses and I felt like I was ten years old and had just gotten caught cheating on a test. "Is that correct?"

I nodded, though her cut-and-dried version was at odds with the way Dad's screams of pain had sliced into my heart, leaving it in shreds. My wonderful, funny, brilliant, loving, and always gentle dad had raised a golf club and ordered me to leave his home. So, yes, her words were correct, but oh, God, that wasn't nearly the way I had felt it. Still felt it. Like a million sucker-punches.

She kept her eyes fixed on me as though assessing if my concern was an act. Or maybe I was just being overly sensitive because I felt so responsible. Her expression dropped. "Okay, you can come back with him. But you'll have to stay out in the hall while we get him into a gown."

I gave her a grateful smile. "Thank you so much."

Dad and I stayed in a small room with a bed and a chair and waited about ten minutes for the doctor to arrive.

She was tiny, hip, and about my age. She gave me a dimpled smile and held out her hand. "I'm Dr. Winfrey. I'll be caring for your dad." I accepted the hand, relieved that she hadn't looked at me with suspicion.

"He's still unconscious," I said. "Is that a bad sign?"

She shook her head. "They sedated him because of the burns."

She grabbed a pair of disposable gloves from a box on the wall and slipped them on over small hands. "Since he fell, I'm going to check for fractures." She began at his feet, and her hands worked their way up his legs.

"Okay, I'm going to order x-rays of his lower body and back just to be on the safe side."

"You think he's hurt worse than the arm?"

"That's why I'm having the x-rays done. His burn is nasty, but not more than surface, so for him to go into shock, something else is probably going on."

"He has Alzheimer's." I breathed out and rubbed my palms over my face. "He thought I was an intruder and came at me with a golf club."

"Did you shove him in defense?"

It was a fair question, but it still twisted like a vise in my gut. "No. I know you have to ask. But I would not hurt my dad."

She nodded. "What happened?"

"I was by the stove about to pour hot water from the kettle. I ducked away from him, and he fell against the stove. His reaction to the hot burner made him stumble and fall. I'm telling the truth, Dr. Winfrey."

"I believe you. Someone from radiology will be back here soon to take those x-rays." She smiled and slipped through the curtain.

An hour and a half later, the x-rays revealed that my dad had broken his hip.

"We'll need to get him into surgery and put in some pins. He's relatively young and his hips weren't that displaced, so I believe pinning will be enough."

"Pinning?"

Dr. Winfrey nodded and spoke more slowly. "We'll put the bones back straight and pin them. He'll be prone to another break, but they'll help him heal. He was lucky. It could have been much worse." She smiled and patted my arm. "Don't worry. We'll take good care of him."

I watched her walk away, the sound of her assurance replaying in my mind, and I started to wonder if I was capable of caring for my dad anymore. Maybe it was time to entrust him to those who were.

No one had bothered to clean up the burn site. Amede studied the charred remains of what had surely been a lovely one-hundred-year-old home. Something about the scene curled her stomach. It was as though Eden's memory was somehow impugned by the lack of respect.

She stepped onto the burned-out foundation, trying somehow to capture the essence.

"Do you want me to come help you, Miss Amede?" Juliette called from the car. "You could get hurt walking in the debris."

"No. I'm fine."

For some unknown reason, Juliette had seemed more at peace the last few days. Amede wasn't sure she liked the logical explanation. Caleb wouldn't leave. He spent his days driving around and making notes as though he were planning to write an article or a book about his time in Abbey Hills.

She walked through the ruins of the home where only a few months before Eden held yoga classes, burned incense, smiled, captured hearts and minds with her easy personality and just a bit of magic—mind control, or whatever it was. Under the influence of drugged incense, there weren't too many men or women who would have been able to resist her.

There was nothing salvageable in the burnt remains. Nothing that spoke of Eden. She continued to walk from room to room, stepping over pipes and other metal. She couldn't imagine Eden dying here. In fact, Eden's presence seemed much less here.

It had been a couple of days since she fed. The root potion had helped with the most intense cravings, but lack of nourishment had weakened her. Her legs ached from maneuvering through the rubble, and when she finally stepped off the foundation, she wished she'd allowed Juliette to help after all.

But as she walked behind the house toward the barn, she was certain she could sense...something.

The cellar door caught her attention and she wondered if anyone had searched there for items Eden might have stored. Just one token or memento, something that might give her a glimpse of the woman her sister had become over the past century.

"Excuse me! Hello?" A female voice stopped her cold and Amede turned to find the red-headed Internet reporter. She had yet to meet the girl face to face.

The girl was all smiles as she approached. "Hi!" she said. "You've been staying at the Inn, haven't you?"

Amede nodded. "That's quite a mouthful." The girl's laughter didn't feel like an insult and Amede took no offense. The girl and her Web site intrigued Amede. There was plenty of truth in the girl's assumptions and theories.

"I'm Miranda. And no one calls me Randi. Ugh, can you imagine?"

Amede smiled. "What are you doing out here on this land, Miranda?"

She gave a one-shouldered shrug. "Following a couple of hunches." She peered close at Amede. "I'm an Internet reporter."

"Interesting." Amede watched the girl, fascinated by the brilliant green eyes. Red hair. She seemed like a walking cliché and yet so fresh and interesting that Amede found her amusing.

Her cell phone rang. "Oh shoot, it's Barney. I'm late again."

Amede glanced around. "What are you driving?"

"I hitched a ride out here." She looked at the Lincoln. "I don't suppose you'd be willing to help a girl out?"

Amede nodded. "We'd be happy to help you."

"Thank you." The girl's smile made Amede smile herself.

Juliette looked up from the journals she was reading, and her eyebrows rose when she saw Miranda.

"Hey, nice to see you again," Miranda said.

Juliette nodded. "You too. What are you doing out here?"

"Research."

"Juliette," Amede said. "We are going to drive Miranda to the café so she can get to work."

"Okay, then."

Amede didn't quite understand it herself. Perhaps it was just knowing the type of Web site the girl ran. Even if the material on the pages seemed crazy and wild to ninety-five percent of the population, there were some who would suspect she was close to the truth. But as long as no one took her too seriously and put Amede at risk, they would get along fine.

CHAPTER FOURTEEN

I started college in Springfield in the fall. I drove home every week-end and cooked meals to last my dad Monday through Friday when I'd be back again. "I'd starve if not for you," he joked but I believed him. And I liked the feeling that I was the only person capable of the task of keeping him fed.

I didn't bother too much with dating. What would have been the point when my weekends were filled with meals, taking care of the house, and helping Dad with the Saturday auctions?

I studied and did well. In the summer I took online art and history classes, and Dad and I would discuss and sometimes even argue over what I learned. I developed knowledge and opinions about appraisals, enjoying my growing role as a business partner.

After all, like Dad said, McBride Auctions would be passed down to me, and I needed to be prepared to run it.

———

Despair filled her, mocking her with images of a terrifying, excruciating death. At least Papa's body had received water and food so while the weakness consumed him, he didn't have the clawing ache in the pit of his stomach and a throat that felt like it had been scraped with sandpaper.

She had known despair such as this only one time before, when she discovered she was carrying Gilbert's child. She grew so agitated at the thought of raising a child that Papa reluctantly found a couple in Georgia willing to raise the baby.

During her labor, Mama gave her a strong potion to make the pain go away. She was alert enough to know when the child passed through her body. "A girl," she heard Mama say. "Ah, a boy." She did not know which her baby was, for Mama refused to speak of it again.

That night, Eden knew despair. Silent and pale and not sure she had done the right thing, she returned to New Orleans with Papa at the end of the week. But she didn't stay long. Her presence thrilled Amede, and Eden loved being back with her sister, but Papa noticed Amede growing restless in Eden's presence. He confided in Mama that he was afraid the blood bond between them would cause Amede to run away. He couldn't bear to lose her. With heartbreak over her baby still fresh, the resentment Eden had once felt for Amede returned with vengeance.

After an impossible evening listening to Amede read to Papa, Eden crept into her sister's room and stole her prized possession—her copy of *Wuthering Heights*. But she didn't stop there. She knew Papa had promised Amede the family ring. She took it from Papa's nightstand.

Then she left the house and never returned while Papa still lived.

But now that the end of her own life was finally coming, she thought of New Orleans. The home on St. Ann Street she had shared with Mama for the first several years of her life. And the last house she had owned for such a short period of time. And her baby. He would have long since died unless by some miracle he had become like her. She couldn't help but wonder if he had married, had children and grandchildren.

These were the things she dreamed as she lay hour after hour, day after day and waited for the flames of hell to claim her.

———

My phone buzzed before Dad was out of surgery.

"You left my baby alone?"

"Cokie?"

"You know where I'm standing right now?" Anger spewed from Cokie and suddenly it dawned why, but Cokie gave me no opportunity to apologize. "I am in your house and my girl is all alone. She said the door was unlocked when she got here after school and that no one was home. That's not the way it's supposed to be. I was afraid for her and asked you to keep her safe, and you didn't even stick around to greet her after school."

"I'm sorry, Cokie. Dad is in the hospital. He had an accident."

Getting the words out was like opening a valve to release the pressure. Cokie hesitated, then asked, "What happened?"

I gave her the *Reader's Digest* version.

"I'm coming to the hospital. We'll be there in half an hour."

Before I could protest, she hung up. The buzzer they'd given me went off. As though I were on the waiting list at Olive Garden. I went to the phone at the other end of the waiting room and punched in the numbers.

A nurse answered and gave me over to Dr. Winfrey. "Well, he came through it really well, like I knew he would."

"When can I see him?"

"He'll be in recovery for a while, and because of his burn and the Alzheimer's, I'll want to monitor him for a little longer. Barring complications, he'll be in his own room within three or four hours."

I thanked the doctor and slowly walked toward the elevators. Cokie found me in the cafeteria a few minutes later. Guilt plagued me as soon as I saw Cara.

"I'm so sorry, Cara!" I said.

The teenager shrugged. "I raided the cabinets. You're out of Doritos." She took some money from her mom and went to the cafeteria line.

"How is he?" Cokie asked. Her face was pale, and worry lines ran deeper than usual. I leaned forward and pulled out a chair for her.

"He's in recovery. The doctor believes he'll be fine. But he'll have to stay here for a few days."

"That's a mercy."

"I know. It could have been a lot worse."

Cokie released a heavy sigh. "I think that's something we need to discuss."

I looked at her, not sure what she meant. I gathered up my insecurity and wrapped it around myself, vulnerable to the criticism of the one person in the world I had to share my burden with.

"My doctor's appointment today was the third in the last three weeks." Cokie often started a topic and then charged into another before tying the two together.

"Is everything okay?"

She looked up, scanning the line for Cara. The girl was still waiting her turn. She shook her head. "I have ovarian cancer and it's bad."

I blinked. "But…" I almost said, "But how will I manage Dad without you?" or "But you're all I have now that Dad barely has any real-time moments anymore." But my mind caught up to my mouth in time to prevent a disaster.

"I'm so sorry, Cokie. What can I do?"

"There's nothing to be done now but to call upon the name of the Lord."

"No treatment?"

"Of course. The doctors can do what they will, but ultimately my life is in God's hands."

I was relieved she wasn't just counting on prayer. "And what will the doctors do?"

"I will have a complete hysterectomy. Then I'll start chemo."

I looked at the woman who had been my rock, my friend, my mother, really. I wanted to hold her close and let my determination that she would not die melt the cancer from her body like ice in summer.

"Oh, Cokie...I'm..."

"Shh. Cara's coming."

Poor Cara.

I watched the girl drop into her chair with a plate of nachos and a large soda. She dug in without a clue about how her world was going to change. My eyes searched for Cokie's, but hers were on her child.

One day you're a kid eating nachos. The next you're watching a parent slowly shrink away. Mind or body, it's all the same.

The constant ache had returned, but Amede didn't tell Juliette. The tea had stopped soothing her, and as much as Amede hated the feeling of reckless compulsion, she had begun to believe that without her strong connection to Eden, she might never find her.

After an uncomfortable dinner listening to Juliette giggle while hanging on Caleb's every word, Amede finally found the opportunity to sneak away alone to hunt.

After burying the carcasses, she returned to the Inn, stronger than she'd felt in days.

She entered the house and headed silently toward the steps.

"Isn't it a little late to be roaming around outside?"

A growl escaped her throat as she positioned herself for defense. She swung around to find Miranda standing in the doorway of the dining room. "Miranda. You startled me."

"Sorry." The redhead nodded toward the front door. "You're a nocturnal creature too, huh?"

Amede narrowed her gaze. "What do you mean?"

Miranda smiled and lifted her shoulders in a small shrug. "You're like me, staying up all night. I can never sleep. It's like I don't even wake up until midnight and then I can just write all night. It always drove my mother crazy. I have some junk food in here, if you're hungry." She laughed. "I'd be starving if I went out for a walk."

Amede stared at the mound of food on the table. "Miranda, what are you doing at the Inn?"

"Oh, my roommate kicked me out because of all the reporters chasing me down, so Juliette offered to let me stay in her room. But I haven't seen her, so I can't get in."

"Deputy Baylor is fine with that?"

"I don't know. I haven't seen him."

Amede shook her head. The girl had more moxie than anyone she'd ever known. "Well, I wish you good luck."

"Thanks." She turned back to her laptop, clicking the keys faster than Amede's hands could even move. The clicking stopped and Miranda met her gaze again. "What's your theory about the weird stuff going on in this town?"

Shaking her head, Amede forced a tight smile. "I don't have a theory." She started to turn. "I don't want to keep you from your work."

"I've sort of come to a dead end if you want the truth." She shook her head. "I heard Charley ran off the night Janine was killed, and when he turned himself in, the sheriff didn't even arrest him."

"Really?"

"I think it must be professional courtesy or something because they would anywhere else. I mean, the guy was almost married to the girl, he takes someone else to the party—no offense—she shows up, throws a fit, she leaves the party, he leaves the party, and lo and behold, he's the one who finds her body. A little too much to be coincidence."

Amede nodded. "Seems pretty cut-and-dried when you put it that way." There was no point in telling her she hadn't been Charley's date.

"I know…right? I just don't get why they haven't taken him in. I do have an idea…"

Heavy boots walking across the foyer floor turned their attention. Charley's eyes flashed. "Maybe because I'm innocent until proven guilty?"

Miranda blushed. "I'm sorry, Deputy." Swallowing hard, she clearly fought back a wave of fear. "I'm just nosy. Always speculating. My mother says I should learn to mind my own business before I get myself into trouble one of these days."

Amede watched the anger sprout across the deputy's face and wondered if this could be one of those days.

"You can just get out of my house."

Miranda stared big at Charley. Her jaw dropped. "You're kicking me out?"

"Under the circumstances, don't you think I'm within my right? Especially since I'm pretty sure you're not even registered." He practically spit the words.

"But..." She stared at Amede for support.

"She was going to share Juliette's room. I'd be happy to pay an added fee to let her stay."

Miranda's face brightened. "Thank you, Amede!"

But Charley wasn't inclined to accept the offer. He shook his head. "You've caused a lot of stir in this town with that crazy Web site of yours. I don't need the extra trouble at my doorstep."

"I'm sorry, Deputy. Please give me another chance. There's no other place for me to stay."

A shrug lifted his shoulders. "That's your problem."

The compassion Amede felt for the forlorn girl came as a surprise. She turned to the deputy but could see in his steely eyes that he would not back down.

He sneered at the girl and walked away.

"Well, that's that." Miranda gave a tremulous smile. She shuffled to the door.

"Would you like me to drive you?"

She drew a breath and let it go, shaking her head. "No thanks." She gave Amede a little wave and slipped out the door.

CHAPTER FIFTEEN

After my dad surprised me on my twenty-first birthday with a check from a trust fund my mom's mom had set up for me before she died, I planned a trip to Italy. I'd always dreamed of going there and thought the summer after my junior year would be perfect. I longed to see the Colosseum, the Peggy Guggenheim Collection, and Vatican City, even though I wasn't religious. I just wanted an experience that didn't scream "small-town girl."

The day before the deadline to put down a deposit for the trip, Dad sat me down and admitted the auction house was in trouble. I did the only thing I could do — gave him the money for my trip to Italy and convinced him he was really saving me from a trip I never wanted to take in the first place. That was the first time I could remember resenting my dad. I spent the summer working for Dad and started my senior year wondering if I'd ever have the chance to breathe.

Eden lay on her cot, peeling back the layers of her life in frenzied flashes of darkness and light.

The war was over and there was excitement and bustle in St. Louis. Eden reveled in the new money and constant change. Each day brought a new excitement, a new party, a new man to love, new blood to spill.

She proudly wore her papa's ring and made up stories about his heroic death in the war. But in her stories, she was Papa's little girl and Amede was the one he had banished.

Her mama wrote long letters, demanding Eden come home. Promising to intervene on her behalf with her papa. But Eden knew it was no use. According to Amede's letters, Papa was changing, refusing to feed. Some religious reason. Mama said he, like Amede, struggled too much with the urge to feed on humans when Eden was near. Eden was the sacrifice, and she felt the rejection more deeply than she would ever admit.

Amede wrote long letters, pouring out her heart to her only sister. The letters continued after Papa died. Finally, Eden had tried to go home. But nothing changed. Amede wouldn't break loose from the ties of Dastillion Court. And Eden could never be held there.

But that was long ago. Now she would give anything to live the rest of her days in her father's house.

Kingdoms are built on the blessing of a father to his child. My dad had been my world for my whole life. I was his princess in this castle built on loss and our need to stick together just to make it one day at a time. And now our kingdom was being ripped out from beneath us, upending my world and making me wonder if it would ever be possible to recover.

My body ached in ways I'd only imagined after three days in the hospital with Dad. I could have slept in a hospitality room on the next floor up, but I didn't want to leave Dad alone in case he awoke while I was gone. And he had several times. But every time he was disoriented and had no idea who I was. He was disappearing more each day.

"Shar?" Dad's pitifully weak voice sliced through me as he called me by my mother's name.

"Hi, Dad." I untangled my legs from the chair and hurried to his bedside. "It's me, Dad. Lauryn."

"Shar. You don't have to go. Please. I'll do better. I promise."

"Shh. I'm not going anywhere, Dad." I smoothed the strands of gray from his forehead. "It's okay. Everything is okay."

"Please don't take the baby." His eyes filled with tears as he looked at me and saw my mother.

The door opened, and to my relief, Dr. Lowell entered. We'd been seeing Dr. Lowell for two years, ever since the day my dad finally admitted his memory lapses might be more than just "senior moments."

The doctor smiled at me, then frowned at Dad's restraints. "What happened?"

"He's declined really fast," I said. "He got violent."

He nodded, and his eyes turned to me with sympathy. "Are you okay?"

I shook my head. "He thinks I'm my mother right now. I can't get him to snap out of it."

My dad's eyes rounded in fright as he stared at Dr. Lowell, and he stretched back as far as the restraints would allow. "Don't hurt me," he whispered.

"Ted, it's Dr. Lowell. Remember me?"

Maybe it was the steady confidence in Dr. Lowell's voice, but Dad stopped midpanic and frowned, staring intently as though he couldn't quite put his finger on it, but he knew the doctor was someone he should know.

"I..."

Dr. Lowell gave his hand a pat. "It's okay. Maybe it'll come to you later." He turned to me. "What medication are they giving him for pain?"

"Something mild. Tylenol 3 maybe?" I wished I could remember, but my lack of sleep had fuddled my brain and I couldn't think straight. "They said it wouldn't interfere with his other medicine."

He nodded as he read over Dad's chart. He warmed his stethoscope with his hand and reached toward Dad.

"Don't touch me." The panic had returned.

"I'm just going to check your heart. I promise it won't hurt."

I stood on the other side of the bed and took his hand. He looked up at me and smiled. I wasn't sure if the smile was for me or my mother, but I smiled back and reassured him until he relaxed enough to allow Dr. Lowell to examine him.

The doctor listened and listened, and it seemed like forever before he stopped moving the stethoscope around on Dad's chest, his ribs, his chest again. Frowning, listening, moving. When I was about to scream, he finally straightened up. He turned to me. "Don't blow this out of proportion."

"What?" I heard the panic in my voice, but that was nothing to the panic swirling in my heart and head. I looked him in the eye as seriously as I could. "Tell me everything you're thinking and don't hold back to spare yourself a hissy fit because I'm the kind that needs to know everything. And I mean everything."

"I'm going to send your dad for an EKG. He's having some irregular beats. I just want to make sure everything is okay before we send him home tomorrow."

I fought hard to stay calm. "Okay, what happens if the EKG comes back and it's abnormal?"

"Then we'll call in a heart specialist to look him over. But try not to worry." He placed a fatherly hand on my shoulder. "Most of these cases turn out to be nothing. His heart could be reacting to the pain medicine."

My dad was crying by the time the nurse's aid came to take him for the EKG.

"Where are you taking me? Stop. You can't do this. I haven't done anything wrong. Don't arrest me. I'm innocent."

His mind flip-flopped between scenarios so quickly it was difficult to keep up.

Tears formed in my eyes and spilled over. I was exhausted and his tears were more than I could bear. I slid down the wall in the hallway and hugged my knees into my chest so tightly I could barely breathe.

I wanted to call Cokie. She would have come right away to take up the emotional slack. But Cokie was dealing with her own level of hell. I could imagine Cara sitting on the floor in her own room, her back against the wall, crying into her knees like I was.

Neither of our parents should be dying. My dad was only sixty-two. I should have another ten to twenty years with him. Cokie was only fifty. Fifty years old and dying of a fast-moving, aggressive cancer bent on leaving her teenage daughter an orphan.

Like me.

Dad had always been my rock. The foundation. The one safe place I could run to when life got dangerous and I felt afraid or lonely or rejected or ugly. He would draw me close, call me "kid," tell me I was the best, the prettiest ever, and I believed him. Now he was fading away from me, and my safe place was fading with him. I felt like I was about to walk off a ledge into no gravity, floating into space with nowhere to plant my feet.

I tried not to think about it. But it was too late and a fresh onslaught of tears began.

"Lauryn?"

I lifted my head from my knees and noticed Jill sitting next to me on the floor. I squinted through swollen, blurry eyes. "Jill? What are you doing here?"

She pointed to her uniform. "Official business."

"Everything okay?" Thinking about someone or something else for a change felt good. "Or too official to talk about?"

"Freddie Morgan was coming home from a date last night and hit another dead deer in the road. He's here with a broken leg." She shook her head. "Guess how the deer died."

I saw fatigue all over her. Charley's situation hadn't made things easier. "Another ritual killing?"

"Yeah. But at least it was only an animal." She rested her head back against the wall. "I just can't believe it's starting again. I thought for sure the fire would be the end of it."

"What do you mean?" I focused on her face, my thoughts flashing to Miranda's crazy theories.

Jill's expression changed suddenly and she looked at me. "I'm just tired and thinking police business out loud. Sorry about that."

"Nothing to be sorry about." Disappointment tweaked my stomach. "So you're here to get a statement from Freddie?"

"Yes." She sipped from the coffee cup in her hand. "What's going on with your dad that has you so upset?"

At the mention of my dad, I felt the tears begin again.

She reached into her coat pocket and handed me a tissue. "There's more where that came from. I think you'll need them."

We sat quietly for a few minutes while I tried to catch my breath.

"Do you want to talk?" she asked quietly. "Word on the street is I'm a good listener."

I made a pathetic attempt at a laugh. "You have enough troubles of your own these days."

She smiled. "Never too much to listen to a friend."

Her words refreshed my tears, and as I leaned into her warm shoulder I gave into my fears, disappointment, struggle. Fresh Kleenex continued to find my hand until by the time I finally sat up, stuffy nosed but rid of some of the pressure, I had a wad in my hand the size of a softball.

"Better?" Jill asked.

I nodded. "Dad's having an EKG. They think he might have some pretty serious heart stuff going on."

"Lauryn, I'm so sorry."

"Two years ago, he was the dad. You know? Strong and protective and involved in everything that mattered."

She smiled. "My dad never was those things, so I actually don't know."

My cheeks warmed. "I forgot. I'm sorry."

"All that's in the past. My dad's been sober for years." She smiled. "And I had a loving mom and a crazy sister who was always in trouble, and that kept me entertained."

Her words twisted something inside of me, squeezing out the pain like a wet rag. "I can't stop thinking that once my dad is gone, I'm alone. I mean the last of the line, Jill. My parents were both only children. If I have an extended family somewhere, I was never told about it. My grandparents are gone. This is it. I don't even know who I am without Dad. If he doesn't need me anymore, there's no reason for me to exist. Seriously, what's my purpose, Jill?"

"That's pretty heavy. But I understand how you feel. For years my sister Nina was gone and we didn't have any contact with her. I kept thinking the same thing. When our parents were gone, it would just be me."

I leaned my head against the wall and rolled it to the side to look at her. "And now you have Barney."

"And baby makes three," she whispered and patted her flat stomach.

I gasped and sat up straight. "Jill, that's amazing. Congratulations. You guys didn't wait around, did you?"

"Honeymoon baby. I swear." Her face shone like only an expectant mother's can. "Don't tell anyone." She smiled. "I'm waiting another couple of weeks just to make sure nothing happens."

"Oh, I'm sure everything will go off without a hitch."

She shrugged. "I have a high-stress job that's getting more stressful every day, and if this new deer slaying is an indication we're headed down the same road as before, I'm just afraid—"

"Jill. Don't think that way. Babies are tough in there. Nature made them that way."

Jill's cell rang. She answered as she stood, using the wall for support. I sat there a minute until she came back. "That was Freddie's nurse. He's out of recovery for his leg and in his room, but they'll be pumping more painkillers into him soon. I better get down there before he's too out of it to know what he's saying."

I stood and gave her a hug. "I'm glad you came by. Thanks for the shoulder. Literally."

"Glad I was here. You going to be okay?"

"Yeah, I'll be fine."

She smiled. "All right. I'll see you later."

The elevator dinged and I turned to find my dad in a wheelchair. He seemed calmer. "How'd it go, Dad?"

He stared but he didn't respond. I turned to the nurse's aid. "Is he okay?"

She nodded. "They had to give him something to calm him down. He got pretty wild for a while."

I stayed in the hall while they settled him back into place. His eyes were closed when I got in the room and soon he drifted to sleep.

I felt my eyes drooping too and my body felt heavier and heavier. I must have slept for hours. When I woke, my dad's heart monitor was screeching. I jumped to my feet and flew to his bedside. Frantically I pushed the call button as he flatlined before my eyes. "No!" I shouted and began to push on his chest. One, two, three. Nothing.

I pressed the button again and again and again. Panicked, I rushed out the door and down the hall, yelling, "Someone help! He's dying. Someone help me!"

My cries echoed off the walls in the deserted hallway. I reached the nurse's station and stopped short, pressing my hand to my mouth, stifling a scream.

The nurses, the doctors, everyone was strewn across desks, chairs, the floor. Their throats had been slashed like a cross and their bodies drained of blood.

I felt pain in my throat from a ripping scream I never heard and I turned in slow motion, sprinting back to my dad. I pushed through the door. Dad wasn't alone.

A woman stood with her back to me, staring out the window. I recognized the crazy red hair and started to walk toward her, but suddenly she whipped around and in the instant it took me to blink, she was next to my dad, her face smeared with blood.

"Miranda," I breathed.

She bared her fangs. "You should have listened to me."

She sprang.

I jolted awake.

I sat still, catching my breath, trying unsuccessfully to shake the dream. My heart raced. And I jumped when the door opened.

I slowly let out my breath as Dr. Lowell walked in followed by a doctor I hadn't seen before.

I stood and faced him, steeling myself. "So," I said, "what's the verdict?"

Dr. Lowell's expression remained grave. "This is Dr. Mayer. He's a cardiologist associated with the hospital."

I started to feel sick, but I took the proffered hand. "I guess this means the EKG showed something?"

Dr. Mayer was not an old man, no touches of gray to give the illusion of wisdom. He was probably in his thirties, and I had to wonder if he was experienced enough to care for my dad.

The look he gave me was professional and sympathetic, and as he began to speak, my concerns over his youth lifted. "An EKG can show us unusual heart patterns. But it doesn't give us details about the reason for the abnormal rhythms. We have to investigate further in those cases."

"And I take it my dad is one of those cases?"

He nodded. "Yes, but at this point, there is no reason to believe we'll find anything."

"But the EKG showed something?"

"Yes, just a little interruption in rhythm. I want to do an EP study to check for blockage."

"What's an EP study?"

"It's a test that should show us the blockage and extent of it. I'll run a wire through a vein in his groin to the heart. The patient is typically awake during the procedure, but in your father's case, he'll be sedated."

My hands began to ache and I realized I had them clenched into tight fists. Slowly, I uncurled my fingers. "When will you do the test?"

"Soon, but it'll take a team and we'll have to set up the room. Your dad can't have any food or water for about six hours prior to the test. He'll have to spend tomorrow night in the hospital too. But if we don't find anything pressing on the test, we'll let him go home the next day."

"And if you do?" My own heart was beating fast.

"We'll have to wait and see."

He smiled again and Dr. Lowell touched my arm. "Don't worry, Lauryn. We'll give your dad the best care possible."

"You know he's been doing worse lately. Mentally."

"Before the surgery?"

I nodded. "He was supposed to see you next week, so I was going to wait. But he mistook me for an intruder the other day, and that's how he burned his arm and broke his hip. He's been fading out more than he's lucid." I gathered in a shaky breath. "I'm concerned. Should he be going downhill so fast?"

"Sometimes it happens that way." He made a note on Dad's chart. "Once we figure out his heart issue, we'll decide how to proceed with treatment for his Alzheimer's. How about you?" he asked. "Are you getting any rest?"

"Some." I thought about my nightmare and couldn't hold back a shudder.

"Not enough." His look was stern, fatherly, which almost became my undoing. "I asked them to call hospitality and get you a room for tonight."

I started to protest, but he held up his hand. "You need to sleep. And you need to eat. How are you going to take care of your dad if you're exhausted and malnourished? Lie in bed, watch mindless TV, and order take-out. Rest!"

"Doctor's orders?" I smiled.

"Exactly. We'll talk tomorrow." The doctors left, their keys jangling in time to their steps. I returned to Dad's side, wondering how I'd ever be able to leave him overnight in the sterile room.

Clouds loomed overhead, but the forecast promised only a thirty percent chance of snow as Juliette pulled the Town Car from the gravel drive. Amede let out a breath she wasn't even aware she was holding.

"You all right?" Juliette asked from the driver's seat.

"Just glad to be out of that inn."

"Me too."

Amede smiled. "What about Caleb? You seem taken with him. I think you'll miss him when we return to New Orleans."

Color rose to Juliette's cheeks. "He's pretty cute."

"Are you being careful?" All they needed was an unwanted pregnancy.

"Miss Amede!" Juliette laughed. "I've known the man for a few days. I don't think I need to be careful in the way you're meaning."

Then she had a lot more sense than Eden when she was young. As if reading her mind, Juliette caught her eye in the rearview mirror.

"I know I'm not a direct descendant of Eden, but I am from her mother's line. Can you tell me anything about her?"

"Of course. What do you want to know?"

Juliette's eyebrows rose, as though surprised by Amede's answer. "Grandmere told me she was banished from Dastillion Court by your father. I have always wondered if she came back after he was dead."

Amede nodded, collecting her thoughts. "She came back several times. The first time she returned, she'd just lost the man she loved. Markus."

Juliette's brow rose again. "*The* Markus of the Chisom house?"

"The very same. But you mustn't tell a soul."

"I won't." She gave a short laugh that made Amede frown. "We are the keepers of your secrets. I would give away my grandmere's secrets before yours. It's called indoctrination."

Amede knew Juliette tended toward the facetious, but sometimes her flippancy worried Amede. This girl was to be her companion for the next forty or fifty years. Amede needed to trust her completely, and so far she didn't.

"I'm sorry," Juliette said. "So when was the last time she came back?"

"Sometime around 1890. The house had been upgraded with modern facilities and we had a telephone. The police chief was assassinated by the Italian mob in October of that year. Eden arrived during all the hubbub."

"Did she say why she'd come?"

"She was heartbroken and lonely. She came home to get her strength. She only got that from New Orleans. Jazz and festivals and the orgies." Amede had never approved of those. She didn't give herself over to any religion. She had always believed her mammy had been killed by voodoo, and she wouldn't go near it no matter how Eden begged her.

"How long did she stay?"

"A few years."

"That long?"

"For us, that's hardly more than a blink. We lived together, ran the house together, and when Eden was home we had parties."

"With humans?"

"Of course with humans. We aren't animals. We can control ourselves. Eden found such pleasure in the gatherings that I couldn't deny her." Of course, later, they hunted on the docks and in the slums. When she and Eden were together, Amede felt alive, wild, and happy.

"It was after a party one night that she left. One of the guests happened to be someone from St. Louis, where she'd been with Markus. He knew where Markus had gone to escape Eden, and he told her. So she was off to find him."

"And did she? Find him, I mean."

"I daresay she did."

"You must have missed her after she left."

The loneliness never went away. "Every day. But we wrote letters." Amede didn't speak the full truth. She wrote letters to Eden. But she never received letters in return. Every now and then a friend, a vampire, in New Orleans for a festival or another reason, would stop by at Eden's recommendation. But by the second World War, those visits by proxy had ended.

Amede faded into the memories as the highway rolled before them. The pungent scent of wood smoke wafted from chimneys along the rural highway.

As she began to recognize some of the landmarks, Amede forced aside thoughts of the past and focused on the task at hand. The thought of the cellar at the burned-out house had not left Amede's mind since the day she noticed the padlock.

"Uh-oh," Juliette said.

"What's the matter, Juliette?"

"Miranda James is here too."

"What's she doing?" She fought the urge to crane her neck.

"The same thing you're going to do, I think."

"What?" Amede scooted forward in the seat. The burned foundation was twenty yards off the road, the cellar directly behind. Miranda was there.

"Pull over and call the sheriff's office and report someone trying to vandalize the ruins."

"Miss Amede, are you sure you want to do that?"

Amede hesitated. On one hand, she hated to kick Miranda when she was already down. But the need to find Eden was growing intense. Sometimes the connection between them seemed lost. As though Eden herself were lost. Other times the hunger gripped Amede, pulling, clawing through darkness, frenzied.

Right now she could barely sense Eden, and that scared her.

As much as she enjoyed Miranda, Eden was the one she loved and Miranda's presence could delay Amede's reunion with her sister. And that would not do.

She turned to Juliette without a trace of humor. "Make the call."

CHAPTER SIXTEEN

During a weekend home my senior year, I ran into Amanda Baylor — now Rollings — at Barney's. She was big bellied and glowing and I hardly recognized the woman she had become. I walked away from her and for the first time in years allowed myself to think about Billy. I slid back into my seat across from Dad.

"Who was that?" he asked.

"Amanda Baylor," I said absently, then laughed. "She taught me to smoke. Ring a bell?"

She got up to leave and we waved to each other. Dad turned and noticed her belly.

"Thank God you were smarter than that."

"Yeah. Thank God."

Eden slowly opened her eyes as the muffled sound of voices came from the world outside her prison. A sob caught in her throat and she raised her fists to the concrete walls, a futile attempt, she knew, and yet she pounded because not doing so meant giving up, and she wasn't ready to give up. She tried to scream, "Help!" But the scream died in her throat and no sound came out. It had been too long now without nourishment. She was too weak. The end must be coming soon.

———

I awoke in the radiology waiting room to the soft sound of my name and a gentle hand on my shoulder. I sat up and the fog slowly fell away as I recognized the cardiologist standing over me.

"How'd the test go?" I yawned, and not in a pretty way. "Excuse me."

He sat down next to me on mauve vinyl. "It's good news."

I blinked. "Dad's okay?"

The cardiologist nodded. Then he raised his eyebrows. "He doesn't need a pacemaker. But we still need to watch him because of the rhythm issues the EKG picked up."

"Okay," I said hesitantly. "What are you trying to say?"

"I want to see him back in my office in two weeks to do another EKG. Just to make sure the heart flutters were from the pain meds and not something more serious."

I nodded, still finding it hard to believe the news had actually been good. "I'll see to it."

"How are you holding up?" He touched my hand and I almost broke down. "I know your dad has Alzheimer's on top of everything else."

"We're getting through it." Even as I said the words, my body rebelled. Lead pipes had replaced my limbs, and four days of little sleep and lots of worry about Dad had caught up with me. I released a heavy breath.

The doctor gave me a sympathetic smile. "Go home and sleep tonight. Your dad will be sleeping from the anesthesia and probably won't be awake until morning. Might be a good chance to rest up before he comes home."

"I'll think about it." I smiled, basking in the relief that Dad wouldn't have to go through surgery to have a pacemaker put in.

He pulled a card from his pocket and handed it to me. "This is a support group for families of Alzheimer's patients. They meet once a month here in the hospital."

"Okay, I'll think about it." I knew full well I'd trash the card, like I had the brochures offered by the nurses and receptionists in Dad's doctor's office. I knew everyone was trying to be helpful, but meetings weren't my thing and even if they were, when would I find time to go?

"My wife leads the meetings. Her mother is in the last stages now."

This piqued my interest. I wasn't completely sure what the last stages were. "Does your wife take care of her?"

His face gentled. "Not anymore. We had to put her in a nursing home."

My chest tightened. "That must have been difficult."

"My wife agonized for weeks, but eventually she had no choice. We found a facility with a separate wing for Alzheimer's patients right in Springfield, so we're able to see her often."

"I don't think I could—"

"I'm not suggesting you do that. But the group would give you a place to go where everyone understands how you feel. They discuss a lot of questions you're likely to have."

"Thanks. I'll think about it if I can find time."

Something in the tone of my voice must have raised his suspicions. He pressed. "The problem with an only child caring for a parent with Alzheimer's is that she usually feels compelled to do it alone. I understand you don't have any other family?"

I felt the knife twist with his words. "Yeah."

"As things progress, you'll need support from people who understand. This is a good place to find those kinds of people."

His kind smile reached his equally kind eyes and I didn't want to disappoint him. "I'll look into it. Thank you for thinking of me."

My cell phone rang, and he stood up. "The nurse will be in later with your dad's appointment time," he said, then left.

I pulled my phone from my jacket pocket and answered.

"Hi, it's Billy."

Did he honestly believe he had to tell me who he was?

I smiled and my heart lifted. "Hi, Billy, what's up?"

"How'd your dad's test turn out?"

"It's good news for once." I hesitated, not liking the way I had just offered up my heart. "I just mean he doesn't have to have a pacemaker on top of everything else."

"I'm glad to hear that." Billy's voice was quiet and gentle. Soothing. "Are you coming home tonight or staying with your dad?"

"The doctor said he'll be out of it most of the night, so...I'm coming home." I hadn't decided until just that moment. "I want to get some work done at the Chisom house and sleep in my own bed." And I still needed to clean up the kitchen from the day of the accident.

"Will you have dinner with me tonight? You do plan on eating, right?"

"I hadn't thought about it, but I'm sure I'll have to eat eventually." I hadn't seen Billy in a few days, and the temptation was too great. I glanced at my watch. "What time does Barney's close?"

"Actually, I meant at my parents' home." He hesitated.

I'd long ago learned to let go of my childish anger toward Billy's dad for telling me God had taken my mother home. But I had never socialized with them. When my grandmother was still alive, she took me to church once or twice, but the thought of spending the evening making small talk scared me.

Apparently sensing my hesitation, Billy spoke up. "We can go somewhere else if you'd rather."

"No, Billy. Your parents' house sounds fine. Do they know you're inviting me?"

"It was Mom's idea."

"Oh." I felt foolish. Was Billy feeling the same connection I felt? His mom made the invitation?

"Let me qualify that." He chuckled. "I told Mom I was going to ask you out to dinner and she thought you might like a home-cooked meal. She assumes you've been eating takeout or cafeteria food for the last four days."

"She's right." My heart warmed toward Mrs. Fuller. "What time should I come?"

"How about if I pick you up at six?"

"I can drive over. I know where your house is."

"I'd rather come get you. That way I can take you home afterward."

"Okay, six o'clock."

As we hung up, I felt lighter than I had in weeks.

Amede's hands shook as something jerked her awake. Her stomach quivered and dread washed over her. Something wasn't right. She slid her sweat-slicked palms across the down comforter to dry them and lay there, terrified. She half expected a horde of demons to fly above her bed, zooming in and out, taunting her. It had happened before, whether in a dream or real life she wasn't sure. Either way, the memory sent her heart racing.

She kept her eyes squeezed together, afraid of what she might see. The clock on the stand glowed with digital numbers, but courage to turn her head and check the time eluded her. She knew it had to be at least afternoon. She hadn't been able to pull herself out of bed all day.

Night terrors had begun the first time she saw Eden attack a man. It was the night of Amede's first hunt. Eden had found her killing a barn cat.

Amede had wept with shame until Eden grabbed her arms and shook her. "Stop sniveling. This is who we are. We are stronger, better than regular humans. Get rid of that stupid cat and come on."

"Where are we going?" she had said, barely able to speak above a whisper so shocked was she at the revelation that she wasn't alone.

Eden's eyes glowed and a slow smile spread across her full lips. "Hunting."

The prey, a gambler who was quite intoxicated, had stumbled upon them, clearly intent on bringing them harm. Eden lured him into an alley and attacked him. "Come before he's dead." Horrified by the look in his eyes as he lay there, helpless, his blood draining quickly from his body, Amede wanted to feel pity, but instead what she felt was bloodlust.

She crawled into her bed that morning, satiated for the first time in all the years she'd craved and didn't know why. But the moment she closed her eyes, the fear gripped her gut, squeezing and twisting. Whenever she was alone, the fear returned. Sometimes it came in subtle waves, cresting and crashing. Other times it collided against her like it was now. Pounding, intruding, seizing her without mercy. Not a day passed that she didn't see the eyes of the man in the alley.

A knock at the door filled her with relief. She dared to open her eyes. Light streamed in from beneath the blinds on the french doors leading to the balcony. The room was darkened still, but enough light filtered in, expelling the pitch of night, to give her peace of mind.

She slipped on her robe and headed to the door. Her eyes hurt. So did her body. Everything ached. "Who is it?" Her voice sounded frail.

"Are you all right, Miss Amede?"

Amede opened the door to Juliette, wishing the girl were Roma.

Juliette frowned as she shut the door behind them. "You don't look well, Miss Amede. Are you ill?"

"I feel strange."

"Strange how? Do you need to hunt?"

"I don't think so. My head is aching terribly. I feel like I need to lie down." She walked back toward her bed and then paused. "Do you need something?"

"The sheriff is here to see you. She's brought another detective with her."

"What do they want?" Fear slid through her again. Arrest and confinement might lead to a revelation of who she was. She couldn't allow that. If they were questioning her again, it meant someone suspected her of this crime. How many of the other guests were being harassed in such a manner?

Juliette helped her to bed and slid the comforter up to her shoulders. "You're shivering."

Amede closed her eyes against the pain in her head. "I feel very... strange."

"It almost seems like the flu." Juliette hesitated. "Can you even get the flu?"

"I don't know. I've never had it. Not even as a child, that I recall."

Juliette placed a hand to Amede's forehead. Her hand was cool and soft and reminded Amede of her mammy's. "You are hot as a griddle."

"Fever?" Her teeth chattered and she opened her eyes. "Th-that's not possible."

"You're burning up."

"It isn't possible. . ." She closed her eyes again and turned, curling up into a fetal position, trying to make the pain go away. "I think you'd better ask the sheriff to come back tomorrow."

"I think that's for the best," Juliette said, her voice soft and low. "I'll check in on you a little later unless you need something right now."

Amede shook her head. "I just need sleep."

Juliette left, closing the door behind her.

Fear gripped Amede again. How could she be ill? She had always been strong and capable. In control. A thought came, terrifying and pleasantly appealing at the same time. Human blood would heal her.

CHAPTER SEVENTEEN

I graduated at twenty-two with a 3.65 GPA. Not a genius by any means, but respectable. And high enough to please my dad and give him bragging rights.

He had helped me secure an apprenticeship at the museum in St. Louis, where he hoped I'd learn enough to become the full-time appraiser for McBride Auctions. I had other plans. I fell in love with city life pretty quickly, but more than that, I fell in love with Ronald Shaffer, a philosophy student who loved art and history. He practically lived at the museum. His parents were from Wyoming and he went home every few weeks on their dime. Within three dates he had moved into my apartment with me, and we started a crazy love affair. It ended after several months when I asked him when he was going to take me with him to Wyoming. Abruptly he told me he was getting married to his high school sweetheart in June. The next month.

I called my dad and he drove to St. Louis immediately, packed me up, and took me home.

Where, he said, I belonged.

After several days he brought her food. She took it hungrily, unsure why he had decided to nourish her, but grateful that he had. He spoke softly, his hands gently brushing back her hair from her face as she ate. She didn't stop to think that as filthy as she was, it didn't really matter. She only knew that for the first time in oh so long, she was gaining strength. Not much. Not enough. But a little.

"Thank you," she whispered, barely able to produce a sound from her shriveled vocal chords.

"Did you enjoy being fed?"

She nodded, dread filling her. The question would more than likely lead to an impossible demand, followed by a wild beating.

But he sat back against the wall, his knees up. "Can poison kill you?"

She shook her head. Had he poisoned the raccoon before bringing it to her? Is that why the animal hadn't put up much of a fight?

"Speak up," he growled. "And don't lie to me."

"I can become ill if the poison is strong enough. But where a human will die in hours, I will recover."

"That must be what happened to her."

Eden did not want to appear curious. He grew angry when she asked questions—suspicious, as though she had ulterior motives. And of course she did. Every answered question gave her insight. And every insight was one step closer to understanding how to overcome him.

He stood and shuffled to her cot. "How many of you are there?"

He meant vampires, of course. She had no idea, but there were many. Most lived in cities where they could blend in and feed without drawing undue attention. What's another unsolved homicide in a city of millions?

His eyes narrowed as she hesitated, and he leaned over her. "Did you hear my question?"

She nodded. The motion sent a rush of blood to her head. "I don't know how many there are. Not many in rural areas. Most gravitate to New York and LA. Some in Chicago. London, Tokyo. Large cities."

"That's what I figured." He gave her a hard look. "So poison can make a vampire weak enough for a human to get close and decapitate it or light it on fire?"

Terror filled Eden at his callous last words. She swallowed hard and nodded.

"That's good to know." Laughter spurted from him as he snatched the raccoon carcass and stuffed it in a burlap bag.

She wanted to call after him. Beg him to let her bathe, brush her hair, change her clothes. If he wanted to keep her here forever, at least allow her to make it livable.

But he was already up the concrete steps. A flash of light slipped in as he opened the door.

She'd had no idea it was daytime.

B illy picked me up at quarter to six. I would have rushed out to meet him, but I noticed through the window he had gotten out of his car and was walking up the sidewalk. Despite the smoky gray sky, I felt my world brighten.

His hands were stuffed inside the pockets of a brown leather bomber jacket. As he approached the steps, I backed away from the door and waited for him to ring the doorbell. He knocked instead.

I counted to fifteen, then opened the door.

His smile at the sight of me made me go warm all over. "Hi," he said. I opened the door and let him in. He reached forward and touched my cheek with his fingertips. It was a brief touch but long enough to make my stomach jump. "You look tired."

I rolled my eyes and snagged my purse from the bench by the door. "Charmer."

He waited for me to precede him out the door. "Sorry. My clumsy way of showing concern."

"It's okay. I know I'm not at my best."

He took my hand and we walked toward the car.

"Is there anything I can do to help?" he asked. I would have loved nothing more than to hand him a list. The kitchen faucet dripped, my heater made a funny noise, and I wasn't sure how I was going to pay for Dad's prescriptions this month, let alone our share of the hospital bill. But those things were my responsibility, and the last thing I wanted to do was burden Billy by whining about them.

He opened the passenger's door for me but held on to my hand, bringing it up to his chest. "You can ask for my help, Lars."

I wanted to ask, "Really? How long before you leave Abbey Hills?" Instead, I faked a smile and thanked him. "I think a home-cooked meal is going to do wonders for me."

Disappointment flashed in his eyes. He gave my hand a squeeze and let go. My chest tightened as I slid into the soft leather seat of his dad's Altima. Our conversation barely dipped below the surface as we drove the few blocks to Billy's parents' home.

"How's Peach adjusting to life in Abbey Hills?"

He kept his gaze on the road, damp from the recent melting. "It's a lot different than Haiti, to say the least."

I laughed. It felt good to have laughter in me. "I can imagine. Can I ask what made you decide to come home?"

"It's a long story we'll have to save for later." He released a breath and I wondered if he was going to elaborate anyway, but he pressed his lips together and focused on driving.

He turned onto Maple Drive, the street where he'd grown up, and I was struck by the contrast between the beautiful homes in this section of town compared to most of the town. "Nice 'hood." Reverend Fuller hadn't done too badly for himself.

The home could have been a showcase, especially with the Christmas lights glowing and the life-size nativity scene in the front yard.

"Stop it."

"What?"

"You know what. Stop acting like you've never been here before. And stop being judgmental about the preacher having a nice home."

I gave up the pretense and smiled. "So I'm not an actress."

"Not by a long shot." He opened his door and I took my cue to exit the car as well. When he walked around to me, he reached out and took my hand, lacing his fingers with mine. My heart raced. "My dad comes from money. And that's the last I'm saying about it."

"Did I say anything?"

"You didn't have to."

I would have replied, but the front door opened. A red door on a white house. His mother stood in the doorway. She was a slim woman of fifty, wearing a snug pair of jeans and a sweater. Her blond shoulder-length hair was straightened and tucked behind her ear. Her smooth skin and an air of confidence cast a striking, youthful appearance.

She welcomed me with a smile that immediately made me feel at ease. "Lauryn, so good to see you." She stepped aside and let us in.

"Thank you for inviting me."

"How's your dad doing?" she asked. "Will has been wanting to go see him, but he hasn't been feeling that well this week."

"I'm sorry. I hope it isn't serious." Or contagious. I had no time to be sick.

A slight frown crinkled her nose and she glanced at Billy. I caught a glimpse of the look that passed between them but tucked it away for later discussion as Mrs. Fuller led us into the dining room. Peach and Reverend Fuller were already seated at the table. I stared at the reverend as he stood and smiled, his eyes crinkling. I didn't remember him looking so gentle. Or so frail. He held out his hand and I accepted it. "It's so nice to see you, Lauryn. You'd think in a town the size of Abbey Hills we'd be able to keep track of people better."

I shrugged. "You probably would if I went to church more than Easter Sunday."

He chuckled, amusement crinkling his eyes. "Easter?"

I felt my face warm, but I allowed the joke at my expense. "Maybe not a recent Easter." I glanced at the food on the table. "Are we late?"

The reverend shook his head and sank back into his chair, breathing heavily. "Just in time."

Billy placed his hands on my shoulders. "Let me help you with your coat." Self-conscious at the closeness, I couldn't meet anyone's gaze as I shrugged out of the leather coat and he slid it along the back of a chair. We each took a seat.

The reverend held out his hands, one toward me and one toward Peach, who sat across from me. I sat dumbly, staring. He smiled. "Shall we say grace?"

I felt stupid. After all, how many reruns of *The Waltons* had I watched growing up? I slid my hand into his. His held a slight tremor. He kept the prayer short.

Mrs. Fuller lifted a plate full of fried chicken toward Billy. My mouth watered at the sight of the meal before me. I hadn't had a real home-cooked meal since Thanksgiving the week before.

We passed the food around, filling our plates. It was typical southern fare of fried chicken, mashed potatoes and gravy, fried okra, and biscuits. I noticed the reverend's plate contained baked chicken, salad, and a baked potato. Not wanting to appear rude, I shoved aside my curiosity, looked away from the healthy meal, and dove into the contents of my own plate.

"This is wonderful, Mrs. Fuller."

She beamed under the praise. "Thank you. I don't get to cook for company very often these days."

"Mom would make five-course meals every day if she could." Billy glanced with affection at his mother and she smiled back at him, with that look found only in a mother's eyes.

A lump lodged in my throat and I had to swallow twice to force down my bite of potatoes and gravy.

When we had finished eating, Mrs. Fuller brought a silver coffeepot and four cups to the table. "I hope you don't mind that it's decaf," she said to me. "Will isn't allowed caffeine anymore."

I wasn't comfortable enough to tell her I despised decaf coffee. So I forced a smile and a lie. "No, it's fine."

Reverend Fuller sighed. "They say you can't taste the difference between decaf and the real stuff, but I have to protest that lie."

Billy spooned sugar into his cup and passed the bowl to me. "Dad drank two pots of strong coffee a day for as long as I can remember. I think giving up his coffee is the hardest thing he's ever done."

"It's definitely the biggest sacrifice I've made."

I was about to ask why all the changes, but Peach spoke up. "Daddy, can I go finish watching my movie?"

"Let's see the plate."

She held up a mostly emptied plate.

Billy smiled. "Okay, you did pretty well. Go ahead."

"What about dessert?" Mrs. Fuller asked.

The little girl grimaced. "I'm too full, Grandma."

Mrs. Fuller smiled. "All right. You can have some cobbler before bed-time. Go on and watch your movie."

Peach pushed back her chair and left the room.

"Has she started school yet?" I asked.

An awkward silence followed and I glanced around, my face growing warm. Obviously I'd said the wrong thing.

Billy's parents had turned in unison to stare at their son. He cleared his throat. "Actually, Peach and I are here on sabbatical from missions. I'm home-schooling her until I'm sure what our plans will be."

My stomach dipped at his words, and all my lofty dreams of becoming Mrs. Billy Fuller fell away. I kept my face stoic. "Oh, I didn't realize." I gave a nonchalant wave. "Or maybe you told me and I don't remember."

"I didn't tell you." Billy's voice remained low and I could feel the tension in him. "I came home for a reason."

"You might as well tell her the rest," Billy's dad said. "We'll have to make it public soon anyway."

Billy's eyes moistened. I reached out and took his hand, and he grabbed on tight. "My dad's heart is failing."

"Oh, Billy, I'm sorry." I looked at Reverend Fuller. "I don't know what to say. What are they doing for you?"

Billy spoke for him. "The only thing they can do is a transplant."

I tried to sort out the information I had from Cokie about the reverend. "But after the bypass surgery, you came out of retirement. I thought you were okay."

The reverend had been retired for two years, but a couple of months ago his replacement got another offer closer to his family and decided to take it. So the reverend came back.

"We thought I was too," Reverend Fuller said. "But last month I started feeling that tightness again and went to the doctor before it could escalate into another heart attack."

I looked at Billy. "So this is why you're home?"

He nodded.

As I stared into his eyes, I knew my face showed every feeling I had tried so hard to deny since his reappearance. "So you might go back to Haiti."

Mrs. Fuller stood. "You know, I believe I'm too full to eat my dessert right now also." She turned her gaze to her husband. "Do you want to go watch *Mary Poppins* with Peach?"

"Yep."

Mortified that I had been so transparent, I couldn't speak as they left the room. Billy took my hand. "The church board has offered me my dad's position, but I haven't given them my answer."

"What do you want to do?"

"I'm not sure. I'd miss our mission if I don't go back. I miss them as it is. But my parents need me." He paused and gave a shrug.

I didn't know what to say, so I said nothing.

"Why so pensive?" he asked, pressing my hand against his chest. "Did I upset you?"

"Upset me?" I shook my head. "Of course not. I'm just surprised. I thought you had moved back to Abbey Hills."

"Would you like that?"

The word *yes* was on the tip of my tongue. "I think you should do whatever makes you happy."

"Don't shut down on me again." His tone was colored with a hint of pleading.

I didn't want to pull away, but I had to face the truth. He had his family to look after, and I had mine. I couldn't expect him to think about my problems when his own father might die anytime.

And there was another reason, although I was a little surprised my lack of religious affiliation hadn't stopped his pursuit so far.

The phone rang in the other room, and I wished it had been mine so I'd have an excuse to back away from the conversation.

"Lauryn..."

I looked up at the sound of my name. Pushing aside my maudlin thoughts, I forced a smile. "Oh, Billy," I said with as much levity as possible considering my disappointment. "Don't get so serious."

His eyebrows rose. "Don't get so serious? Are you kidding? Why are you pulling away all of a sudden?"

"I don't know what you're talking about." I sipped the overly sweetened decaf coffee and had to fight not to gag. "Stop overdramatizing."

He muttered something under his breath, and I had a feeling it wasn't flattering. But there was no opportunity to press for an explanation because Mrs. Fuller came back into the room.

Her face was tense, her eyes troubled. Billy stood and went to her. "Is everything okay with Dad?"

"Your dad's fine." She patted Billy's arm and moved away from him. She pulled out the chair he had just left, sat down, and regarded me with kind sympathy. I started to feel uncomfortable. "Lauryn, we just got a call from Cokie's sister."

"Vernie? I didn't realize you knew her." Cokie's twin sister lived in St. Louis. I'd met her only a couple of times myself.

"She comes to church a few times a year when she visits Cokie."

I could tell Billy's mom was struggling to find words, but my brain didn't want to go there.

"Honey, Cokie passed away a couple of hours ago."

I stared at her, my head spinning as it tried to wrap around her words. "What?"

"I'm sorry, Lauryn. Cokie's gone."

My mind tried to keep up, but something was missing. "Gone where?" Why would she go anywhere in her condition? That didn't make sense.

Billy came closer as his mother spoke the dreaded words. "She's dead."

My eyes tunneled into darkness, lost focus. I saw Mrs. Fuller's mouth moving but couldn't make out the words. My cheeks were wet. I was crying, but I didn't remember feeling tears in my eyes.

Billy knelt beside my chair and wrapped me in his arms, nestling me against his broad chest as reality swept over me. His hands caressed my hair as I buried my face into the curve of his neck. He smelled of wood smoke and aftershave, and I wanted to stay there forever.

Mrs. Fuller pressed a tissue into my hand. Reluctantly I pulled back from Billy and wiped my nose.

I turned to Billy's mom. "But how could she be gone so soon? She was taking chemo…and…she just found out about the cancer."

"Her cancer was already a stage four by the time she went to the doctor."

Mrs. Fuller's hands were cool on mine. "She passed out at home and when Vernie got her to the hospital, they discovered bleeding in her uterus. They tried to stop it, but..."

I didn't hear the rest of her words. Why hadn't anyone called me? My heart began to ache as I realized I was nothing more to Cokie's family than a client. Why should I be more? They didn't know how much I loved Cokie. Or how much we relied on her. "Billy?" I whispered. Billy's arms still cradled me.

"Do you need me to take you home?"

I nodded. "Please."

"I'm sorry, Lauryn," Mrs. Fuller said. "I know how close the two of you were."

No. No, she didn't know how close Cokie and I were. Cokie was the only person I had to talk to. She was more than the person who cooked me dinner and sometimes washed my clothes. She was the only other person who understood my dad. She understood and she was my friend and no one knew how this felt.

Reverend Fuller joined us in the foyer to say good-bye. "Cokie has been part of my congregation for ten years. She was faithful to God and served in the church faithfully as well."

His words sounded like a eulogy. What did I care if she served God or changed diapers in the nursery?

"Thank you for a lovely supper, Mrs. Fuller."

She nodded. "Anytime. I mean that." She turned to Billy. "Please be careful taking her home."

Billy reached over and kissed her cheek. "I will."

"Call us when you're on your way home."

I looked from one parent to the other. What, was he still in high school?

We walked out the door and he steered me toward the car. "Don't say anything," he said.

"Anything about what?"

"About them being overprotective. My parents are just concerned because of the killings. Abbey Hills is a little town."

"They're afraid a guy out alone at night is an easy target."

"Exactly." He opened my door and waited until my legs were inside before closing it behind me.

My head ached from crying, and as I stared out the window I felt tears slipping down my cheeks again.

Billy's hand found my thigh, just above my knee. "I'm sorry, Lauryn. I wish I could spare you another loss. God knows you've had more than your share."

"Why do you think God knows anything about me?"

His eyebrows shot up and he stared at me for a moment. "Only by faith, I guess."

"Well, I don't have that kind of faith, so don't talk to me about God."

God had taken my mother and had stayed absent in my life for twenty-five years. Considering He kept taking away the people I loved, I highly doubted He cared one way or another about my share of loss.

I angled my chin and stared at him. The lines of his face were hidden in shadows. He was suddenly unfamiliar, and my heart started beating faster, almost as though fear had found its way in. I tried to dismiss the feeling as ridiculous but couldn't shake the uneasiness.

He slowed the car at the stoplight. The streetlights illuminated his face and once again he was Billy. He frowned. "You okay?"

I nodded. "I can't get Cokie's face out of my mind. Last week we were having turkey and pumpkin pie and decorating the Christmas tree. And now she's dead."

If he'd said something preacherish, I would have screamed. He didn't, just tightened his hand around my leg. Heat from his palm radiated through my jeans, and I was way too aware of that hand than I should have been, given the circumstances. I covered his hand with mine and he turned his palm, fitting his hand into mine like a puzzle, lacing our fingers. Again my heart sped up.

As my house came into view, I didn't want him to leave me there alone. I gathered my courage as he walked me to the door. He stopped at the bottom of the steps, wrapped me in his arms, and held me close. I slid my arms over his shoulders. "Can you come in for a while?" I whispered into the curve of his neck.

I felt him tense. He pulled away, resting his arms lightly at my waist. "That's not a good idea."

My stomach jumped at the implication of his words, but I played dumb. "What do you mean?" I felt stupid even asking the question when the answer was so obvious.

Billy had mercy and gave me the benefit of the doubt. He bent and pressed his forehead to mine. "Because we'll start making out and I'll be tempted to stay all night. And not innocently."

The image his words evoked wasn't unappealing. "So what? We're both adults."

"Why are you pretending to be so dense?"

"Why don't you want to stay with me? I obviously shouldn't be alone."

"Staying here is too dangerous for me." He pressed a kiss to my forehead and pulled me close again. My pride taunted me to protest, but I didn't. His arms felt too safe and I longed to stay there, for however long he offered the comfort.

"God, Billy, you'd think you have no self-control. Haven't you dated in the last seven years?"

"Yes, and I've been tempted, but it's easy to resist someone you're not in love with."

I swallowed hard. He loosened his hold and held me back a little. I couldn't take my eyes from his as he moved his face close to mine. Even as he drew closer, I knew it would be best if we didn't kiss. A relationship between us would never work. He had to know that. But I had been dreaming of this moment for too long and nothing could have kept me from raising my lips to meet his.

At the first touch of his mouth on mine, I relaxed against him, holding him, matching him kiss for kiss. Passion heightened between us, and I wondered fleetingly if he might change his mind and carry me inside. But in the next moment, he tore himself away and took two steps back. His chest rose and fell. He gave me a sheepish grin. "See what I mean?"

I nodded. "Sorry I can't join in your guilt. I sort of liked it."

"I did too." He regarded me solemnly. "I'll call you before I go to bed to check on you."

"Thank you."

"Wish I could stay with you." He released a breath, hazy in the cold air. "I know it's a hard night for you. I hate that you're alone."

"It's okay. I'm just going to go to bed. Your mom will probably get the news about the funeral service before I do, so I'll call her tomorrow."

"She likes you." He smiled. "They both do. I can tell."

A smile gentled my face, relieving the tension. "I like them too."

"That's important to me. For later."

"Later?"

"Don't act like you don't know where I'm hoping this is heading."

"Maybe this isn't the best time?"

"You're probably right." He stuffed his hands into his pockets and glanced toward his car.

I followed his gaze and my peripheral caught movement. I jerked my head, but the figure was gone.

"What?" Billy asked.

I shook my head. "I thought I saw someone. Just jumpy I guess."

"Are you sure?" He frowned. "Maybe I should stay for a while."

I couldn't help but tease him a little. "And risk being seduced?"

"Don't joke. Do you really think you saw someone? I don't want to take a chance you could be hurt or worse." He scowled. "Maybe you should come back to my parents' house and sleep in the guest room."

"It was just a shadow. Probably from the wind. I'm definitely not spending the night anywhere but here."

He walked back to me, cupped the back of my neck, and pulled me forward. We shared a quick kiss. "Go inside," he said. "I don't want to leave until I know you're safe and locked in."

I kissed him on the cheek. "I'll call you tomorrow."

I locked the door behind me and walked to the window. I pushed aside the curtain and waited until his taillights turned the corner. Before I dropped the curtain, I forced my gaze to the spot where I'd thought I saw movement. The breeze picked up, blowing a branch from the oak tree in the front yard of my neighbor's house across the street. I felt a little silly.

I went back to my room and changed into a sweatshirt and jeans that weren't quite so snug. If I was going to be up all night thinking about Cokie, I might as well get some work done.

CHAPTER EIGHTEEN

First there were the little things. Misplaced documents, forgetting names of people he'd known for years. We laughed about his "senior moments" until he started walking around with his shoes untied because he couldn't remember how to tie them and nearly stripped the gears on the Jeep because he forgot how to drive the standard transmission.

The doctors ran all kinds of tests to rule out blocked arteries to the brain and strokes. Finally the dreaded diagnosis came down to Alzheimer's. An old person's disease at sixty?

We were devastated.

We sat together on the patio that evening staring out at my childhood swing set he'd never had the heart to get rid of.

"What are we going to do, kid?"

"Don't worry, Dad," I said. "I'll take care of everything."

Eden hadn't thought much about her son all these years. But now, now she wondered. Had he succumbed to the thirst, or had he lived a normal life with a wife and children and death at the end? Throughout her endless days and nights with nothing to do but remember, Eden did just that. She remembered the night he was born. Remembered her mother taking him away.

She had never wanted children after that. Not until she met Markus. She would have had as many children as he desired, and she would have gladly stayed home and been a wife to him. But Markus didn't want that. Not from her. She'd lost him in more ways than through his death. She'd lost his heart. That had been unbearable. Now all she wanted was to get free from this prison and go home to Dastillion Court.

But first her captor would pay for his cruelty.

———

Amede's illness left her by evening. But in its wake came a ferocious hunger unmatched by anything she had ever felt. She dressed in a pair of jeans and a black long-sleeved pullover shirt with a V neck and three buttons. She grabbed a short, light jacket—one that would allow for easy movement as she hunted.

Amede had no answers for the afternoon's sickness. Had someone cursed her? She remembered Eden's mother, a voodoo queen, putting elaborate curses on people and then charging them a hefty sum to lift the curse. Had someone done that to her? Juliette? She remembered the look in Juliette's eyes, the resentment. Could she have adopted Roma's ways? Despite the girl's denial, perhaps Amede needed to take a closer look.

But for now, she must feed.

She went out to the balcony, but a knock on the door inside stopped her before she could jump and run into the field. Frustration shuddered through her. Everyone knew she was ill. She had to answer. Otherwise, someone might come in without permission and discover her gone.

Ravaged with hunger, she hoped her eyes wouldn't betray her. They seemed to become more pronounced the hungrier she became. She opened the door to the sight of the sheriff. "Sheriff?" she asked, trying to hide her annoyance.

Sheriff Jenkins wore her uniform, and her expression remained stoic. "I trust you're feeling better?"

"I am. Some. Can I help you?"

"The highway patrol has appointed a special investigator for the case and he is interviewing everyone who was at the party."

"Isn't it a little late?" Amede's hands were beginning to tremble. She could smell the sheriff's scent and fought the rising tide of hunger inside. A door across the hall opened. Thank God.

The sheriff turned at the sound of the door opening, revealing a white neck. She gave the man a cordial smile and turned back to Amede. "We've been interviewing all day. We just left Anise."

Amede grabbed her bag from the table by the door. She had no idea how long she could maintain her control. If Juliette were here, she would have the girl fix her a very strong cup of the tea. Amede knew it would not take away the hunger, but perhaps it would numb her enough to get her through the interview. "I hope we can be brief, Sheriff," she said as Sheriff Jenkins moved through the hallway toward the stairs.

"You seem agitated, Miss Dastillion," the sheriff said.

"Still not feeling well."

Whether the sheriff believed her or not, she didn't know, but Amede had no intention of being bullied.

"We'll be as quick as possible," Sheriff Jenkins said as they took the last of the steps and she led Amede through the foyer to the dining room. A man in a pair of jeans, a button-down shirt, and a sports coat stood as they entered. His boots clacked across the wood floor as he walked to meet them.

Sheriff Jenkins motioned to Amede. "This is Amede Dastillion. She was Charley's sort-of date that night."

He might have been handsome if not for the way he looked at her. His eyes took her in, pausing on her curves. She forced herself to accept the clammy hand he held out. "Detective Townsend," he said.

"Pleased to meet you." Her tone held no warmth.

He motioned toward the dining table. "Have a seat, Miss Dastillion," he said.

"Please call me Amede. I find it's easier for most people."

Sheriff Jenkins took the seat next to her while the detective sat across from them. He had a recorder and a notepad.

"If you don't mind I'm going to go over the information I already have. It'll be redundant and I'm sure you've answered the questions before, but I'd appreciate it if you'd humor me."

He grinned at her, obviously trying to charm her into cooperation. Amede wanted to leap across the table and end her misery. Instead, she closed her eyes, forced away the images, then opened them again. "I'll tell you everything I can remember, Detective. It's time to catch that poor girl's murderer."

He flipped a few pages. "I understand you were in Barney's Café when the body of Jeremy Hildreth was discovered in the parking lot?"

Amede frowned. "Yes. Along with fifty others."

"You didn't leave the building when the others were outside investigating?"

The sheriff gave a short laugh. "You mean milling around and getting in the way."

The detective tossed the sheriff a look that set Amede's teeth on edge. She didn't like this man at all, and if she had to suffer his presence for too long she wasn't sure she could contain herself. She did, however, respect the sheriff, and from where she sat, the sheriff had a lot more intelligence and professionalism than the so-called detective.

He went over the same questions she had answered for Sheriff Jenkins. "Why were you there with Charley? What was your reaction when the girl made disparaging remarks about you? Why did you leave the house instead of going up to your room? Where did you go? You went for a walk in sub-zero weather? Interesting. Who saw you? Your assistant? Convenient."

After fifteen minutes of sarcasm and skepticism, Amede had had enough. She stood. "Detective, I've made every attempt to cooperate with your investigation, but my cooperation ends at being made the object of your bad manners. So unless you are planning to charge me, I'm finished here."

His eyes narrowed and flashed and he stood up, leaning across the table, resting his weight on his fists. He stared her in the eye. "You and your boyfriend are suspects in a murder investigation, so excuse me if I forgot to say please and thank you."

Amede fought back a growl. If she gave in to her instincts they truly would have reason to arrest her. With great effort, she forced herself to remain calm and felt her heart rate beginning to return to normal. She would walk away, go to her room, and resume her plans for a hunt.

But the detective wasn't inclined to end the conversation. "Now listen up, Amede. We have two dead bodies and a slew of dead animals. Not one of the killings occurred until you came to town, so sit yourself back down in that chair and answer my questions like a lady. You can go when I say you can."

The fool couldn't leave well enough alone. Amede felt the growl rising again and wasn't able to fully suppress a small vibration, her anger shoving reason aside.

"Miss Amede?" The sound of Juliette's voice sent waves of relief over

Amede. She turned to find the girl walking into the room, removing her black fur-lined gloves. "Is everything okay?"

"Everything's fine." Sheriff Jenkins spoke up before Amede could. "This is Detective Townsend. He'd like to speak with you and Caleb about the night of Janine's murder."

Juliette's gaze shifted from Amede to the detective. Juliette reached her hand to him, turning on the charm. "Nice to meet you, Detective. I'd be happy to answer any questions you have. Caleb isn't here right now but I'm sure he'll be happy to answer your questions too as soon as he's available."

Amede held her breath, hoping he would back down and not try to prove he had the power to keep her there. He turned his gaze to her, once more raking her with his eyes. Incensed by the obvious disrespect, Amede made a swift turn on her heel. She faced Juliette. "Come and see me when you're finished with the detective." She turned to Sheriff Jenkins. The woman was staring at her, face blanched and brow furrowed in a frown.

"Sheriff?" Amede said. "Is everything okay?"

At the sound of her voice the sheriff shook off her stupor and nodded. She smiled. "Everything's fine. Thank you for your cooperation and I apologize for Detective Townsend's lack of manners."

"Well, hopefully he'll figure out who the killer is and leave me alone."

The detective snorted. "I'd like nothing more."

Amede grabbed her purse and headed back upstairs. She briefly considered going out the front door, but with the detective in the house and the sheriff's odd behavior, she thought better of it. Once in the room, she locked the door behind her and tossed her purse onto the table along with her keys.

Her body still felt weak from the freak illness and she couldn't wait much longer for sustenance. She jumped from the balcony, her body floating. She hit the ground running and raced toward the field behind the house, but nothing caught her senses. She ran for miles until she found herself in the woods above the river.

Whispers as soft as the rustling of dead leaves caught her ears.

She jerked around. "Eden?"

Branches crackled on the ground a few yards away, and she heard the drumbeat of a strong heart. Throwing back her head, she took in the scent of a deer. She crouched, her hair loose and flying into her face. She waited for the right moment. She felt the blood rushing through her veins, and when the animal came into view she paused for just the right second, then leaped.

Juliette's answers to the obnoxious detective were short, concise, memorized, and executed. Yes, Amede had left the party. And, yes, she was angry to have been the object of Janine's verbal assault. But she had walked straight to Caleb and Juliette where they sat cuddled up on the swing in front of the fire pit on the porch. That's when she asked Juliette to come with her while she walked off the anger, which Juliette did after procuring a flashlight from the trunk of the car. Caleb had stayed behind. A little later, Amede had walked back to the inn and to her room. Juliette didn't see her after that.

"So she could have left without you knowing?" the detective said.

"I suppose." Juliette knew the time frame wouldn't match with the murder. But just in case, she had told a small lie to provide Amede with an alibi. And as far as she knew, no one could disprove her words. She and Caleb had gone on their own little adventure, and she was pretty sure no one had seen them together.

The sheriff stood. "I think we're done here, don't you, Detective?"

He gave a lazy, annoying grin and shoved back in his chair. "I suppose. For now."

Juliette showed them out. Then she leaned back against the closed door and looked up as Caleb came down the steps, his hair wet from a shower. Her heart sped up at the sight of him, tousled hair, loose jeans, and a striped button-down shirt.

She often played the "what-if" game. What if she hadn't come with Amede to Abbey Hills? What if Caleb hadn't stopped at the inn? What if she hadn't told him the truth—that she loved him?

She moved to the steps as he came down, and they met at the landing. "I'm sorry you had to endure the questions alone," he said, drawing her close. Juliette's stomach dipped as his mouth met hers.

Amede would never approve of Caleb as a boyfriend, certainly not one she could continue seeing after they returned home. And Juliette could sense things were winding down in Abbey Hills. Amede would have to find Eden soon, or she would have to flee. She couldn't allow the police to arrest her for killing Janine. Juliette had no idea if Amede had fed on the young woman or not. But either way, she was bound by duty to protect all Dastillions.

"Did you find what you were looking for?" she asked Caleb as he pulled away.

"Yes, I did." He smiled and kissed her nose. "Thank you for covering for me."

She laid her head against his chest and closed her eyes. She wanted to tell him how much she loved him. How she would do anything for him. Instead, she allowed him to take her hand and lead her upstairs.

CHAPTER NINETEEN

Most days during that first year after my dad's diagnosis, he experienced memory glitches that were somewhat frustrating at times, annoying at others. He'd ask why we were doing something or where we were headed, then ask the question again an hour later. I religiously studied the disease, focusing on medical breakthroughs, natural remedies, anything that might bring my dad back to the strong, capable hero he'd always been.

But he declined. And while the dynamic of our relationship changed and he grew more dependent, it worked for us like it always had. Where else would I have focused my energy but on my dad?

Eden could sense Amede's closeness. Her heart had begun to pump in wild abandon. She heard a rush in her ears, like the sound of an ocean. Closing her eyes, she transported into the woods. Every sense quickened, every footstep light, as though she floated above the forest floor. A smile tipped the corners of her lips. She sprang. And opened her eyes to the dank reality of the tiny, fetid cell.

"No!" she screamed, though barely producing a noise. "No!" she whimpered, bumping her head against the wall over and over, harder and harder until she bled.

I sat in the driveway at the Chisom house, trying to gather up the courage to leave my Jeep and walk up to the door. My stomach was a cluster of nerves, and my legs and arms felt like lead.

As I sat there staring at the overgrowth, I decided to call the hospital to check on my dad. I was stalling, but I wasn't quite ready to play the role of the stupid girl in a B movie for teens. I could almost hear the eerie music swell at the thought of reaching the door.

Shuddering, I pulled out my cell phone and punched in the hospital's number. I was relieved to learn Dad was fine. He'd had some broth and was able to keep it down. His mind wasn't clear, but otherwise, he seemed okay and hadn't appeared distressed by my absence. The nurse felt sure he'd sleep the rest of the night.

Satisfied that he was okay, I disconnected the call with the assurance that I could bring him home the next day.

I reached into my purse and pulled out the key to the house. I didn't carry it on my key ring for obvious reasons. I didn't want to give a thief any opportunities to take my keys and walk right in.

Reluctantly, I grabbed the handle and opened the car door. I slowly slid from the seat, softly closing the door behind me. Why couldn't there be a big, bright moon and starlight to guide me? I stumbled along the path to the house in pitch black, kicking myself for not grabbing a flashlight from the house. The one in the Jeep had burned out the night of my accident.

I reached the steps and paused, feeling a little guilty for going back on my word to Jill that I wouldn't work alone in the house. But who could I have called? Charley was a suspect in at least Janine's murder, and if he was arrested for that, he'd most likely be charged with Jeremy's murder too. I found it hard to believe that he could have done such a thing, but I didn't want to be naive either.

I slid the key into the lock and twisted the doorknob. My heart pounded in my chest and I nearly turned around and made a run for the Jeep. What was I thinking?

Shoving aside my cowardice, I stepped inside, shivering. My breath was visible and it felt colder in the house than it did outside. I headed straight to the thermostat and pressed the up arrow on the digital box. I liked the idea of old look, modern convenience. Markus had outfitted the house to run like a newly built home. That would be a huge selling point. It could have easily sucked a person dry financially just trying to heat the old dinosaur.

I stood in the middle of the foyer, trying to decide where to start. I had been working on crates in the living area where my desk sat, but I was curious about the ring Amede Dastillion was hoping to recover. I still wasn't clear on the relationship between the Dastillions and Markus Chisom, but my curiosity about the ring led me toward the stairs.

I tried not to look at the carvings on the railing. Since Dad had pointed them out to me, the hellish, demonic images gave me the creeps. Those images and the recent events in Abbey Hills pressed me as close to the wall as possible while I climbed the stairs. Each step filled me with a deeper sense of foreboding. I should never have come here alone at night.

I slipped my hand into my jacket pocket and clutched my cell phone in case I needed to make a hasty call. Jill's number was on speed dial. But that made me feel only a tiny bit better. What was it about walking upstairs in an old, dark house that evoked my childhood fears? When I reached the top, I switched on the light and headed toward the master bedroom at the end of the hallway.

I stopped short at the sound of water running in the bathroom. My chest tightened. I ducked into the first room on the left and dialed Jill.

"Lauryn?"

"Jill," I whispered. "Someone's in the house."

"Your house?" Her tone had immediately gone from friendly to professional and cautious.

"The Chisom house."

"Okay, are you inside, or did you see a light or movement from outside?"

I could have kicked myself for not paying attention when I was still outside. Would I have seen a light? "Inside. I'm upstairs and someone is running water in the bathroom."

"Running water?"

"I know it sounds odd."

The water shut off in the bathroom.

"Where are you?" Jill asked.

"Upstairs in one of the guest bedrooms. The water just turned off."

"Okay, stay hidden. I'm on my way."

I crawled toward the closet but didn't want to make noise with the door, so I made myself small against the wall, tucking my legs to my chest.

I cowered in the corner, imagining all the brave things I'd do if I was packing a Glock. A board creaked in the hallway as soft footfalls moved closer to my hiding place.

A high-pitched screech summoned a scream from my own throat. I jumped to my feet just as a figure leaped around the corner, baseball bat raised high, ready to be used as a weapon on me.

I closed my eyes and waited for the blow, my mind shifting to thoughts of my dad as it had the night of my accident. What would he do without me?

"Oh thank God, Lauryn, it's just you."

My eyes popped open. It took a second to twist my mind around the sight of Miranda James standing in front of me in a fluffy white towel, her hair wrapped turban-style. She lowered the bat and dropped it onto the floor. She seemed as relieved as I felt.

"Miranda, what are you doing here?" Irritation shot through me. "I swear, you could have knocked my brains out."

"Lauryn, I'm so glad it was you." Her hand was out, palm forward.

"What are you doing here?" I repeated through clenched teeth, still shaking from the near-death experience.

"The deputy kicked me out of the Inn. There's nowhere to go in this town. I thought about sleeping in the park, but come on. Is that really safe? I mean, a woman was just murdered days ago. Besides, it's freezing out there. I mean, not to downplay all the homeless people sleeping under bridges in this weather, but I've never done it and I'm sensitive to the cold. But I guess now I'll have to do it anyway."

"Stop talking!" I finally said as she was gathering a breath for what I presumed was a new onslaught of words. "Back up. Now *slowly* tell me why Charley kicked you out. That doesn't sound like him." Not because he was a kind soul but because filled rooms meant money in the bank.

She glanced toward the door. "How about I get dressed first?"

"Yes. Go ahead. Come to the kitchen when you're done. And then you can tell me why I shouldn't have you arrested for breaking and entering."

I headed back down the steps, shivering a little, as the furnace had only just begun to warm the place. How could she stand to shower in this freezing house? I called Jill. "False alarm. It was just Miranda."

"Miranda! Barney's Miranda?"

"A lot of wives might be jealous of a beautiful free spirit working at their husband's restaurant. Especially the way Barney puts up with her crap."

Jill chuckled. "Do you know something I don't know?"

"No. Sorry. Barney is true as a golden retriever."

"Why is she there?"

"Charley kicked her out of the Inn."

"Why was she at the Inn? What about her apartment?"

"I don't know. We didn't get that far. She was showering—thus the water running—and was wearing a towel when we discovered each other."

"Well, I'm coming over to talk to her, but it'll be awhile. I just got another call about a dead animal."

My stomach sank at the news. "Be careful, Jill."

"Keep the doors locked. I'll use my key."

In the kitchen I put on the teakettle, glad I had thought to bring it along with some mugs and tea bags.

The kettle was whistling by the time Miranda returned. She was dressed in a pair of skinny jeans—figures she could wear those, no muffin top around her middle. Her wet, crazy red hair was twisted up and clipped in back. She looked gorgeous, even without makeup. She started talking before she was even fully in the room.

"Look, I know I shouldn't have just broken into the house. But honestly, you should be glad it was me."

"Oh really?" I couldn't believe her audacity. "Why do you say that?"

She shrugged and dropped down into a kitchen chair. "Who would you rather have here, me or a crazy bloodsucking killer?"

"Hmm...I'll have to think about that for a while." My mouth twitched. Irritated as I was, I couldn't resist teasing. I didn't bother to ask if she wanted tea. I put two tea bags in two cups and poured the water, then set one in front of her.

"Thanks." She grinned. She bent her knee up to her chest and pulled on a thick sock, then did the same with the other foot. "Sharing your tea with me. Does this mean you're not having me arrested?"

"No, it means I'm not drinking mine alone while I try to decide. And for the record, Jill's coming soon." I sat catty-corner from her. "Okay, spill it. What happened at the Inn to make Charley kick you out?"

"Well, I'm investigating the murder story, of course, and I was asking Amede about the murdered girl. So of course the topic naturally headed to Charley since he's the prime suspect."

"Not necessarily."

She shrugged. "In my opinion he is. Anyway, he overheard me telling Amede I wasn't sure he was innocent. And he got mad."

I shook my head. "I can't believe the audacity," I said facetiously. "Accuse a guy of murder in his own house and he kicks you out."

"Well, it isn't like I was the first one to think about the motive and opportunity. The highway patrol investigator only needs one tiny piece of evidence or some kind of reasonable doubt to arrest him. I'm surprised he hasn't decided to hold him for questioning."

"Maybe he's trying to lull Charley into a false sense of security." I was being sarcastic again, but she missed it this time.

"I was thinking the same thing. Give him just enough rope to hang himself."

Exasperated, I fingered the top of my cup as I waited for the tea to cool. "Okay, that explains the being kicked out part. Why are you here?"

"There's no place to get a room in this town except the Inn."

I gave her an incredulous look. "So you thought it'd be okay to move into a beautiful Victorian filled with priceless antiques and paintings?"

"Well, I couldn't sleep on the park bench, Lauryn. I already told you that's not safe."

Her faulty logic reminded me of a selfish two-year-old trying to get out of trouble for pulling the dog's tail. "What happened to your apartment?"

Taking her mug between her palms, she scowled. "I was asked to leave because of all the press over my Web site." She sipped, keeping her eyes on me over the rim of her cup.

I had a hard time drumming up sympathy for the teenager in a grown woman's body. "Well, that's your own fault."

"Why can't I stay here? If something turns up missing, you know who to blame."

"First of all, this isn't my house, so I can't decide who can or can't stay." I spooned honey into my tea and stirred. "Second, even if I could decide, I would say no. Why would I let you snoop around when all you want to do is disparage this man's memory with crazy claims that he's the undead?"

I grinned at my own choice of words.

"You think by trying to prove he was a vampire I'm disparaging his memory?"

She almost seemed offended. I thought maybe she'd been studying vampires a little too long.

"Considering that the recent murders seem to mimic the murders from before, I think it does border on accusing him of being a murderer."

She sipped her tea again. "I happen to think it's a compliment." She'd definitely been living in her blog world too long.

"Okay. Listen, I have work to do." I abandoned my thought of starting with the jewelry. No way was I leaving crazy Miranda unattended downstairs. I walked into the living room and scowled. "Miranda, how about getting your computer off my desk?" I called.

"Oh, sorry. I'm coming."

Her computer was opened to her Web site and I couldn't help but read. If nothing else it *was* entertaining.

Things That Go Bump in the Night

Seriously, how many more people and animals will be found slaughtered and drained of blood before the police get a clue? Personally, I
believe vampires can coexist with humans. It just takes a little bit of
cooperation. Blood drives maybe. I don't know the solution. But
forcing them to become murderers is just wrong.

I know some people think I sound crazy, and that's the point.
We have to stop being in denial about their existence. That's the first
step.

Will you add your voice to mine in this fight?

"What do you think?"

I jumped at the sound of Miranda's voice. I couldn't hold back a smirk. "I think Martin Luther King would be proud of you for standing up for vam-pires' rights."

She scowled. "I wish people wouldn't make fun. This is serious."

I looked into her green eyes and realized she wasn't just doing this Web site for a stunt. Miranda was about as crazy as they came.

Amede loved the smell of the night air. She'd forgotten just how much the fresh, crisp scent of dirt and wind could send her emotions soaring. Tonight's hunt had been wild, frenzied. It had taken awhile to be satiated and clean up the mess.

Not ready to go back to the Inn, she found herself at the charred site of Eden's house.

It angered her that no one had attempted to clean up the site. She walked to the cellar, hoping to find some evidence of Eden's whereabouts. She didn't feel her as strongly as she had earlier. Perhaps because she'd recently fed.

As Amede approached the cellar she noticed the lock had been broken and the door flung open. Vandals? Surely Miranda hadn't come back last night after the squad car had arrived and scared her off.

Outraged but curious, Amede climbed down the steps. The cold, dank cellar burned her nose. New Orleans didn't have cellars or basements. The city was too far below sea level, so these underground rooms always fascinated Amede.

A cot sat in the corner, and shelves held old paint cans and pieces of dry wall. But nothing that would lead her to Eden. Disappointment set in. She had been certain she would find at least some small clue. With a sigh, she turned and started to walk up the steps. A shadow appeared. She started to call out just as the door slammed shut. Fear gripped her. She raced up the steps, pounding on the door above. "Someone is in here!" she called. "Open the door."

The lock clicked.

Her stomach knotted.

"Hello?" she called, a sickening feeling that someone had purposely locked her in settling in her stomach. "Let me out, please."

"How does it feel to be hunted?"

Amede heard the raspy voice from above. "Why are you doing this? You can't kill me the way you killed the others."

He laughed. "I know what you are."

"What do you mean?"

"I know there are others like you. One right here in Abbey Hills."

Amede's heart pounded in her ears. "Eden?"

A howl of laughter rose from him. "I knew it! I knew you came here looking for her. That's why you haven't left. They all think she died in the fire. But you know better. Can you feel her?"

"Yes," Amede whispered hoarsely. "Do you have her?"

"Locked away just like you."

"How did you find out about me?" Amede needed to keep him talking to find out where he was keeping Eden.

"Did you recover from the poison?"

The memory of her illness swept across her and she almost felt the ache, the nausea all over again. "You?"

"No. You've obviously been betrayed by the ones you thought you could trust. I wonder if your victims felt that way about you."

Amede sat on the steps and listened to him stumble away. *He must be drunk.*

She laughed at her momentary panic. She still felt strong. Thank goodness literature had the idea of vampires wrong. She'd never survive a night in a coffin.

When Amede was sure her assailant was gone, she turned, dropped down a couple of steps, and flung herself forward. The door cracked and fell open.

Her relief didn't quite coincide with the short time she had been locked away. She couldn't force her heart to slow.

She walked along the highway, ducking out of sight when headlights came into view. She thought about the man who had locked her in. He said he had Eden. She had to find him. Eden was slipping away.

CHAPTER TWENTY

What are the chances that Amanda would have not one but two kids before I even found a man interested enough not to cheat on me? She called me one day and invited me to lunch at her house. Curious, I went. Abbey Hills might be a small town, but if you didn't go to church or attend town meetings you could easily go months without seeing a friend.

When I arrived, carrying a loaf of french bread and an olive oil dip, I recognized the setup. Amanda's younger brother, Charley, who had graduated with me a year after Amanda, was there wearing his police uniform.

"What about Janine?" I asked Amanda. Everyone knew those two were on-again, off-again and usually lived together either way.

"He says they're broken up for good." She smiled, rubbing her bulging stomach. "He's had his eye on you since high school."

I had no time for dating. Even if I had, Charley wasn't my type.

"My dad and the auction house keep me too busy to date."

She grinned. "I understand. It was worth a try. But, Lauryn. . . I bet you'd have time to date if Billy Fuller came back to town."

Me? Date Billy?

I wished he'd come back to town so I could show him just how much I didn't care about him.

The end was coming. Nothing mattered anymore except for the trembling deep inside. She'd never feared God. She knew about God and sin and believed deeply in angels and demons. But the idea that she should bow to anyone felt wrong. Why shouldn't she be as she was inclined to be?

Markus had hated his way of life. But he'd fallen for Eden almost immediately the night they met at the theater. She'd been the mistress of Mr. Blakely, who owned the largest shipping company on the Mississippi. They'd met at intermission, and the next day flowers filled her rooms—rooms paid for by Mr. Blakely. Markus and Eden were infatuated with each other. She left Mr. Blakely in less than a week.

Eden had fallen in love for the first and only time in her life.

They'd been together fifty years when he disappeared the first time. She couldn't bear to be without him. Her love for him went far beyond every emotion she'd known. Each time she found him, she cajoled him into returning to her. The last time he had hidden well, so tired, he said, of hurting people. He'd become a vampire with a conscience. Pathetic. No better than Papa and Amede. When she discovered he had come to Abbey Hills, anger, more than love, had brought her to town. She'd killed and left the bodies to be discovered, knowing Markus would come after her. And he did, but he betrayed her. Eden closed her eyes against the memory, too weak, too tired to care.

Now Markus was dead and she was the captive of a maniac. She would die here, punishment for her many sins.

———

I stared at the screen in front of me, trying to find the value of what appeared to be a first edition of *Wuthering Heights*. An inscription inside may or may not have decreased the value, but otherwise the book appeared to be in mint condition.

To Amede it would be priceless. The inscription was to an ancestor with the same name. Amede. Must have been a family name. I clicked on a link that showed a price as high as a quarter of a million dollars. Amede Dastillion would have to pay a small fortune to have the book returned to her family's estate. If she chose not to purchase it, someone else surely would.

Making a few notations in my database, I slid the book into a plastic sleeve for protection and added it to a crate where I was storing the priced items.

An instant message popped up.

Check this link if you don't believe me.

Miranda. I rolled my eyes but clicked on the link. It was a newspaper article from the *Abbey Hills Daily Record*.

Local philanthropist Markus Chisom donates $100,000 to the Abbey Hills local library to repair damages caused by last month's tornado.

I clicked on the messenger screen. *What am I supposed to be looking at here?*

The date.

I squinted and scanned the article until I found the date. I still didn't get what she was trying to show me. *Okay, June 1995. So?*

How old was Markus when he died?

Thirty or so?

Does he look fifteen in that photograph?

I clicked away from the instant message and studied the photograph. Mrs. Abernathy, the head librarian, definitely looked fifteen years younger. The town mayor at the time, Mr. Crane, who was now retired and had joined the group of old-timers for their daily ritual at Barney's, also looked fifteen years younger. But Markus Chisom looked thirty years old.

"See my point?"

I jumped as Miranda stuck her big red head around the corner.

"What I see is that Mr. Chisom had good genes," I said after catching my breath.

"Now you're just being stubborn. I'm this close to posting this link on my blog with a copy of his obit photo."

I shrugged. "That's your call, I guess."

The front door opened and closed and I tensed until Jill called out, "Lauryn? It's Jill. You here?"

"At my desk, Jill."

"Don't show her the picture," Miranda whispered.

"Whatever."

Jill's face was screwed up into a scowl when she entered the room. "I thought you promised you wouldn't come to the house alone."

"I know, Jill," I truly felt bad, but I was just so far behind. "I have so much work to do, I didn't really think about it."

"Besides," Miranda piped in. "She's not alone. I'm here."

Jill's eyes narrowed and she gave her a firm "cop" stare. "I don't think trespassing your way into the house constitutes the buddy system."

At least Miranda had the good grace to blush. "Yes, but for a very good reason." Without waiting for an invitation, she launched into the diatribe about her unfortunate popularity among the media (which, of course, she had nothing to do with) and her expulsion from not only her apartment but also the Baylor Inn. "I mean, this house is just sitting here and I figured I could kill three birds with one stone."

Jill appeared more entertained than irritated and I wondered if Barney's infatuation with Miranda's antics had rubbed off on his wife. "Okay, three birds. What are they?"

"Well, I figured, one"—she kept count with her fingers—"I could protect the place because it's pretty simple to break into. Even with the alarm."

I made a noise of protest and she turned. "Just sayin'." She turned back to Jill. "Two, I could use a place to stay, of course."

"Of course," Jill said, her sarcasm lost on Miranda.

"Three, I am doing research on this guy and other vampires like him, so this is the obvious place to find what I'm looking for." She angled her head toward me. "And don't worry, I'm not a thief and I wouldn't break anything either. So can I stay?" She addressed the question to Jill.

"Sorry," Jill said, smiling. "I can't allow you to do that."

Miranda's cheeks puffed as she blew out her disappointment. "Darn."

"But I have another idea."

The look on Miranda's face was priceless as her red eyebrows lifted in surprise. "What sort of idea?"

"Barney and I live next door. Why not stay with us until the press dies down and your roommate lets you back in?"

I don't know who was more surprised, Miranda or me. Then I saw it from Jill's perspective. She and Barney had hearts of gold. Miranda worked for them and had no place to go. I supposed Miranda was harmless enough.

This way there was little chance she could get into trouble. Theoretically.

Miranda broke the silence. "Are you sure?"

"Definitely."

"Is Barney okay with it?"

Jill nodded. "I wouldn't have mentioned it to you otherwise."

My eyes traveled back to the screen. "Jill," I said. I could feel Miranda tense but didn't bother to placate her. "Take a look at this."

"What's up?" she asked, walking around to look over my shoulder.

"That's Markus."

She paused a couple of seconds. "Hmm. That's a pretty old article. How'd you find it?"

I tilted my head toward Miranda. "Ask middle-aged Buffy over there."

Miranda slammed her hands on her hips. "Hey! No need to get personal."

"Her theory is that Markus never aged past this fifteen-year-old photograph. I have to admit it's pretty compelling when you think about it. If he died at thirty, he would have been fourteen or fifteen in 1995. Right?"

"I'm afraid I don't have an explanation." Jill's voice was shaky, but she seemed to be forcing levity. I didn't believe the levity, and the shakiness gave me pause. Jill knew something. Vampire? I highly doubted it, but there had to be an explanation that went beyond good genes. A fifty-year-old looking sixty I could believe. A fifteen-year-old looking thirty? Not so much.

"Jill..." I said, but she cut me off.

"Okay, here's the plan," she said. "I'm taking Miranda to the café to help Barney clean up. He's been short-handed since Janine was killed. Barney will drive her home afterward."

Miranda shrugged. "Fine by me. Do I get overtime?"

Jill chuckled. "Yeah, it's called a warm bed and a full belly."

"That sounds fair."

The two of them left, but I didn't miss the long look Jill gave me. "I'll talk to you later, Lauryn."

Twenty minutes later my cell phone buzzed. The caller ID said Jill.

"So, what was that all about?" I asked without the typical phone etiquette.

She breathed out. "I just got off the phone with Nina and I think we need to go to her place and chat awhile."

I glanced at the clock. It was midnight and I had to be at the hospital by ten to pick up my dad.

"Can it wait until tomorrow evening?"

"It can't." Jill's voice was starting to break up and I suspected she was already near the reserve where the trees sometimes interfered with reception. "Nina is leaving tomorrow to go back to Dallas. She's remarrying Hunt the day after."

"Is a conference call out of the question?" I knew I was being difficult, but it was all I could do to hold my eyes open. The thought of driving out to the reserve to speak with Nina filled me with dread. Exhaustion wound through me, tightening its tentacle grip and dragging me to a moment very close to collapse. I wasn't positive I could even make it out there without falling asleep at the wheel.

"We can't risk someone with a scanner listening in." She paused. "It's important that you come hear what we have to say. It's about that photo."

"Okay, I'll lock up here and head out. Give me fifteen minutes."

"Watch out for ice fog. It's pretty nasty out here."

Wearily, I pressed my palm to my forehead and began the process of cleaning up. I slid my laptop into my bag, slipped my purse over my shoulder, and set the alarm. An eerie, gray feeling overtook me as I stepped onto the porch and pulled the door shut. I fantasized about my nice warm home and pillow top mattress. I wanted to be anywhere but plodding through the cold fog. My peripheral vision wreaked havoc with my imagination and I kept seeing things that went bump in the night. I was more than a little scared by the time my shaky hands unlocked the car door. I jumped in and locked the door as quickly as humanly possible.

I started the engine, not bothering to wait for it to warm up before shifting into reverse and pulling out of the driveway. As I turned the wheel I saw something move. This time I was convinced enough to pause and look. A figure stood at the top of the driveway I'd just exited. He, or I suppose it could have been a she, wore a long, heavy coat.

My heart slammed against my chest as he walked toward me, but there was no way I was waiting around to find out if it was someone I knew.

I slammed the gearshift into drive and stomped the gas. When I looked in the rearview mirror, he stood in the street, watching me drive away like the coward I was.

Rather than feeling weary from the long walk to the Inn and the ordeal of being locked in the cellar, Amede was invigorated. The incident only confirmed that Eden was alive. She would have endured any hardship to have concrete proof. Amede walked inside, knowing her jeans were ripped and caked in mud, her shirt torn at the elbow.

The night manager raised his eyes curiously but said nothing. Upstairs, she knocked on Juliette's door.

Juliette's eyes widened at the sight of her and she accompanied Amede into her room. "Miss Amede, what happened?"

Amede waved aside the concern, stripping off her shirt. "Oh, most of this happened during my hunt. It was out of control." She smiled thinking about it. "I haven't felt that way in years."

"Since you hunted with Eden."

She wiggled out of her jeans and grabbed her robe while Juliette gathered up her clothes.

"Yes, since I hunted with Eden. It was like we were part of each other again. As if we were sharing the same cravings, the same thrill when we found our prey."

Juliette stopped and regarded her quietly. "Human prey."

The soft condemnation in Juliette's tone clouded Amede's euphoria. She sat on the edge of her bed. "Yes, but not tonight or any night in my recent past." She peered closer at Juliette. "Do you think I killed Janine and the man in the truck?"

Juliette hugged the clothes against her and dropped into the desk chair. "No…well…it has crossed my mind. Eden's nearness has turned you into someone I've never seen before. Even Grandmere's tea stopped working pretty quickly. I just can't help but worry."

"I would have nothing to gain by lying to you or Roma. You two are honor bound to help me cover it all up."

Juliette's eyes flashed but so briefly Amede thought she might have imagined it. The girl stood. "I'll get rid of these."

"Wait. I wanted to ask you something." Juliette paused. "Where is Caleb tonight? Has he gone? Or are the two of you quarrelling?"

A barely perceptible blush crept up Juliette's cheeks. "We're not arguing. He left earlier to get barbeque and I felt I should wait for you to come back in case you needed me."

It gratified Amede to know the girl considered duty before romance. She nodded her approval. "I am going to tell you something, but you must promise not to reveal it to anyone."

"Of course. Like you said, we Morioux are forever honor bound to keep Dastillion secrets."

Something in the way Juliette said the words raised Amede's suspicions. Her voice was edged with just a hint of resentment. Not enough to pinpoint, but subtle, like a festering wound.

"On second thought," she said, smiling so Juliette wouldn't feel as though she had done anything wrong, "I think I'll keep it to myself for now."

"Okay. I'm going to get rid of these clothes and turn in. Caleb should be back soon. Barney's closed two hours ago." Her eyes grew wide as though her statement betrayed her fears.

"I'm sure he'll be back any minute. Maybe he drove into Branson for some barbeque."

The sparkle had left Juliette's eyes, and Amede felt a rush of tenderness.

"Do you want me to run out and look for him?"

Juliette shook her head with quick jerky movements. "No. I'm sure you're right about him going to Branson. He's pretty obsessed with barbeque."

"All right then. I'm going to give your grandmother a call and check on your grandpapa, and then I'm going to soak in the tub."

Dropping the clothes on the floor next to the door, Juliette walked toward the bathroom. "I'll run your bath. You want the Jacuzzi tonight or bubbles?"

"Use the salts. I think I want the jets." She reached into the minifridge and pulled out a bottle of Merlot. She'd already downed a full glass and poured a second by the time Juliette returned from the other room.

"It's ready. I used some new salts I bought in a little bath-and-body shop downtown. I think you'll like it. Smells like spicy lavender."

"Thank you." Carrying her phone and her wine, she walked barefoot toward the bathroom. "Sleep well, Juliette."

"Please give Grandmere my love. I didn't have a chance to call her today."

"I will." She paused before going inside the steamy room. "Juliette. I intend to let your grandmother know that you are the perfect choice to succeed her."

The news should have overjoyed the girl. She should have blushed with pleasure and pride at being chosen. To be the lifelong companion of a Dastillion was a great honor. But the look of dread on her face was insulting to say the least, infuriating to say the most. Amede felt the monster in her beginning to rise. "Well?" she huffed. "Have you nothing to say to me?"

"Thank you, Miss Amede. I appreciate the honor and look forward to serving you as well as my grandmere has served you all these years."

She spoke the right words, but Amede couldn't fool herself into believing the girl was sincere. And when Juliette looked Amede in the eye, she knew the last thing Juliette wanted was to be Amede's companion.

"Juliette."

"Yes, Miss Amede," the girl murmured, and it was obvious tears hovered just below the surface.

Amede smiled. "Leave the clothes until morning. They'll be all right."

"Thank you, Miss Amede. Good night."

The door closed firmly behind Juliette.

Amede slipped into the hot water and turned on the jets, still unable to get Juliette's expression out of her mind. It reminded Amede of the way she had felt when the cellar door closed, locking her inside, alone.

Juliette felt trapped.

Amede closed her eyes and breathed in the spicy scent Juliette was hoping would please her. Instead, the bath salts smelled almost pungent. She didn't care for the scent at all.

Deciding to call Roma from bed rather than the tub, she downed the second glass of wine and stood. She stumbled in the water as a wave of dizziness overcame her. Carefully, she slid into her terry robe and concentrated on staying upright. But the lightheadedness persisted. As she fell across the bed, the thought occurred that Juliette had purposely given her something to harm her.

She fingered the numbers on her phone, pressing 1 on speed dial.

Roma answered.

"Roma?" Her hands were beginning to tingle.

"Amede." Roma's voice sounded very far away. "What's wrong?"

"Juliette...I think she's poisoning me."

"Juliette knows poison can't kill you. Besides, we don't do that to Dastillions."

And yet the familiar ache in her bones returned like before. "She doesn't want this life, Roma." Her voice trembled as her body began to shake.

"She knows her duty. Don't you worry. Whatever is happening to you, we'll figure it out, but don't go blaming my girl."

"My eyes hurt." Amede moaned as the pain seared through her eye sockets all the way to her skull. "If she has done this, she'll have to be killed."

"She would never harm you." A tremor of fear laced Roma's hard tone. "But I'll question the girl myself. Don't you touch her. If you have no proof, you'll be the one to invoke the curse."

As if she were strong enough in that moment to harm the girl anyway.

Blackness swirled about her. Even as she lay on her bed the dizziness refused her any reprieve.

The phone fell away from her palm, and she succumbed to the darkness.

———

Rage gripped his chest, threatening to explode out from his rib cage as he stared at the open cellar door. He fought the rising tide of emotions until his palms bled from his fingernails. If she thought she could make a fool of him, she was sorely mistaken.

He knew where to find her. She wouldn't know what had hit her until it was too late and she was sharing a tomb with her sister.

CHAPTER TWENTY-ONE

I went out on three dates with Daniel Chadwick, an attorney who had overseen a client's auction. He had a shy smile and told great stories. Each attempt to eat dinner together ended with an "emergency" phone call from my dad. After the third time of rushing home to find him completely unaware he'd even called, Daniel and I agreed it wasn't a good time for me to date. Well, he agreed more than I did. A few months later, after Cokie came along, I swallowed my pride and called him to ask him out. His new bride answered.

It could have been me. . .

Tears flowed down her cheeks and sobs shook her frail shoulders as she listened to his raging.

"I had her! I had her and she got away. She is so much stronger than you are. Look at you. Pathetic. At least she put up a good fight."

"You leave Amede alone, you. . .monster." She cringed as she braved the words, knowing his next action would make her pay.

Surprisingly, he laughed. "Leave her alone? She escaped and went right back where I wanted her. No, I won't leave her alone. And tomorrow you'll have a roommate."

I didn't like the blackness of the wooded driveway up to the vet's cabin. The General lived next to Nina in a little cabin of his own. He ran the horse sanctuary that everyone still called the reserve from when it had once been a refuge for exotic wild animals.

Jill's patrol car was parked in the circle drive and I parked behind her.

Mustering all the courage I possessed, which wasn't much, I hurried to the cabin door and knocked, relieved when someone called, "Come in!" rather than making me wait outside while Nina walked to the door.

The small kitchen and dining area opened to the living room, where an extremely handsome man sat holding a little boy who had fallen asleep in his lap. Jill sat at the kitchen table.

Nina Parker smiled a hello. "Go ahead and sit with Jill. I'll be right back," she whispered. She walked softly to the chair and touched the man on his shoulder. She bent down and her long black hair grazed his face. She spoke. He jerked awake, looked up, and smiled at her.

He stood, mindful of the child in his arms. Nina kissed them both and walked back to the kitchen as the man exited the living room through a hall in the other direction.

"Coffee?" Nina asked, holding up the pot.

I shook my head and she offered tea, which I also declined. "I'm good," I said, hoping they would take the hint and get on with whatever they felt they needed to tell me.

Nina brought a mug full of coffee to the table and eased into a chair. Jill leaned forward, clasping her hands in front of her. "I've brought Nina up to speed about Miranda and her latest claim." Jill looked at me. "I'm only telling you this because you seem to be putting two and two together. In that photograph, Markus was thirty. And when he died he was also thirty."

"At least that's how he looked." Nina sipped her coffee.

It felt like I was sitting in a room and my parents were about to tell me I was adopted. Something surreal washed over me and I stared, open-mouthed, while they spoke.

Nina swallowed hard as she met my gaze, demanding my attention and my trust. "Markus was two hundred fifty years old."

I laughed. Surely this was a joke. Only not a very funny one to lure me all the way out here.

But Jill and Nina weren't laughing.

"Come on. You two are both intelligent women. There's no way you believe this guy was a vampire."

Nina regarded me with serious doelike eyes that seemed to speak a hundred things at once. Though I couldn't understand why, I was suddenly believing every word that came out of her mouth. "He was born not far from here in the mid-1700s before the Revolution. His father was a mountain man. When Markus was a little boy he watched his father drain the life from his mother. Literally."

"So you're saying it runs in the family?" I shuddered but couldn't quite wrap my head around the fact that these two lovely, accomplished, intelligent women had bought into Miranda's fantasy. But as I began to work with the rational part of my brain, I realized Miranda didn't have these facts. Nina must have firsthand information.

"The propensity for bloodlust is passed down genetically. It's a hunger that begins around puberty and continues to grow until the person gives in."

"What if the person doesn't give in?"

She shrugged. "I don't know. I suppose he or she lives a normal life and has to make a choice every day, just like the rest of us."

Jill stood and grabbed the coffeepot. "Markus Chisom was in love with Nina."

Nina nodded for a warmup and Jill tipped the pot. "Love is a strong word. Infatuation is more like it."

"Well," Jill said, setting the pot back on the warmer, "whichever it was, thank goodness for it, considering the outcome."

Sisters have a way of finishing each other's sentences, living in a world all their own. But I've never had a sister, any sibling for that matter, so I didn't understand, and their behind-the-scenes banter was starting to annoy me. I tried to uncloud my thoughts. "I'm lost here. First, why are you telling me these things? Miranda would appreciate this information a lot more. I just want to sell his house and take care of my dad. Second, what do you mean by thank goodness Markus was infatuated with Nina, considering the outcome? What outcome?"

Jill gave an exasperated shake of her head. "I know you have a lot going on, but don't you think it's time to get out of your little bubble?"

I stared at her, hurt.

"My bubble includes my father, and he comes before anything else. And if that means I'm not up to speed on the local gossip, so be it." I kept my voice even. I liked Jill too much to snap at her.

Nina held up her hand to Jill, then turned back to me. "I know you don't want to think about these things. It's hard to hear that creatures of the night actually exist. But we aren't crazy. Markus Chisom was a vampire and so was Eden, the woman who was obsessed with him."

I jerked my chin up at the sound of the familiar name. "Who is Eden?"

"Haven't you paid any attention to Miranda's blogs?"

I was tempted to be sarcastic, but these women didn't deserve the sharp edge of my tongue. I shook my head and tried to be civil. "I've skimmed it from time to time, but I don't have enough hours in the day as it is. I don't waste those minutes on Miranda's sort of entertainment."

"Fair enough." Jill sipped her coffee, then set the cup down. "Why does the name Eden stand out to you? Other than the obvious?"

"Amede Dastillion's letters mentioned someone named Eden."

Nina's eyebrows rose. "Amede? Who is that?"

"A guest at the Baylor Inn," Jill said. "She's also under investigation for Janine's murder." She looked at me, now in sheriff mode. "Are you sure about the letters?"

I nodded. I had scanned them into my computer. I had felt bad about my duplicity to Amede, but I couldn't give up historical documents like that so easily. I never planned to share them with anyone.

"The letters were written to Eden or Dearest Sister. Signed Amede. I assumed the Amede from the letters was an ancestor. And I never put two and two together with the yoga instructor Eden."

"There's no reason you should have." Jill stood and paced in front of the sink. "But here's the scoop. Eden came to Abbey Hills looking for her long-time boyfriend."

I had the horrified feeling that everything I used to know about reality was about to be replaced by things I didn't want to know.

"But he had cast his lovely eyes toward my beautiful, troubled sister."

Nina tossed a dishtowel at her sister. "Don't gussy up the story, okay? Let's just keep it real."

"That's not real?"

"Well, he had become a little infatuated." Nina's eyes revealed she was not proud of this. "But Eden couldn't let him go. Apparently they go back a long way. Like to just after Civil War times."

I couldn't fathom the things they were trying to convince me were true. Civil War times? "I know you couldn't possibly have brought me out here for some sick joke. But this is more than a little hard for me to believe."

Leaning forward, Nina placed her hand on my arm. "Everything we've said is true. And if what you've said is true, Amede is Eden's sister, which means she's a very old vampire. And she has probably already killed twice."

I liked Amede. She seemed vulnerable and kind. Not at all the woman Nina had just described. Certainly not a centuries-old vampire.

Nina looked at her sister as she paced. "Jill, what is the excuse Amede gave for staying in Abbey Hills?"

I answered. "She's waiting for me to appraise a couple of heirlooms she thought might be in the house."

"What heirlooms?"

My phone vibrated. I glanced. Billy. He would have to wait.

"A family ring and a first-edition copy of *Wuthering Heights*. I found the book. It's in mint condition except for the inscription." I smiled at the irony. "To Amede, from your loving father. December 1855. Suddenly that takes on a whole new meaning."

Jill and Nina each nodded gravely. "I'd lay odds that a couple of mementos are not all Amede is hanging around for. She's looking for Eden."

Nina's beautiful olive-toned skin turned pale. "And we were directly involved in her killing."

"If she's even dead." Jill leaned against the counter and crossed her arms.

"The last time I checked, she was in the house when it burned." Nina reached back, pulled her hair up, and let it drop. "I should know. I was there."

"Under normal circumstances I'd agree," Jill said. "But the fact is, forensics found one set of bones in the house after the fire burned out. And they were from a thirty-something male."

"Markus."

Jill nodded. "Yep."

"And you didn't see fit to tell me that after what she tried to do to my daughter?"

"We thought it best not to. We figured she had left the area and wouldn't be any trouble."

Nina groaned. "So that crazy woman is alive and Markus died for nothing."

Listening to these two, I was beginning to think there was something really wrong in Abbey Hills.

Jill walked to Nina and placed her hands on her sister's shoulders. "Looks that way. I'm so sorry, Nina."

"Even after the deer was left on my porch you still didn't tell me, Jill?"

"You were getting ready to leave for Dallas for Thanksgiving. I hoped to catch whoever did it before you got back."

The sheriff's cell phone buzzed and she stepped away to answer. I felt shy in Nina's presence. But she smiled, putting me at ease. "Do you have a sister?" she asked.

I shook my head. "It's just me and my dad."

"You live with your dad?" Her voice held a bit of a lift, betraying her surprise.

The question always made me a little defensive. "I moved back home two years ago when he was diagnosed with early-onset Alzheimer's."

Her expression softened. "I'm sorry. He's lucky to have you."

I remembered back to my conversation with Jill at the hospital. Nina left home when she was seventeen, so of course she wouldn't be able to understand someone sticking with her parents. Or maybe that was my wall talking. "I'm lucky to have him too. It keeps me from being alone." As soon as I spoke, I wished I hadn't. So much for the wall of protection. I felt like the first and second little pigs. I'd been such an emotional wreck lately that my house was ready to fall with the smallest burst of wind.

My phone vibrated. Billy again. I decided I would wait to call him until I got home. I knew he'd be ticked that I'd left my house after he'd seen me safely inside.

Jill looked positively ill when she returned from the other room.

"Everything okay?" Nina asked.

She shook her head, stepping toward the door. I stood and grabbed my purse from the chair. If she was leaving, so was I.

Nina stood too. She reached out and stopped Jill with a hand on her arm. "Hey, what's up?"

Jill's eyes filled with tears. I'd never seen the sheriff tear up when she was in sheriff mode, and the chink in her armor frightened me. If the sheriff wasn't confident, who among us had any reasonable right to feel safe?

She straightened her shoulders, gathering her strength. "Detective Townsend, the special investigator I requested to help with this case, was found murdered." Nina and I stared at her, waiting to see if she would elaborate. She expelled a heavy breath. "Charley found him."

"Was it the same kind of killing as Janine and Jeremy?" I knew the answer before I asked the question.

She nodded. "He was investigating out by Eden's house tonight. I should never have let him go alone. But I needed to get back to the Chisom house and talk to Miranda. I just left him out there."

Nina slipped her arm around Jill's shoulders as she walked to the door. "Don't beat yourself up about this, Jill. You stopped them before and you'll do it again."

I watched the sisters, wondering what it might be like to have that kind of support. My phone vibrated again as if to answer my question. Billy wanted to be a support for me, but I couldn't trust my feelings for him right now. His own life was too uncertain.

"I'll walk out with you, Jill," I said. "Thank you for telling me all this." I stepped out onto the porch. Nina joined us. I paused. "What happens when Miranda proves she's right about the vampires?"

Jill shook her head, her eyes filled with determination. "That's part of the reason we discussed this with you, Lauryn. You're smart and have the common sense not to share this with anyone else."

"You definitely don't have to worry about that." I gave a short laugh. "Miranda might be right, but she's still as crazy as they come under all that red hair." I felt a little guilty saying it when she had been right all along. Her bulldog faith in the truth of her words was actually sort of inspiring and gave me a new respect for her. I resolved to be nicer to her as I told Jill and Nina good-bye and got into my Jeep.

I made sure all the doors were locked and waited for Jill to pull out before I put the Jeep in gear. The fog had rolled in thicker than during the drive here and that, combined with a five-degree drop in temperature, made roads dangerous again. I couldn't see Jill's taillights ahead of me.

The road under my tires might as well have been a hundred miles away. I couldn't see it through the fog, but I could feel the Jeep slide as the fog froze on the hard surface. The phone vibrated several more times. But I couldn't risk answering while driving on such a treacherous road.

My childhood nightmares came rushing back to engage my overactive imagination as I crawled the five miles toward town. Jason, Freddy, and bad-boy vampire Lestat took turns tormenting me. By the time I pulled into my driveway, my nerves were shot. I wasn't prepared for Billy to be there waiting. He jumped out of his truck as soon as I shut off the Jeep.

He grabbed me and pulled me close, holding me tight. "Why didn't you call me back? I thought you were dead."

"I'm sorry, Billy. I was in a meeting and couldn't answer."

"A meeting? What kind of meeting could be so important this late at night?" He pulled away and held me at arm's length. "I thought something had happened to you. There's a murderer on the loose and you had to go to a meeting? How stupid is that?"

Anger flashed in me at the word *stupid*. "What are you doing at my house, Billy?"

"What am I doing?"

I didn't give him time to answer. "If you don't stop speaking to me in that tone, you can leave."

He gathered a deep breath, steadying himself, and then released it. "Okay, I shouldn't have yelled. Can I come in with you?"

I slid the key into the lock and opened the door. "I thought you couldn't control your hormones."

His eyes narrowed. "I think I'll be okay."

Still harboring a grudge over his attitude, I shrugged. "Come in, but I'm exhausted, so I don't know how long I'll be awake."

I yawned and let him lock the door behind him. I shrugged out of my jacket and tossed it onto the chair by the sofa. I sat and he sat next to me. He slid his arm along the top of the cushions. "When you dropped me off earlier, I realized I was too keyed up to sleep, so I decided to get some work done at the Chisom house."

I told him everything. Even the vampire parts, which I probably shouldn't have, but I was so tired. I lay my head on his shoulder halfway through the story and told the rest with my eyes closed.

"So Miranda was right all along?" His voice sounded as shocked as I'd felt an hour ago.

"Appears so." I yawned and settled in against his shoulder. Billy encircled my arms and pulled me in.

"I think the sheriff is in over her head. She should call in the FBI or someone."

"Or maybe the VTF."

"What's the VTF?"

I grinned, so weary I couldn't even open my eyes to see his reaction. "Vampire task force."

He chuckled. "Funny. But seriously, she is going to have to call in reinforcements."

I couldn't argue with him. If the law enforcement team couldn't keep themselves safe from the killer, how could Abbey Hills citizens expect protection?

I tucked my legs up under me. Darkness pulled me in and I dozed off. I woke up thinking about my dad. My eyes popped open. How could I bring him back home until Abbey Hills was safe again?

"You okay?" Billy asked, giving me a gentle hug.

"I was just thinking about my dad. I'm not sure I want to bring him home right now." In my mind's eye I could see him, alone with a caregiver we didn't even know.

I closed my eyes again. I couldn't think about it anymore. Something about Billy's arm holding me close released my stress, and I finally gave up trying to stay awake. Morning would have enough stresses and worries. God only knew who the next victim would be.

CHAPTER TWENTY-TWO

*Amanda's murder shook Abbey Hills. I grieved for my high school
friend but found myself so busy running the auction house alone and
caring for Dad in the evenings that I simply didn't take time to
allow it to reach my heart, until Charley showed up at my door,
completely wrecked.*

"Will you say something at her funeral?"

"Me? Charley, I've hardly seen Amanda since high school."

He looked at me, hard. "She considered you her best friend."

*The church was full the day of Amanda's funeral, but only
Charley, the preacher, and I spoke. Very few tears were shed that I
could see.*

I guess Amanda was my closest friend too.

*She was gone now, so who would speak good things about me
when I died?*

She paced the cubicle, back and forth, back and forth so many times her legs
ached, her arms wrapped about her hollow middle. Amede was coming today.

Eden's mind jumped from one thought to the next, torn between hoping he would bring Amede to her and hoping Amede would never let him take her captive.

No. He couldn't bring her here. This was no life. Amede would watch her die, and then she would die alone.

But if he did bring Amede, at least Eden's solitude would end. She had spent most of her life feeling alone. She had almost had a daughter last spring.

Little Meg. At first Eden had merely meant to use the girl as leverage to convince Markus to come back to her. But eventually, the idea of having a daughter, someone to love her, to depend on her, became an appealing thought. And she had almost had Markus and Meagan both. They could have been a family. But Meagan, that ungrateful, conniving girl, had run away, and her mother, Nina, had bewitched Markus so he no longer wanted Eden.

Tears ran down her cheeks and a wail exploded from her throat like the howl of a wolf.

When she escaped, she would not only kill her captor; she would find Nina and take her daughter away. Then she would never be alone again.

For the first time since her father died, Amede wished for death. After his funeral, she had refused to eat for weeks. Finally, Eden came home from wherever her travels had taken her, yanked Amede out of bed, forced her into her prettiest gown, and took her down to the docks to hunt. Amede followed after Eden for a while. She regained her strength and shoved their father's death far into the back of her mind.

But in due time, Eden moved on to the next man, once more leaving

Amede alone. The more she thought about her father, the more she realized that even though she wasn't ready to die for his convictions, she couldn't bear the thought of killing. That's when she had resolved once and for all not to feed on humans.

She felt weaker physically but somehow morally and emotionally stronger. She had something to live for. Principle.

But believing Juliette could have caused this pain, taking her to the brink of a death she couldn't pass into, sent Amede into despair. If she couldn't trust a Morioux, there was no one left in whom to place her confidence.

Roma refused to believe it. But the salts had to be the catalyst for Amede's sickness. She couldn't explain the earlier illness, but who else other than Juliette had access to her? Who else could be doing this?

She lay in her bed, grateful the effects had begun to wear off after a gallon of water and several hours of sleep. Weakness and dizziness still clung to her, but she was hungry.

Dragging herself out of bed wasn't easy, but she knew from the last time sickness had wracked her body that only feeding would return her strength.

She reached for her robe as someone knocked on her door. A growl hung in her throat. Black dots clouded her vision as she carefully made her way across the room and opened the door.

"Oh." Her eyebrows rose and she heard the surprise in her own voice. "Sheriff Jenkins. What can I do for you?"

The sheriff's expression was hard. "I need you to get dressed and come with me to the station."

"The station? What is this about, Sheriff? Are you arresting me for something?"

"Not exactly. I'm asking you to come down for questioning." Sheriff Jenkins seemed on guard, her body tense and ready to...what? Strike? Defend?

"Sheriff, I don't mean to be difficult, but I seem to be ill again." She grabbed hold of the doorknob to steady herself. The sheriff started and her hand shot to her pistol.

"I...I didn't mean to threaten. I'm simply a bit unsteady." She gripped the doorknob tighter as the dizziness waved over her. "Would you mind coming in and conducting your interview inside?"

The sheriff shook her head. "I need you in the office."

Amede didn't understand the sheriff's sudden sternness, but she recognized resolve when she encountered it, and since the sheriff was the one with the power, Amede felt she had no choice. "I'll only be a few minutes. Please excuse me."

"I'll be right here," the sheriff said, and Amede closed the door.

There was no warmth in her voice like Amede had sensed before. She believed the sheriff didn't seriously consider her a suspect in Janine's death and that knowledge had given her a sense of peace. But now it seemed as though she had changed her mind. Amede couldn't imagine what had occurred to alter her status so drastically.

Hunger gnawed her stomach as she dressed in a pair of jeans, a body shaper, and a long-sleeved tee. She put on a pair of boots, pulled her hair up in back, and clipped it. She didn't bother with makeup but hastily brushed her teeth. Her reflection showed smudges under her eyes. So unusual for her and others like her. She shouldn't be ill.

As she grabbed her purse, another knock at the door drew a sigh from her. "Yes, Sheriff, I am coming."

"Miss Amede," Juliette called. "It's me. May I come in?"

Amede opened the door. She could barely look at the girl. But she was still bound by the blood oath. "I'm ready, Sheriff."

"Where are you going, Miss Amede?"

"Don't concern yourself." Amede stared at the girl, her eyes searching her face for any trace of guilt. "I spoke with your grandmother last night, and we agreed you should go home. Immediately."

A frown creased Juliette's perfect brow. "I'm not sure I follow. What's going on?"

"Two things. The sheriff has some questions for me, and I am no longer in need of a companion. That's all there is to it." She closed her eyes against a shower of black stars.

"Are you okay? You don't look well. Are you ill again?" Juliette's voice seemed sincere, but Amede knew better.

"Use my credit card to book your plane home and ask Caleb to take you to the airport."

"Did I do something wrong, Miss Amede?" Juliette's voice was shaky, but Amede remained unmoved. "I don't want to leave you when you're still under investigation."

"Please be packed and ready to go or already gone when I return."

She sensed the girl's wide eyes following her but felt nothing but anger.

The sheriff drove the Blazer and allowed Amede the dignity of the front seat. "You were a little hard on Juliette, don't you think?"

Tensing at the very sound of Juliette's name, Amede stared out the window. "I have my reasons." Her aching muscles and throbbing head attested to the truth of her words. She turned to the sheriff. "As I'm sure you have your reasons for bringing me into the station on such short notice."

The sheriff nodded. "Why are you really in Abbey Hills, Amede?"

Overnight, icicles had formed on the branches of the pine trees along the road. Amede was forced to close her eyes as the sun shining off the ice stabbed at her sockets.

"I came to speak to Lauryn McBride about some things from my family's past that she will be selling in the auction. I'd like the chance to make a preemptive bid." Irritation welled up. "Haven't I already mentioned this several times? To you and to the other investigator?"

"I guess I just don't believe a family quest is your only motive."

"Well, unless you have any evidence to the contrary, I suppose you'll have to believe me, Sheriff. I don't know what else to say."

The sheriff remained silent the rest of the icy crawl to the police station. When they arrived, she seemed as though she might jump out of her skin. Amede's suspicions grew as they stepped inside and Jill hung back in. . .fear?

Inside the small concrete building that looked as though it had seen better days, Jill motioned her to a chair on the opposite side of a metal desk.

"Sheriff, I truly don't see the necessity of this humiliation."

"I apologize if you feel that way, Miss Dastillion, but new evidence has given me reason to take this next step."

"Evidence?" Someone had seen her hunting last night? Or another night, perhaps.

"Coffee?" Jill held up a half-empty pot.

Amede shook her head. The very thought of the oily brew made her stomach draw up. Whether from nerves or the effects of whatever Juliette had poisoned her with, she wasn't sure.

The sheriff sank into a faded office chair with wheels that squeaked and scooted up to the desk. She pulled out a statement form and dated the document. Then, pen in hand, she looked up and regarded Amede with a blank expression. "I need to know where you were last night between ten and midnight."

Amede felt the blood drain from her face. Normally she would rely on Juliette to be her alibi, but the girl had proven her disloyalty, and for the first time in many years, she had no one to back her up.

"I was…" She swallowed hard. "I don't know how to explain."

"How about if I try for you?"

Confused, Amede shrugged. "If you'd like."

"You raced, on foot, to the old house where your sister almost killed my niece and sister…" Her eyebrows rose. "Any of this ringing a bell?"

There would be no pretending now. It was time for Amede to lay out the truth and hope the sheriff believed her. "Please continue. These questions must be due to more than my need to hunt."

The sheriff's nostrils flared as though she fought for control from a rising anger. "My objection isn't your need to hunt but the object you chose to hunt. Or, should I say, the man you chose to murder."

"Sheriff, let me be clear." Amede drew a breath, wishing for her usual mental clarity. But knowing this was a critical moment, she had to speak up, regardless. "I am what you are implying. I did hunt, on foot, last night. And I did end up at the site of my sister's burned home. When I got there, the cellar door had been thrown open. I believed by vandals."

The sheriff's attention didn't waver, and she seemed to forget to write as her eyes fixed on Amede's. "Go on," she said in a hoarse whisper.

"I went down the steps, and the door was shut and locked after me. A man's voice mocked me and told me he had my sister locked away somewhere else."

The sheriff's face drained of color, but otherwise her demeanor didn't change. "Eden was burned in the fire last spring. I was there."

Amede shook her head. "Sheriff, there were no bones found. We both know that isn't possible. They found Markus Chisom's remains but not Eden's? How likely is that?"

"All right, Amede." The chair squeaked back and Jill crossed one leg over the other. "Let's get this out in the open. Say what you are. Eden was a vampire. And so are you."

Amede's heart pounded in her ears. "Yes," she said softly.

"You admit you were at your sister's property last night."

"I was locked in the cellar, but I escaped."

"How did you do that?" Her tone betrayed her skepticism and she folded her arms across her chest.

"I'm stronger than the average human. Not as strong as I would be if I fed on humans, but still a good deal stronger."

"You don't feed on humans, but Eden did?"

Amede nodded. "We are half sisters. She has a wild streak in her that comes from her mother's side. Our father was like us, but toward the end of his life he became convinced that consuming blood was an abomination, and he believed he could be reconciled with God. So he stopped feeding."

Jill's eyebrows lifted. "He stopped feeding on humans, you mean."

"My father stopped feeding on blood altogether. He became more and more frail as his many years began to catch up to him. It took him two years to die. Two agonizing years."

No mercy found its way to the sheriff's face. "But you still drank blood."

"Not human blood. Not in many, many years. Almost a century." She pressed trembling fingers to her temple. "I wasn't strong enough to join him in death, but I chose animals only."

Jill's eyebrows went up and she began to write again. When she finished scratching whatever she was writing, she dropped the pen and leaned forward.

"Here's the thing, Miss Dastillion." She steepled her fingertips. "Last night between ten and twelve, Detective Townsend was murdered. His throat was ripped out and his body drained of blood. And he was dumped into the cellar."

"And you believe I'm the one responsible."

"Based on your testimony today, I have enough evidence to hold you for at least twenty-four hours."

A chill moved over Amede. "You want to lock me up?"

"Wouldn't you, in my position?"

As much as she admired the sheriff, Amede couldn't allow herself to be confined. Especially now when she needed to feed. Her hunger was growing by the minute as her emotions grew more volatile. The more the poison wore off, the more she felt Eden's hunger too. "Sheriff. You know what I am. So you know I can't possibly allow you to lock me up."

"You don't have a choice, Amede."

A slow smile spread across Amede's lips. "I respect and admire you, Sheriff. But I do have a choice."

"Nope."

Amede turned at the sound of the familiar voice. "Charley." He held a rifle in his hand. "Guns don't kill me."

"We don't want to kill you, Amede," Jill said.

Charley fired, and Amede's neck stung almost instantly. Anger flared and her eyes felt like fire as she stared at him, not as a man, but as a threat to be eliminated. A guttural scream rose at the same time she leaped toward him. He fired again. Her head began to swim, and her arms and legs lost strength. And instead of falling on Charley, she fell at his feet. "What...?"

Barely conscious, she felt her arms being yanked nearly from their sockets as she was pulled along the floor.

"Good grief, Charley. Don't just drag her across the floor. Carry her."

"No," Charley said. "Have you forgotten her sister killed my sister and almost killed yours?"

Amede couldn't move, couldn't respond, but she could hear everything, and she knew where she had heard that angry voice before. She had stayed at the Inn for weeks and never suspected Charley Baylor had Eden hidden away. And now that she knew, she was powerless to do anything about it.

She and Eden would both be at the mercy of a madman.

⸻

I awoke to the smell of breakfast and smiled. Cokie must have gotten here early. The smell of bacon, my favorite breakfast, sent my stomach into a frenzy. I smiled, then remembered, and pain squeezed my heart. Cokie was gone. Dad was almost gone. What was there to fight for if I was all alone?

Why had I slept on the couch? I sat up, pushing aside a blanket that I couldn't remember covering myself with.

"Hey, sleepyhead."

Billy. And then I remembered.

He stood behind the couch, smiling, looking too good for morning, but then he didn't have crazy curly hair like I did. I reached up self-consciously and tried to smooth the unruly locks.

"Don't bother," Billy said. "I think you're adorable."

I snorted. "Then you must be blind."

"Blinded by love." His eyes flashed with his teasing.

I tossed a pillow at him, which he caught easily. "Yeah, right."

"If you're not ready for love, would you go for 'strong like'?"

"Whatever." Embarrassment forced my gaze away from him and I stood, folding the blanket. "You're not burning the bacon, are you?"

He smiled. "No, but I'll leave you to wake up and recover from your embarrassment if you want." He walked toward the kitchen, then looked over his shoulder. "Breakfast in ten. Don't be late."

"Aye aye, captain."

My BlackBerry sat on the table beside the couch, and the light flashed red to indicate I had a message. I'd forgotten to turn the sound back on after I got home. I snatched it up and noticed several calls from the hospital. The voice mail asked that I call the hospital, which I did without hesitation.

I called the direct line to the nurse's station on Dad's floor. "This is Lauryn McBride. I had messages to call regarding my father, Ted McBride."

I waited on hold for ten minutes, and then the head nurse got on the line. At the same time, Billy walked into the room carrying a plate. "Time's up. Come and get it."

Though it wasn't fair, irritation shot through me. I held up my hand for silence. A jerky movement that raised his eyebrows. He retreated to the kitchen. I felt a little guilty.

"Lauryn?" she said.

"Yes."

"We've been trying to reach you for several hours."

"I know. My phone was on vibrate and I fell asleep without turning my ringer on. Is he okay?"

"He's better now. Let me go over his chart here." She clicked her tongue. "He spiked a fever around midnight."

"Spiked?" Guilt washed over me.

"He was up to one hundred and three before we finally got it to go down around three o'clock."

"I'm so sorry. I'll get dressed now and head that way. Is he still going to be released?"

"Wait, go where?" Billy interrupted again. Clearly he hadn't gone too far into the kitchen. I glared at him to be quiet, but he shook his head, walked to the window, and pulled back the curtain.

The nurse spoke as I stared out the window, mouth agape. I'd slept through a major ice storm.

"He won't be going home today and probably not tomorrow. His doctor wants him to get twenty-four hours of this antibiotic and not have a fever for a day before he goes home."

Ice-laden branches sagged from every tree along the street. Several had broken under the weight. My stomach dove. The back highways wouldn't be drivable. There was no way I could go to my dad. But how could I leave him at the hospital alone for two days?

The nurse sensed my hesitation and softened her tone considerably. "Lauryn, you've spent almost every second in that room with your dad. Even if we could have gotten ahold of you last night, there would have been nothing for you to do."

"I would have tried." But now it was impossible.

"Leave your dad in our hands. We'll take good care of him. Call us anytime you need an update. We're here."

"Will you call if he asks for me? Maybe I could talk to him on the phone."

"If he asks for you I will call, but he's been pretty out of it. I honestly don't think he even knows you're gone."

"Well, I'll check on him in a couple of hours anyway."

I disconnected the call and walked to the window. I sympathized with the trees. As beautiful as the ice was, the destruction it caused would hardly be worth it. As if feeding off my thoughts, the electricity flickered. I held my breath, and the lights brightened and stayed.

Billy came out of the kitchen. "Was that my imagination or is the electricity trying to go out?"

"I better go to the basement and bring up the oil lamps."

"Is everything okay with your dad?"

"He spiked a high fever in the night, so they have him on a regimen of antibiotics." I walked past him toward the kitchen to the basement door.

"Hey." Billy reached out and took hold of my arm. "You okay?"

I shrugged. "I just wish I could be with my dad today."

"I'm sorry," Billy said, his tone soft, filled with sympathy.

The lights flickered again. "I best get down there before the electricity goes out altogether."

As I walked down the basement steps, I replayed the conversation with the nurse in my head. Everything was changing so fast. I wanted my dad to be well cared for, but the house seemed so empty without him. It had been just Dad and me for so long that without him I felt like half of a broken whole.

As I climbed the steps back to the kitchen, arms around a box of candles, oil lamps, and kerosene, the electricity gave up to the heavy ice.

"Here, let me take that," Billy said.

"Thanks."

Together we placed the candles around the room. I set one on the bookshelf in the corner. A photograph of Dad and me from my high school graduation stared out between my collection of Charles Dickens and Dad's Louis L'Amour. I lifted the photo. Dad's eyes were filled with pride, mine relieved and a little scared. I remembered that day. So excited at the possibility of college, but dreading that I would be leaving Dad alone, even if I was only going to Springfield and would be home every weekend.

"Look at you," Billy said over my shoulder. "I remember that night."

Part of me resented Billy's intrusion into my memory. I released a sigh and put the photograph back on the shelf. "Yeah, that was humiliating."

"It was sad," he said. "I wanted to stay but knew I had committed to something bigger than a romance. Even with you."

I didn't know what to say. I had revealed enough of my heart, so I simply nodded.

"Come on," Billy said. "I have some tea for you, and breakfast is getting cold."

I followed Billy into the kitchen, cursing the crazy icy winter. I thought back to my conversation with the nurse. How could she have thought I would find comfort in the fact that my dad hadn't asked for me?

CHAPTER TWENTY-THREE

After Amanda's funeral, Charley became a fixture in my life. And to be honest, I needed him there. He listened to my sob stories about Dad and applauded my victories at work. On the other hand, he shared his sorrow over Amanda's death and her husband taking the kids away. Ours was a relationship of necessity. I knew there was a part of Charley I'd never understand, but I didn't have the time or energy to try to figure it out. We were friends because each of us needed a friend.

Too bad it never went heart deep.

I wasn't sure I even had the capacity for a real friend.

Juliette didn't have to convince her grandmother that she hadn't poisoned Amede. Grandmere had already dismissed Amede's order for Juliette to leave Abbey Hills and given an order of her own: a Morioux never left a Dastillion unprotected.

After a tense drive through a winter not-so-wonderland, she and Caleb arrived at the police station. She paused before getting out of the

Mustang. "We can't leave without her. Amede won't survive being locked away."

Caleb bent and gave her a quick kiss. "Whatever you need, I'm here."

Sheriff Jenkins looked up from her desk as they entered.

"Juliette. I thought you were leaving."

"I'm not going anywhere while Amede is in trouble." She pulled at her gloves, hoping she appeared more confident than she felt. "Besides, all flights are cancelled today because of the ice on the runway." Heat rushed to her face at the memory of Amede's accusation. "Amede isn't herself these days. She didn't mean what she said."

The sheriff's eyebrows rose. "She seems adamant."

Caleb squeezed her hand.

"Sh-she thinks I gave her something to weaken her. But my family would never do anything to harm a Dastillion. We've always..." She bit back the words.

In the corner, Charley Baylor lounged, his elbows resting on the arms of a vinyl chair, fingers clasped over a flat stomach. He narrowed his gaze and stared, his eyes colder than the ice hanging from the trees and clinging to the roads outside. "I can't figure out why you're such a loyal puppy to this bloodsucker."

Juliette whipped around. How could he know? "What do you mean?"

Slowly, Charley stood. Caleb moved forward, shielding her with his body. "Are you a vampire too?"

"Come closer and find out," Caleb said, his tone deathly still.

Juliette placed her hand on Caleb's arm. "It's okay, Caleb. The deputy is clearly delusional." She turned her attention to Charley. "You've known us for weeks. Why are you treating us this way?"

From her desk, the sheriff expelled a breath. Her chair squeaked as she pushed back from the desk and stood. She leaned on her palms. "Juliette, we know about Amede. The question is, how much do you know?"

Defeat sliced through her like a wielded sword. "I really don't know what you mean. I'm just Miss Dastillion's assistant."

"Bull," Charley said. He stepped closer to Caleb. Juliette could feel Caleb tense. If she didn't take control of the situation, something unfortunate might happen. She squeezed Caleb's hand and he relaxed, though Juliette was certain it took great effort to force himself not to react to the deputy's goading.

"Sheriff, is Amede allowed visitors?"

"No," Charley answered, his voice deathly still.

"Charley." The sheriff motioned toward the chair along the back wall by a door. "Why don't you let me talk to Juliette for a while?"

Charley scowled and retreated to the chair.

The door at the back of the room was closed, but through a small window, Juliette could make out a cell. "Is that where she's being kept?" she asked.

The sheriff nodded kindly. "Yes, but no one else is in jail right now, so she's alone."

That was a mercy. "May I see her?" She addressed her appeal to the sheriff.

"I need to ask a few questions first. Some might be...difficult." She angled her gaze at Caleb and back to Juliette. "Do you want to do this alone? I'm sure you can guess what sorts of questions we're going to ask."

Turning to Caleb, Juliette slipped her fingers from his. "Would you mind waiting outside?"

He bent and gave her a quick kiss. "Call my cell if you need me."

Juliette nodded. "I shouldn't be long."

"Unless we arrest you too." She had never noticed what an unpleasant man Charley was. Her patience was running out fast.

"Enough, Charley," the sheriff insisted. "Go get us some lunch and hot coffee. I'll be fine."

"Yeah, right." He stomped across the room. A cold blast of air blew into the room as he snatched his coat from a hook on the wall and left the building.

"All right, Juliette," the sheriff said, motioning her to a seat in front of her desk, "have a seat."

"Thank you." She lowered herself into the chair.

The sheriff leveled her gaze and Juliette wished to be anywhere but here. She had never been to a police station before and she felt dirty and ashamed, even though she knew she'd done nothing wrong. Except, perhaps, keeping secrets about someone society would never accept, despite the waitress's crazy Internet claim that vampires and humans should find a way to just get along.

Jill's demeanor remained subdued, nonthreatening, but this just put Juliette on guard. She prepared mentally, determined not to give anything away that might endanger Amede. The sheriff took a breath. "Let me tell you what I know, and then you can tell me if I need to worry about you too."

Jill leaned forward and fingered a mug as she spoke. "Amede is a very old vampire. She came to Abbey Hills under the guise of wanting to find family heirlooms, but in reality she wanted to find her sister, Eden, another very old—and very evil—vampire. I knew Eden and was among the first to know what she was. Those things are not up for discussion or denial. I have a feeling you're with Amede to, what, protect her? And of course to serve her." She paused for a breath. "Am I right?"

With a jerky nod, Juliette betrayed centuries of secrets. Tears formed in her eyes. "My family has served the Dastillions since before the Civil War."

"Are you a vampire?" The sheriff's voice was soft but had an edge as though she wouldn't hesitate to take action if necessary.

At least the truth was on Juliette's side. "No. My grandmother was Amede's companion, and her mother and her mother before her. Over one hundred and fifty years ago a covenant was made between the Morioux family and the Dastillions."

"What sort of covenant?" the sheriff asked.

"We care for them, and they don't allow harm to come to us."

"What do you mean, they don't allow harm?"

"During Katrina, my family and quite a few friends stayed for a couple of weeks at Dastillion Court, which is Amede's home." Of course, the relationship was about more than simple generosity or monetary compensation. The protection extended to physical help as well. But this was so hard to explain that Juliette chose instead to stop right there.

"Given the circumstances, I'm not going to allow you to see Amede. But I'll tell her you were here."

Disappointment seized Juliette. How could she do her duty if the sheriff wouldn't allow her even a glimpse of Amede? "Will you also tell her that I didn't do anything to her bath salts? I'll even have them analyzed if that will help convince her."

"Okay. I'll tell her."

"I called her lawyer and he'll be here tomorrow if he can get a flight out."

"She's not under arrest. We're just holding her for questioning while waiting for the results of DNA testing."

"DNA?"

"I'm sorry, but I can't reveal the investigation details to you." The sheriff walked her to the door. "If Amede is innocent, there's nothing to worry about."

"Thank you for your time, Sheriff," she said, reaching out her hand. The sheriff took it.

"You're a good kid, Juliette. Don't stay wrapped up in this craziness."

Juliette's boots crunched on the salt-treated walk. Caleb saw her and hurried from the car. "Why didn't you call me? I'd have come up to the door."

"I'm fine. The salt's melted the ice."

"They wouldn't let you see her?"

Juliette shook her head. "They're waiting for DNA samples to be analyzed."

"Well, don't worry. Once they come back, they'll prove she's innocent."

He waited for her to climb into the car, then closed the door. Juliette watched him walk around to his side. She wished she could be half as confident. Although she'd never believed Amede would hurt a human, her recent behavior *had* been volatile.

One thing was certain; she had to call Grandmere as soon as she got back to the Inn. These people knew about Amede. And that was simply too dangerous. Charley would need to be dealt with, but Jill? And who else? Even Miranda was getting awfully close to the truth. Good thing no one took her seriously.

Caleb slid his arm along her seat and massaged the back of her neck. "Let's take it one minute at a time. I'm going to buy you some lunch at Barney's and hopefully the salt truck'll make it to the highway before we have to head back to the Inn."

Caleb's nearness and care didn't make her feel better, but he was right about the road.

She hoped that by some miracle, the DNA test didn't reveal that Amede was two hundred years old. The world wasn't ready for that sort of truth.

Juliette paused her train of thought. Why should she care when Amede had made her life miserable for the past couple of weeks? She'd even had the gall to accuse Juliette of trying to poison her. Still, duty was stronger than resentment, and she had promised Grandmere. Besides, there was no time to nurse a grudge. Not when Amede's DNA could be telling all at this very moment.

———

I couldn't get over how Barney's seemed to explode with activity whenever bad weather closed the rest of the town. It was as though the residents needed to band together to prove they were still in control of their own destinies. The destinies in question being the ability to eat barbeque and fried catfish if they wanted, icy roads be damned.

Cokie's mother and sister had come and taken her body back to St. Louis to be buried among her people. I felt the weight of this. The utter slap. Hadn't she told them how special we were to each other and how she was practically family? Why didn't her daughter mention it at least? I had to find out about her death through Billy's mom.

With Dad's condition so precarious right now, I couldn't attend the funeral. The most I could do for Cokie now was send a plant with a card, a polite gesture that didn't come close to representing our relationship.

Miranda and a teenage girl—Janine's replacement—dashed around the restaurant trying to look after the customers. I elbowed my way to the window. "Hey, Barney!" I yelled. "Is my order ready?"

His red face popped up and he scowled. "It'll be ready when it's ready."

Embarrassed, I pulled back. Miranda rushed up to the counter. "Barney, where's that catfish salad for the General? He's biting my head off."

"Give him a free cup of coffee and tell him to hold his horses." He tossed some filled plates into the window. "After you deliver those."

Miranda rolled her eyes. She angled a gaze at me from enormous green eyes that always made me uncomfortable. "For a guy who thrives on work, he gets awfully worked up when he's actually in the middle of it all."

"Well, it gets a little intense when he's the only cook." I gave her a dry smile. "But at least you're here today."

She grabbed four plates, balancing them like a pro, and didn't respond to my sarcasm.

I waved at Charley as he blasted in through the cold. He pushed through the group waiting for a seat and strode toward me with attitude.

"Bad day?"

He shrugged. "I've had better."

"Well, judging from your uniform, at least you're off the hook about Janine." I assumed Jill had reinstated him when she learned about Amede.

"Yeah." He scowled toward the pick-up window. "Why does it always get so stinking crazy in here when we have bad weather?"

The question was both angry and rhetorical, so I didn't bother to answer.

Barney popped up and tossed a few plates into the window. "Miranda!" He glared at Charley and me. "Don't even ask."

"Wasn't going to," I lied. I pulled Charley into the hallway between the two rest rooms where there were fewer people milling about.

"We're never going to get out of here," he complained. "I wish we'd get some new restaurants in this stupid town."

"Okay, Charley. What's your problem?" I leaned against the wall and folded my arms across my chest. "Seriously, you're more of a grouch than usual."

"It's Jill." He faced me, leaning against the other wall, breathing out a frustrated breath. "She just doesn't get it."

"Get what?"

He hesitated, and I thought he might open up. Instead, he changed the subject. "Where's Billy?"

"Home, I guess. Why?"

A shrug lifted his shoulders. "He stayed the night at your place. I just figured you'd be together today."

My mouth dropped open as I stared at him. "What...are you stalking me?"

"No. I drove by on patrol at five and his car was there. It had an inch of ice on the windshield. Doesn't take a genius to figure out that the two of you spent the night together."

My cheeks grew hot. "He stayed the night, but only because I fell asleep on his shoulder."

His knowing grin bugged me, especially since he knew nothing.

"He was there when I got home and yelled at me for not staying there after he dropped me off. We sat on the couch, and I fell asleep with my head on his shoulder. He settled me on the couch and covered me up and then he spent the night in Dad's ratty old recliner."

"Figures. Loser."

"Charley!"

"What? Hot girl in his arms and he lets you fall asleep?"

I didn't take the bait. "He's not that kind of man."

"Whatever." His gaze moved over me, giving me a shuddery feeling.

"Why are you upset with Jill?"

"She wants to play nursemaid to the inmates." He kicked the wall with the flat of his foot. "Especially certain inmates who wouldn't hesitate to kill her."

"What's wrong with you all of a sudden? Is this about Amede Dastillion?"

His eyes flashed. "What do you mean?"

I stepped across the narrow hall and stood shoulder to shoulder with him. "I know about her and her sister." I kept my voice to a whisper. Just thinking about the truth made me cringe, and I definitely didn't need anyone listening in on the spooky truth. I felt a sense of foreboding move across me as Charley's gaze darkened. He looked ready to say more, but Miranda interrupted.

"There you are. I thought you got tired of waiting and bailed." She handed me a bag. "One pulled pork sandwich and a side salad—on the house per Barney's orders." She handed another bag to Charley. "And it goes without saying that the sheriff's lunch is on the house. And yours too, Deputy Baylor." She smiled at him, and he seemed to forget all about Amede.

Barney's bellow broke the spell before Charley could make a fool of himself. "Miranda!"

She wrinkled her nose. "Gotta go."

Charley watched her go, then turned back to me. "I'll walk out with you."

We carefully made our way through the icy parking lot to my Jeep. "So," I said, "Jill arrested Amede?"

"No. Not yet." He held my lunch while I unlocked the Jeep. "We're holding her for twenty-four hours. Pending a rush DNA job at the Springfield lab."

"Surely you have all the evidence you need." I slipped into the seat and took the bag, setting it on the passenger's side.

"She's a vampire. She's had centuries to learn how to cover up her messes."

I knew what he meant, but I'd never had a bad feeling about Amede. How could I have not known?

"What will you do if you have to let her go?"

Charley stared across the top of my Jeep so long and so intently that for a minute I thought he hadn't heard. I cleared my throat.

"Sorry," he said. "I was just thinking. And the answer is, I don't know." He shrugged. "Wasn't your dad supposed to come home today? Jill mentioned it."

My stomach tightened at the memory of the nurse telling me they didn't need me at the hospital. "He got sick in the night and they kept him." I felt my tension rising at the thought of him alone. "I couldn't go because of the ice."

"Well, there's probably nothing you could do anyway."

"I don't know." Why was everyone trivializing the importance of my presence by my dad's side? Who else did he have to love him and attend to his needs? "I would be there if I could."

"I think they can handle your dad without you there making unreasonable demands and getting in their way."

"You're a jerk, Charley." I grabbed for the door handle, but he slapped it back with his massive hand.

"Hey," he said. "Look, I'm sorry. I didn't know you wanted to be there that much. Personally, I'd rather be anywhere other than a hospital, and I don't care who's lying in the bed."

Did he have a filter at all? Or a brain for that matter? "What's your point?"

"My point, Lauryn," he said, "is that I'm sorry I said a dumb thing. Okay? Your dad needs you. He just probably doesn't know it, so there's no point in beating yourself up for not being able to get to the hospital."

"Just stop, Charley." I shook my head.

"Sorry."

"It's okay. I'll see him tomorrow."

"What are you doing now?" he asked, still blocking the door.

"I'm going to get some work done at the Chisom house. I'm so far behind because of all the..."

"Murders?"

"Yes, those, of course, and other things. It's been a bizarre couple of weeks." I grabbed the steering wheel, hoping he'd get the idea that not only was it freezing out here but I really just wanted to go to work.

He stepped back. "I better go. When Trent comes in later tonight, I'll come by the Chisom house to check on you."

"Thanks, Charley. Be careful."

"What's there to be afraid of?" He laughed. "They're all locked up now."

He closed my door and waved good-bye before I could ask what he meant.

I made the slippery drive at a crawl the few blocks to the Chisom house. For the first time in my life I didn't love Abbey Hills as I drove along the brick streets between Victorian houses that predated everything else in town except for Amede Dastillion. The unwelcome guest had turned safety into danger, peace into fear. This wasn't the town I knew and loved. It was dismal and frightening.

Even the cold bit deeper.

Without Dad home, I couldn't even enjoy the Christmas decorations. When I pulled up to the Chisom house, all I could think about was the fact that Markus had been a vampire. I wondered, had he brought his victims inside the home I was about to enter?

Amede sat quietly in her cell staring at the bars. Her wrists chafed in the cuffs Charley had insisted putting on her.

Whatever Juliette had given her had finally left her system and her head had cleared. But now that she was fully awake, her hunger gnawed painfully, worse than the effects of the poison or the tranquilizer dart.

It was all she could do not to pace, threaten, yell, beg, cry. She didn't know if the sky still spat ice, or if night had fallen. Time eluded her completely. Finally she lay on her cot and faded in and out of disturbing dreams and restless wakefulness.

The door to the cell room opened. She tensed and sat up as Charley walked in, keys in hand. "What do you want, Charley?"

He stared without words. He stepped aside and jerked his head for her to get up and walk out.

"I'm not going anywhere with you." Instinct and common sense told her he didn't have her best interests at heart.

His eyes flashed and an eerie smile, scarier than a frown, tipped his lips. He stepped forward and grabbed her arm, jerking her up without any attempt to be gentle. "We're going," he said. "Don't you want to see your sister?"

"Don't you think someone is going to see us?" she asked, hoping to speak to his reason.

"It's nine thirty. You know this town rolls up the sidewalks at nine. Especially during ice storms. I could take you to the middle of town and burn you at the stake and no one would notice."

And she could easily snap his neck, but Amede kept her mouth shut for one reason only. He was taking her to Eden. Why hadn't anyone ever noticed that Charley was a madman? He muscled her out the door toward his truck. There were no cars anywhere on Main Street, and the only lights to counter the cloud-covered sky were the streetlights on the corners.

Charley forced her in through the driver's side and shoved her across the seat so he could get in. He fired the engine and Amede felt her first real sense of fear.

As they drove through town, Charley repeatedly tightened, then loosened his grip on the steering wheel. Amede eyed him, remaining cautious. Finally, he turned to her. "What makes you think you can kill humans like we're animals?"

"I don't think that, Charley," Amede said, keeping her tone low and calm. "I don't drink human blood."

"Your sister killed mine. Her name was Mandy. And she never hurt anybody." His voice trembled. "She had two kids and a husband. A family."

"I'm sorry. I don't know what to say."

"Admit that you are a killer."

The tires slipped, and Charley set his attention back on the road.

"I've killed in the past, but it's been a century. And I never killed a mother with children."

"Keep telling yourself you're not a monster, sweetheart." He kept his focus forward.

Amede kept talking. Her nerves were on edge, not because she was scared of this moron, but because the idea of being hunted, chased down, captured, and thrown into a pit seemed so barbaric. Inhumane. "Eden wasn't like me— not inside, where it counted. She had a different mother. One who was a voodoo priestess. Eden didn't think there was anything wrong with a vampire consuming human blood. She believed we'd been put on earth to dominate."

He bristled.

"We were a family of vampires, Charley. We lived by instinct for many years, but then my father stopped drinking blood altogether, even animal blood, because he wanted to be with God and believed it was a sin."

"It is a sin. An abomination."

"That's what he came to believe. I watched him waste away day after day as the things our bodies gained from blood began to wither away. He grew increasingly older—many years flew by in a week. He became weak, sick. Finally he died."

"Good," Charley spat. "Don't think I'm going to feel sorry for you."

He left the road and followed a trail high above the river. She'd hunted these woods. And she remembered the feeling of unbearable hunger, like now. The sense of wild craving. She should have realized how close Eden was. If she'd only persevered.

"Are you planning to kill me, Charley? Because that's not so easy."

"I know how to kill you. I could cut your head off right now or burn you to death. Of course that doesn't always work, does it? Sometimes a vampire escapes the fire, only to become an ugly, scarred freak."

Amede shuddered. "My sister escaped the fire but with scars." She must not have been able to feed right away or her body would have healed.

"I told you, she murdered my sister, Amanda." He angled his gaze at her. "I couldn't let her get away."

"Eden acts from instinct."

He slammed his booted foot down on the brake and the truck fishtailed, slid forward, and finally stopped. He jumped out of the truck and stomped around to her door. "Let's go," he demanded and yanked her from the truck. His fingers bit into her with bruising strength as he dragged her to a cave. His flashlight bounced around in the dark, briefly revealing a door in the ground. He had buried her sister underground.

"You're the one who locked me in the cellar of the burned house."

"That's right." He scowled at her. "The detective might still be alive if you had stayed put."

"What are you saying?"

"He was snooping around and found the doors broken through. Apparently I had dropped my lighter in the cellar. He was taking it to the crime lab."

"That wouldn't have been proof of anything, Charley."

"Maybe not, but it was another piece of the puzzle." He shook his head. "He was searching for clues to link you to Janine's or Jeremy's murders. It was just dumb luck that I dropped the lighter."

"You've committed three murders to frame me?"

He shook his head. "Only Townsend. You know that."

He jerked opened the door.

"You've been looking for your sister. Well, guess what? You're about to see her again. I hope you enjoy the reunion."

CHAPTER TWENTY-FOUR

By last summer my dad had very few moments of lucidity and Cokie began hinting at permanent-care facilities. "I won't always be here, hon," she said. "You need to stop closing your mind to the future."

My defenses rose. "Are you planning to leave, Cokie? Because if you are, just say so and I'll find someone else to look after Dad."

It would have been much more effective if my lips hadn't trembled and my eyes hadn't spilled over with tears.

She wrapped me in her arms. "Honey, I am not leaving you yet, but please start thinking about the future."

Dad had called for me then and I pulled myself together, happy and hopeful for a moment to connect with my dad. But when I got back to his room, he'd forgotten why he called and was engrossed in a nature show.

How could I think about the future when the present consumed every bit of me?

The door above opened. He was talking to someone. She strained to hear. She crouched by the stairs, looking up. Was it Amede? She could feel the wild in her growing stronger, her instincts heightening, her breath moving through her throat in spurts. Yes, it had to be Amede.

"Eden!"

A sob caught in Eden's throat. "Amede? Is it really you?"

"I'm coming, Eden. Charley, take off these stupid cuffs."

"I'll see you in hell first." The snarl Eden had grown to fear and hate shattered her hope. He couldn't be defeated. She had tried so many times, but he was too strong. Maybe he was God, here to bring judgment and avenge the innocent dead.

Amede gave a sigh and started down the steps. Panic welled up in Eden at the thought of seeing Amede. It had been so long. As her sister's legs came into view, Eden reached up and touched the scars on her face. Shame sent her cowering into the corner.

Amede reached the bottom of the steps and turned around. "Eden, darling? What are you doing?"

"Don't look at me. Th-they burned me."

"I know, but I'm here now. Everything is going to be okay. I promise."

"I'll be back in a few days," Charley called. "Then I'll think about uncuffing you."

The door above them closed with a loud thud.

"Eden?"

"I'm hideous." Eden could see her clearly. Her eyes had long adjusted to darkness. Amede appeared to be a beautiful, modern woman of thirty. How Eden envied Amede's smooth skin.

"Eden." Amede's voice broke. "I've been looking for you for such a long time."

The soft, gentle tones of Amede's voice swept over her like a warm Gulf wind, drawing her closer, giving her courage to step from the shadow. "I can't believe it's really you."

Amede smiled, her eyes misting. "It's me." She strained and jerked her hands free from the handcuffs. She reached out and touched Eden's face. "What did they do to you?"

Eden walked into Amede's embrace and laid her head on Amede's shoulder. "I'm so hungry."

"Poor darling." Soft hands caressed Eden's filthy, matted hair.

"We're going to die here," she whispered.

"No, we're getting out of here." Amede squeezed Eden and held her out at arm's length.

"I've tried so many times, Amede." Eden's voice cracked around the wretched words.

Once more, Amede placed her hand on Eden's cheek. "I'm getting us out of here. Right now." She walked toward the steps and turned. "He'll never hurt you again."

I worked by oil lamp and candlelight, trying to make a dent in the crates Charley had brought upstairs from the basement before Thanksgiving.

My mind flashed to images of pierced necks and vampire teeth. And I swear I heard creaking and groaning every few minutes. I had to keep reminding myself it was nothing more than ice on the roof and the sounds of an old house settling on its foundation. Why had I ever read Bram Stoker's *Dracula*?

Despite my growing hunger, I didn't bother with supper. If I had left the house, I never would have returned, and there was a ton of work to do. My last meal had been nine hours earlier and my stomach protested against the neglect.

My laptop battery gave out after three hours, so I took photographs and cataloged by hand for the better part of the day. It was dusty, creepy work and if I'd had a girlfriend to call, I would have asked for company and maybe a sandwich. I missed my father desperately. My heart broke to think of him alone in his hospital room.

At nine o'clock, Billy called. "You still working in the Chisom house?"

I dropped into my desk chair. My body ached from the bending and lifting and sitting on the floor. "I am."

"Are you hungry? My mom fixed lasagna tonight. I could bring some over."

The thought of lasagna brought out my inner Garfield. "Do you even have to ask?"

He chuckled. "Peach is sound asleep, so I'll be over in a little while."

Carrying a candle, I walked through the foyer, avoiding the stairs. The carvings of demons fighting humans suddenly made sense. Markus used art to portray his conflicting feelings. Good versus evil. Human versus vampire. I wondered if I could spin that in a way that could help with the sale. As if anyone in the Bible Belt would want to purchase a home with scary carvings from the inferno.

I walked into the kitchen and pulled out two plates. Lasagna by candlelight, I imagined. Romantic. I could use a distraction from the work and the vampires, the unreality of Cokie's death, and the fact that as my dad slipped away I was losing myself, my role in life, and the person who had always defined me.

I set a kettle of water on the stove and lit the gas burner.

By ten o'clock, I'd consumed two cups of tea, and the candle I'd carried into the kitchen was beginning to fade. I didn't want to call Billy and sound needy or, even worse, demanding, so I checked my phone for a text or e-mail. I didn't like feeling cowardly, but I was beginning to wish I'd left this place before the town had gone to bed.

If I had to leave the house alone, I'd be terrified. Especially considering the man I saw standing outside last night. I hadn't told Charley or Billy about him. And I'd been trying all evening not to think about him, but in my tired, scared mind that man standing in the dark street had become Freddy, Jason, and Michael Myers all rolled into one, with a little Dracula tossed in just because it seemed appropriate, considering...

At ten fifteen, I sat paralyzed in the kitchen chair, watching candle wax drip onto the paper I'd set it on to keep it from ruining a very expensive kitchen table.

A knock at the door nearly sent me through the ceiling until I realized it had to be Billy. I walked through the foyer to the door. Flung it open without verifying.

It wasn't Billy. For a second, my heart drummed in my ears. Then the man's face came into focus.

"Charley!" I said. "You scared me!"

"Why didn't you ask who I was before you opened the door?"

"Because I thought you were Billy," I countered. "Why didn't you use your key?"

He reached out and jiggled the storm door handle. "Because you locked the storm door, genius."

"Oh, duh." I flipped the lock and he stepped inside, shaking his head. I frowned at his disheveled appearance. Charley had never been GQ, but he'd always respected the uniform. "What happened to you? You're looking a little off."

He waved away my comment. "Had to pull the Alexanders out of a ditch on the way over. It's as thick as pea soup out there."

I glanced out at the fog. "Great. More ice fog and black ice."

"Are you ready to leave? I'll drive you home if you want," Charley offered.

I shook my head as he closed the door. "Billy's supposed to bring me supper, but he's later than I thought he'd be." I realized I sounded whiny, so I gave a nonchalant wave to divert Charley's attention. "Do you want some tea?"

He cringed a little, then shrugged. "I guess so, if you don't have coffee."

"I don't."

"Tea then." He hesitated when I waved him to a chair. "Do you want me to run out to the Inn and bring you some food?"

"Thoughtful." I smiled and set the kettle back on the stove. "But I'm sure Billy will eventually show up."

I thought I saw his eyes flash irritation, but considering the poor lighting, I gave him the benefit of the doubt. He dropped into a chair as I pulled another cup from the cupboard and another tea bag from the box.

"I thought you were working at the jail tonight. Jill stopped by earlier and said—"

"I'm taking a break," he said. "Trent's there. We're still on the two-to-a-shift schedule."

"Is Amede still in custody?"

"In a manner of speaking." He stretched his long legs out in front of him and folded his arms across his chest.

The kettle whistled. "What do you mean? She either is or she isn't." And God help us if she wasn't still in jail.

His face softened in a slow grin. "Let's just say Abbey Hills is once again safe from killers."

"So the DNA came back?"

"Not yet, but it'll show she's guilty of murder." He cleared his throat. "I'm sure of it."

Charley seemed nervous. I glanced at the clock.

As if by design, my phone rang just as I poured the steaming water from the kettle into Charley's cup. I hurried to pick it up from the table. "Hi," I said.

"Everything okay?" Billy's voice came across the line. "You sound out of breath."

"No. Just getting Charley some tea."

He hesitated. "Charley's there?"

I grinned. Was Billy a little jealous? "Yeah, he's keeping me company since someone is so late."

He breathed out. "Listen carefully, Lauryn, and don't say anything that Charley might think seems off." My gaze darted to Charley.

He frowned a "what's going on?" frown.

I shrugged.

"So, what's up, Billy?" I tried to sound as natural as possible.

"Something's wrong with Charley. You need to be careful, not let on that you know. Say something about how late I am."

Without missing a beat, I picked up the cue. "I hope you're bringing enough lasagna for three. Charley looks hungry too. He's been working all night at the jail."

"Trent is dead and Amede is missing from her cell. And before you ask, the answer is no. Amede isn't the killer. Trent died by strangulation."

"Oh." I still tried to sound natural, but my voice shook. "That's odd."

"Jill couldn't get an answer at the jail or on either deputy's cell phone, so she drove over there and found him dead. That's why I'm so late. She called me and asked if I could go with her to tell Trent's wife."

Charley's eyes had narrowed. My face had always registered every emotion I felt. I could only guess the story my expression must be telling.

"They found Trent, didn't they?" Charley said.

I gave a slow nod and disconnected from Billy without a good-bye, hoping he would think Charley had forced me to hang up. I didn't believe Charley would actually hurt me, but it would bring Billy faster if he believed it.

"What happened, Charley?" I set his tea down and shoved the sugar bowl in front of him. "What did Trent do?" I tried to sound natural, as if I understood that Trent had given Charley no choice.

He shook his head. "He wouldn't let me take that thing out of the cell." The look he gave me chilled me more than the ice outside. "What was I supposed to do? I had to take him down."

I sipped my lukewarm tea, trying to gather courage and wrap my brain around the fact that my friend had just murdered a man. A good man with a wife and family. "What about Amede?"

Charley leaned forward. "I'm going to tell you something because I know I can trust you. It's why I came here. I need help getting both vampires out of town. But if Jill already found Trent, I guess I'll have to move faster than I thought. You'll help me, won't you?"

"Of course." I fought to control my fear. I had to keep it together. If Charley could turn on Trent and justify killing him, he could turn on me. And where would it leave Dad if something happened to me? I hid my trembling hands in my lap and smiled.

"You were right. Amede and the vampire witch who killed Mandy last spring are sisters."

I nodded. "I just found out last night." I couldn't believe how calm and natural I sounded. But this was Charley, my only friend for a while, and I hated the thought that he was going off the deep end. I wanted to help him. "Jill took me to talk to her sister. They told me about Markus and Eden and everything that happened last time."

He stood and walked to the threshold, glancing at the front door. "When you talked to Billy, did he say if they were coming here?"

The question startled me. "He didn't say. He went with Jill to tell Trent's wife."

He whipped around suddenly. I tensed, ready to defend myself. "I never wanted to hurt Trent. But he kept coming at me, yelling at me about justice. I would have tied him up and left him for Jill to find, but he fought too hard and I…"

"You had to kill him." I said it matter-of-factly, but barely masking my horror.

"Exactly. I knew if anyone could understand hard decisions like this it would be you."

"Of course." I hoped my smile was convincing.

"I want to tell you something else." He stared at me with a frightening intensity.

Just then, the front door opened. We stared at each other and listened, unmoving. A woman's voice called out, "Lauryn? Are you here? The door was open."

Charley shook his head and pressed his finger to his lips. His face had twisted into something almost unrecognizable. More than rage, somewhere between outrage and pain, as though the sound of that voice was beyond his ability to cope. I reached out and gripped his arm, hoping to calm him.

"It's Amede," the voice said.

I swallowed hard, looking for a place to hide.

"Lauryn?" she called again. "I saw your Jeep. I know you're in here."

Charley jerked his head toward the foyer, indicating I should go see what she wanted.

"I'm coming," I called, trying to sound friendly and unconcerned.

I stopped short as I walked into the spacious foyer. The oil lamp gave enough of an eerie glow, but the dark feeling I got imagining a vampire walking into this house crawled all over my skin. "Amede," I said. "What can I do for you?"

"We came to get my ring."

"We?" And then I noticed a frail figure by the stairs. I could tell she was a tall woman, but her body was hunched over. She crept along next to Amede. Her emaciated body looked like something from a horror film.

As she walked into the glow of the oil lamp I couldn't hold back a gasp. Her sunken face was beyond description. More than scarred, it looked as if it had melted.

"Stop staring at me," she hissed.

I averted my gaze, my face burning. I turned to Amede. "I'm afraid I didn't find the ring."

"Eden knows where it is." Amede turned to her sister. "She gave it to Markus when he left for the war."

I looked at Eden, focusing on her perfect, all-consuming eyes and doing my best to ignore her skeletal figure and grotesque face. "Go get it then." I tried to sound professional and not like I was barely able to stand on my weak-kneed legs.

She headed toward the stairs, grabbed the railing with both hands, and ascended, one excruciatingly slow step at a time. "I'll come with you, Eden," Amede said.

Eden turned. "No. I want to be alone with his things."

She labored to climb the stairs and I almost felt sorry for her. Amede stepped forward. Startled, I stepped back. She frowned. "I'm not going to hurt you, Lauryn. And neither will she. I made sure she fed before we came over."

That wasn't exactly reassuring and I couldn't believe she thought it would be. Still, I nodded.

"She fed on a deer," said Amede. She watched Eden finally reach the top step. "She's still so weak. Like Papa before he died."

"Your father was a..." I hesitated. Somehow saying the word *vampire* bordered on the ridiculous. I felt as foolish as Miranda just thinking it.

"Yes," she said quietly. "He was."

"He's gone?"

"I watched him starve to death." The pain in her voice sounded familiar. It reflected my own. I stopped short of reaching out to her.

A muted yell from upstairs crescendoed into a scream. Amede's eyes widened in horror. She sprinted toward the stairs and took them two at a time. Charley burst through the kitchen door, his pistol in hand.

"What do you think you're going to do with that?" I asked.

He sneered. "I don't know. But we better get out of here while they're gone."

"Okay, but I need my phone and computer and purse—"

"Maybe you don't understand the concept of get out of here, Lauryn. There are two vampires upstairs who would think nothing of ripping you open. And I don't have any way to protect you in here. We have to go now!" He grabbed my arm.

"Before you go, I have a couple of questions for Lauryn." Amede seemed to appear out of nowhere. I jumped.

Charley turned on her. "Leave her alone if you know what's good for you." Considering our circumstances, his threat seemed nothing more than a childish pomp.

"Or what?" Amede's eyes flashed. "You have no tranquilizer darts. No poisoned wine."

Charley gave a short laugh. "You figured that out, huh?"

She nodded.

"I knew you liked your glass of wine before bed."

Seeing this side of Charley was horrifying, and I was shocked at my own blindness to the pain that was clearly driving him insane.

He grinned as though the two of them were the best of friends sharing a laugh. "I planned to take you straight from the Inn, but Jill came by and arrested you instead."

Amede's face twisted, and for the first time I saw the evil in her. I trembled as she came closer and stood nose to nose with Charley. He tensed.

"Amede," I said softly. "Charley hasn't been himself since his sister died. What he did was wrong, but he needs help. If there's any humanity in you, let the law administer his punishment."

She turned to me and her pupils were almost as big as her irises. I wasn't sure she'd heard my words.

A whisper, like the hiss of a snake, came from Eden, who clung to the banister. "He deserves to die after what he did to me. Kill him, Amede."

Charley sneered. "You'd be dead if not for me, you stupid slut. Who do you think put out the flames when you ran from that burning house?"

Sucking in a breath, Amede reared back and slapped him. The force of preternatural strength flung him across the room. He landed on his back next to the wall.

I tried to wrap my head around the information flying around the room. "Charley, what did you do?"

Amede kicked him, hard, far from the gentle southern belle she'd portrayed thus far. She walked away from Charley. I got the feeling she did it as a method of control. "He locked her away in an underground prison and kept her there, starving, filthy, in pain. He locked me in there tonight too, but I was stronger than he knew."

Cautiously, I walked across the room to where Charley still sprawled on the floor against the wall. I'd seen enough vampire movies that I could imagine them stalking toward us, teeth bared, thirsty for our blood. Clearly Charley had brought this on himself, but regardless of that, I couldn't just leave him alone to face that sort of fate.

His breathing was labored as he angled his gaze upward to Amede's. "Eden killed my sister and you killed my girlfriend."

"I didn't kill anyone, Charley." Amede's icy tone made me shudder. "Yet."

Charley hauled himself up off the floor, only slightly more subdued than five minutes before.

He walked slowly as though in pain, but then he quickly grabbed the oil lamp and in a flash he raced to the staircase. He yanked Eden by the arm before anyone could react and pulled her up the steps.

CHAPTER TWENTY-FIVE

Amede knew one of them wouldn't make it out of the house alive. Charley held Eden fast with one arm and carried the oil lamp in the other.

She took a step toward him.

He waved the lamp precariously in front of Eden. "I swear I'll smash this thing at her feet and hold her here until she burns to death."

Amede held her breath. Charley was a man unafraid of his own mortality. The most dangerous kind. He slowly backed her up the steps until they reached the landing.

"Amede!" Eden cried out. "Please don't let him take me."

"Did my sister beg for mercy before you killed her?" Charley asked.

Lauryn moved to the stairs. "Charley," she said. "What are you doing? Jill knows Eden is guilty. Let's just turn her in and let Jill deal with it. Don't make things worse."

"She's not human, Lauryn. She's a monster."

"Charley, look at her. She's not a monster anymore." Lauryn's gentle tone seemed to have a calming effect on Charley. Amede could tell his breathing had slowed. "Think about what you're doing. Amanda wouldn't have wanted you to do this. You know she wouldn't. So don't pretend you're doing this for her."

"She took every drop of blood from my sister's body, Lauryn." Tears dripped down the deputy's face. Amede watched, waited, poised to rush the stairs if necessary—but there might be another way to stop him.

Opportunity seized her and she grabbed Lauryn from behind, gripping her shoulders. She could feel Lauryn's fear.

Amede trailed her index finger along the side of Lauryn's neck and stared Charley down. "I'll kill her."

Charley focused on Lauryn, and it seemed he had loosened his grip on Eden. Eden must have thought the same thing. In an instant, she whipped around and lunged for Charley's lamp. She grabbed at it, but Charley snatched it and it flew from his hand over the staircase and set fire to the rug below. A cloud of smoke rose instantly.

The world seemed to slow, and Amede shoved Lauryn aside and sprang into action.

But she couldn't get to her sister fast enough. Charley sidestepped as Eden lunged for him, and they both collided into the banister. The banister broke under Charley's weight and the impact of Eden's fury, and they crashed through the splintered wood.

I watched as Charley and Eden fell through the smoke. I had an odd feeling of déjà vu just before I screamed, "Charley!" I knew his neck was broken the second he hit the ground with a sickening thud.

Fire engulfed Eden. Her screams filled the room as she burned.

Amede leaped onto her, rolling her until the flames were out. The rug still burned and I rushed into the kitchen where I knew a fire extinguisher hung in the pantry. By the time I returned and doused the remaining flames,

Eden lay still and though I wasn't sure what it took for a vampire to die, I had a feeling she wouldn't live through this. Her chest rose and fell in short spurts that suggested death was imminent.

Tears rushed down Amede's cheeks as she knelt beside her sister, her hands and face blistering where she'd forced out the fire. "Don't leave me again, Eden. I just found you."

I felt out of place. Every inch of Eden's skin had been burned and her hair was completely gone. Her clothes melted into her skin. The smell of burning flesh turned my stomach.

A wail rose up from Amede. Eden must have taken her last breath.

I lifted my phone to call Billy just as he and Jill walked in on the scene. Billy came to me and slipped his arm around my waist, fitting me close against his side.

Jill stared at Charley, lying on the floor. She glanced up. "What happened?"

"He kidnapped Amede. He's been holding Eden all these months." It was all I could muster the strength to give at the moment.

"Why did the two of you come back here?" Jill asked Amede. "You could have gotten away."

"Eden believed she knew where Markus had placed Papa's ring. She gave it to him many years ago." Amede turned to me and I shivered. "Please forgive me, Lauryn. I wouldn't have harmed you. I was desperate."

I couldn't look her in the eyes. No matter what she said about not harming me, I still felt her cool breath against my skin, her finger sliding down my neck as though marking the spot for her bite. I would not soon forget the choking fear.

"What happened?" Billy asked. He looked at Amede and his tone dipped lower. "What did you do to her?"

I relished the protective outrage, but nothing productive would come of it. "Billy, calm down. It's over now."

Jill let out a long breath as she looked around the room. Pain clouded her eyes at the sight of Charley's twisted body. She turned to me. "Lauryn, can you tell me everything that happened here?"

Amede stayed on her knees next to her sister and didn't deny anything while I gave Jill my statement. Billy bristled when I recounted Amede's threat. I left out the part where terror weakened my knees and I prayed my dad would never know how I died. It seemed melodramatic at this point.

Jill's tension was almost palpable as she placed her hand on her pistol and addressed Amede. "You know I have to take you back to the jail until that DNA report comes back. You are still the primary suspect in the murders. Are you going to force me to use the tranquilizers again?"

Amede shook her head. "I won't fight you. But the DNA will not implicate me. I didn't kill them—and Eden couldn't have."

Jill called the coroner, then Barney. When Barney came over, Billy offered to take me home. It was well after midnight and I was more than ready to leave.

The air outside was bitterly cold, but it was still a relief from the stench of burned flesh and the horrifying events of the evening.

Billy drove me home, holding my hand the whole way. "I was so frantic to come to you," he said. "And that's when I thought you only had Charley to worry about."

I slid over and nestled into his shoulder, my cheek resting on his leather jacket. He pulled into my driveway and parked the car. His arms went around me and he drew me close, pressing his mouth to mine first gently, then with more fervor, almost frantically. My heart sped up and I surrendered.

I was breathless when he tore his lips from mine. He stared into my eyes and I didn't have the slightest desire to look away. He smiled. "I got a little carried away."

"It's okay. I liked it."

"Stop looking at me like that." He kissed me firmly but quickly. "I'm only human."

"Thank God. I'd hate it if you weren't."

He chuckled. "Okay, let's go. I could use some icy air."

He walked me to the door, and I knew better than to ask him to come in with me.

Billy cupped my face and kissed me again. "I'd like to come to the hospital with you tomorrow."

The offer surprised me. I nodded, grateful for the support. "Thanks, I'd like that."

He waited for me to get inside. "And stay put this time," he teased, but I could see in his eyes he meant what he said.

"Don't worry. I'm down for the count. See you in the morning."

I locked the door and watched out the window until he drove away.

Amede didn't protest when the sheriff placed her in the familiar cell and locked it behind her.

Jill's husband, Barney, had insisted upon accompanying them. "You're not staying at the jail alone with that thing," he'd said. Now he stood poised to spring if Amede made a move.

"I am sorry about Eden, for your sake," she said. "What Charley did to her was unconscionable."

Amede remained silent.

"I'll leave you alone for now," Jill said softly. "I'll be in to check on you later." She left, closing the door behind her.

Amede sat on the cot, staring, replaying Eden's fiery fall over and over until her brain hurt.

Papa had spoken of death so many times during the last few years of his life. He had a hope that somehow he'd be forgiven and reconciled with God. She wondered about Eden but couldn't allow her mind to travel there.

She lay on the cot, forcing away image after fiery image until sometime after sunrise, when the door opened. The sheriff entered with a breakfast tray. "Hi. I hope you can eat. It's just oatmeal and toast. And I've brought you a cup of tea as well."

The intense hunger brought on by Eden's presence had abated somewhat, but she still had a sense of urgency twisting inside her. She attributed the feeling to being locked away. Sitting up, she waved away the food. "I couldn't eat, but I'll take the tea."

Barney's hulking presence hovered as the sheriff unlocked the cell and passed the tea. After the door clanged shut once more, the sheriff said, "Lauryn is here to see you. I told her it would be okay. But it's your choice."

Surprised but curious, Amede nodded. "Of course. Send her in."

Barney, still standing in the doorway, made a motioning gesture, then stepped aside while Lauryn entered. She carried a package in her hands.

"I found something of yours." She cleared her throat. "Jill has already inspected it and okayed my giving it to you." She slid the package through the bars. "I remember you saying how special the book was to you. The inscription from your father is still clear."

Amede frowned as she stared at the bag. She opened it up and drew in a sharp breath. She slid the plastic-protected book out of the paper bag.

"Wuthering Heights," she whispered. Tears pricked her eyes. "Are you sure? It must be very valuable."

Lauryn nodded. "There are more priceless antiques in that home than I've ever seen in one place. The town will make out just fine. The book belongs to you."

Amede opened the cover and the tears dripped down her face as she traced over the familiar handwriting.

"I better go. Traffic is going to be backed up today with everyone finally getting out after the ice."

"You're leaving town?"

"Just going to Branson to get my dad."

"Lauryn, may I offer some advice?"

The young woman lifted her eyebrows but nodded. "Okay."

"I know you love your father, but make sure you take time to have your own life."

Lauryn nodded and began to retreat toward the door.

"Don't misunderstand. I'm not suggesting that you don't care for him. Only that you make sure that at the end of the day there's someone or something to offer you a place to land."

Amede noted the resentment in Lauryn's eyes, but after a sleepless night of reflection, she felt like she had experience to offer the young woman. And nothing to lose. "I sat by my father's side for years while he declined mentally and physically. I got nothing out of it but loneliness. He hardly even knew I was there.

"When he was gone, I was left with nothing but heartache because I'd spent my life holding on to him. After that I lived for the times Eden and I were together." Amede gathered a breath and held her book close to her chest.

"There has to be something more. My father believed that something more was God."

"What do you think?" Lauryn's voice held no mockery and Amede could see she was listening.

"Think? You mean do I think reformed vampires get to go to heaven?" She shrugged. "Maybe. Perhaps it's time to put Thomas Aquinas's theory into action. Better to believe in a redemption and go in that direction—and by that I mean stop drinking even animal blood and let myself die like my father—than to not believe and find out in the end after it's too late for forgiveness."

Lauryn observed her silently. "I truly hope you find what you're looking for, Amede."

"And I hope the same for you, Lauryn McBride."

After she left, Amede sat on her cot and opened *Wuthering Heights*.

Juliette trailed after Miranda as the two of them and Caleb walked up the steps at the jailhouse. "I still don't see how you could possibly know it was Eden."

"Because I eavesdropped when Jill was talking to Barney. Plus, they live next-door to the Chisom house and I watched who went in and out, including the two bodies the coroner took."

Caleb held her hand tightly as she continued questioning Miranda. "Stop. Don't go in yet."

Miranda rolled her eyes. "What else is there to say, Jules? Charley broke Amede free so he could kill her and Eden together. Instead, Eden and Charley were killed together, and the sheriff took Amede back to jail—which I personally think is an injustice."

Caleb smiled at Miranda, and Juliette felt a tinge of jealousy. She didn't like the feeling, but the two of them seemed oddly close for recent acquaintances. Because they were closer in age and because of Miranda's unique beauty, Juliette couldn't help but feel a little threatened.

As though sensing her mood, Caleb squeezed Juliette's hand as he responded to Miranda. "She hasn't been proven innocent yet, so the sheriff really didn't have a choice."

Miranda gave a little shrug and opened the door. The sheriff looked up. Barney scowled. "Miranda, why in the heck aren't you at the café? You're supposed to be opening for me today."

"Kellie has it covered. And Dave's your right-hand man in the kitchen." Miranda patted his meaty shoulder. "Don't worry, big guy. Everything is going to work out fine."

The sheriff walked across the floor to her husband. "Honey, go check on the café. I will be fine." She stood on tiptoe and kissed him. "I won't open Amede's cell until you get back or until the DNA analysis—which should be coming any time—proves her innocent."

He eyed Juliette and she felt her cheeks warm, so she spoke. "I couldn't help Amede escape if I tried. The sheriff is stronger than me, plus she has a gun. I'm not like Amede. All the sheriff has to do is shoot me to stop me."

He glanced at Caleb. "Keep an eye on them."

Chauvinism aside, Juliette couldn't help thinking how great it would be to someday have a man who cared about her as much as Barney cared about Jill. True, Caleb was good to her, but that was after only a couple of weeks together. Who knew what would happen once she returned to New Orleans?

Caleb reached out and offered his hand, which Barney shook. "You can count on me."

Juliette could see Barney's reluctance as he walked out the door. Jill smiled after him. "So," she said, "what can I do for you?"

Miranda spoke up in her irritatingly pushy manner. "We want to see Amede Dastillion."

"Why?" The sheriff maintained an air of professionalism while sizing up the three of them.

Miranda and Caleb exchanged glances. Caleb cleared his throat. "I'm here to support Juliette."

"And you?" the sheriff asked Miranda.

Miranda narrowed her too-large green eyes, and her face darkened to a blush. "Is there a rule against my seeing her?"

"I kind of make the rules, and to be honest, I'm not in the best mood, seeing as how both of my deputies died last night."

Caleb stepped forward. "We heard about that, Sheriff. Please accept our condolences. Miranda came to the Inn this morning to give Juliette the details of last night since she works for Amede. Is there a chance that Juliette at least can see her?"

Juliette held her breath as Jill considered the request. "I'll have to go back and check with Amede. She might not want more visitors."

"More visitors?"

The sheriff didn't see fit to elaborate, so Juliette fell silent and waited until she returned.

"She'd like to see you."

Miranda stomped her foot. "I can't go back there? I want an interview. Considering last night's events, I think the people deserve some answers."

"Take it up with your congressman," the sheriff shot back. "Amede is being held as a possible suspect in three murders. Until DNA evidence comes back exonerating her of all three, I'm not letting you talk to her. Juliette is a longstanding employee and I'm letting her in." She fixed Miranda with a glare. "You, not so much."

Juliette rolled her eyes as she followed the sheriff to the back. Seriously, Miranda had to be half-crazy.

Amede looked surprisingly serene as she sat on her cot, a book on her lap. She set the book down and walked to the bars as Juliette entered the room.

"It was good of you to come, Juliette."

"I'm sorry about Eden. I know how much you loved your sister."

Gathering a breath, Amede nodded. "Thank you. Have you spoken to your grandmother about all of this?"

The thought had crossed Juliette's mind, but she was too ashamed to tell Grandmere that she had let Amede down. She averted her gaze. "Not yet."

"Well, there is no sense worrying her until we find out whether or not I'll be charged."

Relieved, Juliette peered closer, dropping her volume. "Miss Amede, you aren't guilty, are you?" She hated to ask, but after witnessing Amede's episodes of anxiety and hunger, she felt like the question was warranted.

"I haven't fed on a human in many years."

"Then if Eden has been locked away, who killed the waitress from Barney's and the EMT? I just don't get it."

Amede closed her eyes and opened them. She hesitated just a minute before leaning closer. "I'm feeling the presence of other vampires. I don't feel them like I did Eden, thank God. But I know they're here."

Amede jerked her head up.

"What is it?" Juliette asked.

"Something isn't right in the other room."

"What do you mean?"

The door opened and Caleb and Miranda entered. "Don't worry," Caleb said. "We didn't harm the sheriff. Just cuffed her to a chair for a few minutes."

The room closed around Juliette as his words sank in. "Are you crazy? What do you think you're doing?" She glowered at Miranda. "Seriously? She talked you into this?"

"Careful, little girl," Miranda said. "You really don't know what you are talking about."

"Juliette." Amede's cool voice brought her back. "I think we've found our vampires." She turned to Caleb. "I should have known. But Eden's presence eclipsed everything and everyone else."

Miranda held the keys to the cell. "Before we let you out, we want to tell you who we are." Her lips quirked up as though about to tell an enormous joke. But Juliette saw nothing funny about the situation they were in.

Caleb stepped forward and slid his arm around her. "I'm sorry I couldn't tell you, sweetheart. We couldn't risk exposing who we are until we were sure our mother was in Abbey Hills."

Amede stared at them. "Surely you don't think I—"

Miranda laughed. "Of course not." She paced a little. "I hate being so closed in. How can you stand that cage?"

Ignoring the question, Amede focused her attention back to Caleb. "Explain what you mean. Who is your mother?"

"Eden."

A condescending smile curved Amede's lips, and even Juliette couldn't help but give a little laugh. "Why would you think this?"

Caleb leveled his gaze to her. "I have her diaries, stolen from the Chisom house, and I have the diaries from our adopted mother. Eden became pregnant in 1857 and her father sent her away to deliver. Our adopted parents lived in Georgia and were friends of your father."

"Do you mean the DuShanes?"

Juliette jerked her head to look at Amede. Disbelief gave way to incredulity.

Miranda stepped forward. "We were raised by Miranda DuShane. She named me after herself. Isn't that quaint?"

"If you wanted to find Eden, why not just come to Dastillion Court?"

"We tried. Once shortly after our mother died in 1892, but a woman said there was no Eden there and we should try St. Louis. We assumed she must have been one of the Morioux."

Miranda turned to Juliette and smiled. "Your family line has been extremely loyal."

Juliette didn't respond. "Why not ask to speak with Eden's father or Amede?"

Picking up the story from Miranda, Caleb moved away from Juliette, leaving her back cold where his palm had been. Why had she never noticed how gracefully he moved or how elegant his hands? She had been involved with a vampire for weeks and had not had any idea.

"We didn't know Amede existed, and the woman at the door indicated he was dead."

Miranda gave a laugh. "We almost barged in and demanded our rightful place as Dastillion heirs, but Caleb insisted we find Eden first so we could substantiate our story. DNA tests weren't around back then." Miranda addressed the last statement to Juliette, as though she were an idiot for being the only nonvampire in the room.

"No kidding." Sarcasm dripped from Juliette, and Miranda's eyebrow rose.

Amede raised her palm and Juliette turned away from Miranda. Clearly,

Amede had the floor. "So this is about the Dastillion name and fortune, I assume." Her tone was harsh and Juliette knew she wasn't buying their story for a second.

"We have the diaries as proof, Amede, and there is always DNA if you want," Caleb said. "You know as well as I do we don't need money; there are ways to be rich when you're like us. But this is about family. Mostly we wanted to know our mother. Miranda did, especially. But you're family too."

"Enough to kill two humans for it?"

Miranda gave a nonchalant wave. "Oh, Amede. What difference does it make? We had to find a way to get your attention and keep you here. Janine was an unfortunate necessity."

"The EMT, well, that was more impulse..."

Juliette looked at Caleb as though she'd never seen him before. She certainly didn't know him. "You killed a human?"

"It's who I am, Juliette." He stepped toward her but she held up her hand and shook her head.

"Amede doesn't kill humans."

Miranda frowned. "I thought that was just a story."

A wry smile appeared on Amede's face, but Juliette knew she was anything but amused. "It wasn't. I am not a murderer."

"I don't consider what we do to be murder," Caleb said. "They consume animals for food, and we are just doing what comes naturally."

Juliette knew Amede had heard that line of reasoning before. She had heard stories from her grandmere.

"Am I sensing that you disapprove of us?" Caleb asked Amede. His eyes flashed disappointment regardless of the rueful smile on his perfect lips.

"I disapprove, yes. And if you are Dastillions, then I am sorry Eden didn't see fit to raise you. Although you were probably better off with the

DuShanes. Funny how Papa told me Mrs. Dushane had finally given birth to twins and I never gave it a thought." She sighed. "Those were days of innocence."

"Do you mean to tell me you don't want us?" Miranda sprang forward and gripped a bar in each hand. Her dramatics were comical.

"That is precisely what I'm saying."

From the corner of her eye, Juliette noticed a figure appear in the doorway. Two shots rang out in succession, each hitting its spot. The sheriff stood as Caleb and Miranda stumbled.

"Rule of thumb, never handcuff a sheriff without checking for an extra set of handcuff keys."

Caleb tried to lunge, but she shot another dart into his chest. Then another dart into Miranda's arm. "For the record, not only are you under arrest for assaulting an officer, but I heard your confessions, so murder is also on the table."

Caleb dropped to his knees and fell face forward. Miranda slid down the bars and fell back.

"Are you okay, Sheriff?" Amede asked.

She nodded, stepping over Caleb to open the cell door. "It looks like you're free to go, Amede. I'd like your statement about their confession first." She turned to Juliette. "Both of you."

She grabbed Caleb's hands and pulled him into the cell and did the same with an unconscious Miranda. "I guess I'll have to wait to read them their rights."

Within half an hour, they were in the Town Car headed back to the Inn to pick up their bags and leave town.

Juliette stayed silent, allowing Amede to reflect on the recent events. To lose her sister and learn her niece and nephew existed and were killers...it had to be too much.

Once, as she looked in the rearview mirror, she thought she saw a tear roll down Amede's face. "Miss Amede? Is there anything you need?"

Amede turned and caught her eye in the rearview mirror. "No, thank you. We've been through a lot together, haven't we?"

"Yes. And I am sorry for your loss."

"Juliette, I've never thought to ask this of any Morioux. Are you happy serving in my house?"

Juliette felt her face go flush at the unexpected question. "I haven't exactly served in your house yet."

"You evaded the question. When we get home, I'm dismissing you to return to school."

Almost missing a curve, Juliette jerked the wheel and righted the car. "Grandmere is going to kill me if I've been that inadequate."

"Don't worry about Roma." She stared out the window. "I was thinking about what a waste of life it is to live for someone else. I don't want that for you." She smiled and briefly glanced toward Juliette. "After you become an interior designer, maybe I'll hire you to redo Dastillion Court."

"Are you sure this is what you want?"

"It is. But I hope you'll stop by for lunch every so often and let me know how you're doing."

"I will."

They fell silent again as she came to grips with the incredible gift Amede had just given her.

The highway dipped and curved ahead of her, but all she saw was a straight path and wide-open road.

CHAPTER TWENTY-SIX

I stood next to Dad's bed as he slept, still forced to receive IV antibiotics for recurring fevers and therefore unable to return home again. They'd had to sedate him because he kept trying to pull on his IV. He just couldn't grasp the concept that he needed it there. To him, it caused him pain and therefore must go.

Billy stood next to me, holding my hand as we watched my dad's chest rise and fall. How could his body be functioning exactly like it should at his age but his mind be digressing so rapidly? It didn't seem fair.

Billy expelled a breath and moved behind me, encircling my waist. He rested his chin on my shoulder. "I hate seeing the look of pain in your eyes," he whispered.

"It's sort of inevitable from here on out, I'm afraid."

"You're not alone, Lauryn. And I can't believe God would want you to be in such pain for the duration of your father's illness."

His words brought back my last conversation with Amede.

"Amede said I can't just live for Dad." I leaned back against Billy's chest. He kissed my neck, just a flutter of butterfly wing. "She advised me to make sure I have time for something more."

"What kind of something more?"

"I got the feeling she meant something that makes me center on contentment no matter the responsibilities." I smiled, remembering an episode of talk TV. "Oprah says that is the place where you find God, or whatever you think God is. That 'something more.'"

"I think God is God. I don't think you can find Him in such a narrow place. He's definitely not just in contentment. But I believe He's definitely something more than you. More than me. He's indescribable."

"My relationship with Dad has always been such a close thing." Dad stirred a little and I lowered my tone. "We never really needed anyone but each other. In hindsight it wasn't that healthy for either of us. He should have remarried a long time ago."

I remembered my history teacher and cringed a little.

"My relationship with Dad clouded my vision of God, I think."

"How so?" His breath tickled my ear and I shivered a little.

"Well, first of all, I was really mad at God for taking my mom."

"That's pretty typical."

"I know, but instead of getting over it, Dad sort of stepped in and took every place where I was empty, including the God space. There just wasn't room for anyone in my life who didn't somehow connect to Dad. And he was just as mad at God as I was."

Billy turned me in his arms and stared into my eyes. "There are some places no one but God can fill. And if you try to fill them any other way, things just get really hard." He bent and pressed a light kiss to my lips, then pulled back. "I want to be there for you. I've decided to stay in Abbey Hills, for my dad and Peach and myself. And I don't want to lose you again."

"Things are complicated," I said. "I don't know how long I'll be busy with Dad and work, but I'd like to try, Billy."

I turned back to my dad. There was a lot to figure out about his care. I knew I couldn't do it alone. And like Billy said, no human would bring the sense of calm I so desperately craved.

So maybe God was that "something more." Indescribable, and yet when He's there, you know it. When you fall into nothing and find yourself held. Maybe that was the something more I'd been missing.

In my dream—my recurring, "Is someone trying to tell me something?" dream—I float blissfully through a wall of gray, wafting, vaporous smoke, blind to what lies beneath the dark expanse of haze. In this dream, I'm aware that I'm falling, falling far, and yet I'm not afraid.

Strong arms encircle me as I fall, and I realize I'm not alone. I've never been alone. I'm falling, yes, but there's someone with me who understands the art of falling together. His arms are strong, His experience vast, and we're falling. . .tandem.